D1110269

after
nirvana

after nirvana

a novel

lee williams

william morrow and company, inc.
new york

RD1052 97879

Copyright © 1997 by Lee Williams

"Toilet Training (The ABC's)" appeared in Men on Men 5: Best New Gay Fiction, ed. David Bergman (New York: NAL-Dutton, Plume Books, 1994).

All rights reserved. No part of this book may be reproduced or utilized in any form or by any means, electronic or mechanical, including photocopying, recording, or by any information storage or retrieval system, without permission in writing from the Publisher. Inquiries should be addressed to Permissions Department, William Morrow and Company, Inc., 1350 Avenue of the Americas, New York, N.Y. 10019.

It is the policy of William Morrow and Company, Inc., and its imprints and affiliates, recognizing the importance of preserving what has been written, to print the books we publish on acid-free paper, and we exert our best efforts to that end.

Library of Congress Cataloging-in-Publication Data

Williams, Lee. 1967–
    After nirvana : a novel / Lee Williams.—1st ed.
      p.   cm.
    ISBN 0-688-15215-5
    1. Street youth—Northwest, Pacific—Fiction.   2. Narcotic addicts—Northwest, Pacific—Fiction.   I. Title.
PS3573.I44972A69   1997
813'.54—DC21   9711220

Printed in the United States of America

First Edition

1   2   3   4   5   6   7   8   9   10

BOOK DESIGN BY BRIAN MULLIGAN

For my mother,

Violet Williams,

All apologies

after
nirvana

Mid-July X-Out in Portland

It was dark and I was hungry and we were scrunched on a bench in a corner of the Square, twenty or less yards away from the Arctic Circle on Yamhill, hamburger-smell on everywhere, and somewhere, not real far from the Square, Jody and James were waging a deal for five hits of Ecstasy. My stomach went off and Nikki said, "Don't think about it—X works better on an empty stomach, anyway."

Branch said, "Here they come," and we all moved around and looked up—checked out their faces. James's face was cool, but Jody's face said that they got a good deal.

Jody said, "It's all five hits—we're gettin' them at the City-club," and Nikki got out a cigarette and passed it to Jody and she lit it.

Branch said, "Fairly cool."

James said, "Ten a hit."

Branch said that was "Fairly not cool," then, "We should've got it from Max," and I knew that we didn't have that much that night.

James pooled the money, recounted, but I was right and we were short.

"We shouldn'ta strayed from Max, Max's got it cheaper," Branch said.

"*When* he's got it," James said and Jody said, "Hey, *hey*, okay? We can still make this deal."

James said, "The guy looked, you know, reliable," and Branch said, "Reliable—some dumbass outta the park . . ."

"How much we got?" Nikki said.

"Enough for three," James said.

"What's the fuckin' point, then?" Nikki said, and Jody backed her with, "Ooh, that's true, the whole thing is that we, like, *all* do it," and then James said, "Well, duh, fuck, the dumb dude that's got it won't have it tomorrow."

And then everybody looked at each other and everybody's face said, "We need bucks—fast—and you know what that means," which meant me and James because we were out of Jody and Nikki's territory, and Branch—because he was oldest—had to stay with Jody and Nikki.

"We have to be at the Club at ten," Jody said. Then James said, "*I* could make it all fast—in one shot—if I run back to the crash pad, borrow a Jody dress, do me up in drag," and me and Nikki laughed but Branch and Jody said at the same time that there wasn't any time—to get to the Dead Hotel and back—so me and James started out of the Square, heading for Southwest Third. I kissed Nikki—my girlfriend— a goodbye.

"Wait," Branch said, rechecking the funds, "James—what about the A? You and Jody had a quarter-sheet to sell."

"Sold it," James said, "Then we got some McDonald's," and my stomach went off.

* * *

From Sixth we crossed Yamhill—already picking up stares out of a couple cars—two yellow cars and a black truck playing loud hoe-down tunes—and James was hum-singing Guns N' Roses—"Paradise City"—only changing the lines from "Take me down to Paradise City/ Where the grass is green and the girls are pretty," to "Take me down to Sin City/Where the men are trolls but you can sure make a livin'," and I said, "You're snuffin' him," and he said, "Snuffin' who?" and I said, "Branch, duh, fuck," and he said, "Just his stupid L.A. head-banger shit." He hum-sang more, went through it maybe three more times, and then we were just yards from the real thing, the real Sin City coin-op adult bookstore on Third, and James stopped singing.

"Prime time," James said, and it seemed like the car action outside was picking up with every step we got closer to inside.

I said, "Not too much competition"—single-old-men cars, family cars, cars with bald-head drivers, and the guys hanging under the big SIN CITY sign all had beer bellies.

Right before going in, James pointed—"Check it out"—to a big, baby-blue Volvo station wagon that was coming up. When it passed, I couldn't see what James was talking about and then it stopped in front of us, opened a front door, and let one of the beer bellies in. When it pulled off, I could see that there were a couple of kids' car seats—close to brand-new—in the backseat.

James jingled the door open, and "Paradise City"—the real version—went off in my head.

Inside, there was no one up front—the only lighted part of the place—except a counterguy. The rest of the place was halls, mazes of doors to booths, and planks to other halls, and from the front, we could make out the sounds of the things further in—feet clanking on the planks, quarters clanking behind the doors, and another kind of clank—belt buckles hitting the floor, maybe.

I heard James humming in front of me, but then figured out it was the video-machines whirring up, a lot of them going on all at once, down the halls, James said sounding like a mile-long zipper that somebody wouldn't quit pulling down.

In the halls, the bald-heads were all over and there was room for me and James and them but they were crowded. James looked back—video flicker-light was the only light—and said, "You still think you're hungry?"

I said, "Anybody yet?" and James said low, "Eyes up," and there was a guy with some hair, not-real-stained T-shirt—staring us down, looking us up. James turned back and I nodded that it was cool, and so we backed into a booth in the back of the hall—me and James in first. A video was playing, just going out because end-names were flashing—a flick called *Bad Boys Dormitory*—and a guy fucked a guy in back of the words rolling up and the music was warbled and James kicked a wad of Kleenex that'd been floor-stuck onto my shoe and I kicked it to a corner.

The guy said "Hi," and dropped quarters into the slot on the wall, and in the flicker-light of *Bad Boys Dormitory* I couldn't see what he looked like, just saw a mustache and stubble.

His hands got on us—left on James's butt, right going down my front—and the guy said, "Time to play with the doggie," and we rubbed him, then James jingled the change in the guy's pockets.

"It's gonna take more of this," James said.

"Both?"

"Two for one," I said.

"How much?"

"Sixty"—James looked quick at me, then the guy looked at me.

"Fifty," the guy said, and me and James said "Okay," at the same time.

James already had him unbuttoned, and the guy was playing with my hair and then holding and then pushing, pushing my head down hard—and I caught a big whiff of everything in the booth—old shoes and old Kleenex and old come and Old Spice and bleached-out concrete—but he pulled on my hair and stopped my head at his crotch and then he whipped it out. "Pet the doggie. Play with the fuckin' doggie."

James put his mouth on the guy's mouth and the guy quit talking and then a couple of seconds later there was a whiff of something else and I looked up and the guy was sniffing from a little yellow bottle—sucking Rush—and he passed it to James, then down to me. I smelled in the bottle, got some, handed it back up and slowed sucking the guy, put a hand up, out on the video-screen, kept steady.

The guy said, "I got better shit than this."

James stopped feeling him and I stopped, took a big breath. "Cola?" James asked.

"Crystal."

I caught James looking at me in the video-flicker, looking and thinking, and he said low, "Crystal goes good with X," and we started back up.

"For bucks and dope," the guy said, "I'm gonna need more."

James nodded at me and got over, took my spot in front of the guy, and James pushed his jeans down to his ankles and the guy grabbed my hair, pulled my face into his while he tried to get into James, James squeezing my other hand, making noise but not saying anything.

The guy said, "Goddammit!"—dug into his pants and stuck a pock-etful of quarters into my other hand, then said, "Nope. Goddammit. Your friend's just too cherry—get me some more of that Rush, would you."

James let my hand go and got the door open and I got out and it went closed and I leaned back on a hall-wall and stood and rubbed my face and then I heard the video flicking off, then coins dropping, falling behind me.

Through the hall and past the bald-heads that stared, and hands that came out, and past the men going in and out of the doors—through the whole way up to the lighted counter part—there was that clanking and whirring, the vid-machines starting up, more going on again.

I tripped on some rug at the counter, and the counterguy looked at me and said to come up front, head of the line, past a fat black guy in running shorts who was scoping out fag-mags, handfulling the free rubbers. Counterguy pulled up a Rush and I spilled the quarters onto the glass top—silver-tipping black, pink, and red dildos under-neath. The black guy watched me go back and the bell on the door kept going off. The place was crowding more, some more jingling pockets, some more eyes in bald heads, coming in, pouring out of the hall, roaming.

In the hall, I popped open the Rush—sucked—guys roaming and jingling by me. Then I started moving and kept moving because they'd pull on the crotch, crush the butt, suck your neck when you weren't looking and I looked at doors, all the doors down the hall, and I rubbed my head and stopped in the hall and rubbed my eyes.

Guys came by close and I pushed things out of my hands—other hands, money, a dick, and heard, "Lookin' for me?" "Lookin' for fun?"

and, "C'mon boy, c'mon boy," and clank, clank, clank, clank—but no "Pet the doggie, play with the doggie."

Then, for a second, the hall got clear and I got to our door, pushed it and inside it was empty.

Empty.

Dark.

No *Bad Boys Dormitory* flicker-light.

And somebody pushed after me—said, "Son, you're blocking the—" then two, three more guys were pushing in—one saying, "In or out, sweetie"—one saying, "Shit're get off the pot"— and change went on the floor, and then two, three more guys after that and the Rush hit the floor and Rush-smell flew, and I said, "James—fuck, you fuck— where're you at?"

I dodged the hands, made it to the hall again, and mazed the other halls, looking, circling around, and in a couple seconds saw the same faces—then stopped because I was in the back part—darkest part of the place—all open booths, where some old guys stood, standing and shaking and jacking off and crowding each other in.

I bolted—mazed out of there—for anywhere outside, passed the counterlight—stopped at the counter and looked at counterguy— counterguy put a finger up, pointed at the door. The black guy in the running shorts had a stack of fag-mags, a little pink dildo, and was staring and I said—*"What the fuck're you lookin' at?"*

Counterguy wrapped up the dildo and I booked out.

Back on Third—outside—I looked around, took some big breaths and ran. I ran to Sixth, crossed Taylor toward the Square, jammed on till Stark—where two cop cars—a state trooper and a Metro-cop—

were parked and lit up in front of O'Bryant Square—blocking my shortcut, so I had to cut back, take Park Avenue to Burnside—to down-downtown—and dodge all the Burnside night traffic-scene—cars coming down from Washington Park—and I breathed hard, said loud, "Don't be in one of them."

Somebody yelled, "Boy!"—yellow car, real small, before Tenth or Eleventh, at a stoplight—and my breath came out fast and there was sweat on my nose and my eyes and I spit—nailed the driver's-side windshield and crossed the street, then heard him screeching back till he almost sideswiped me before I could touch curb.

Maybe three blocks from the City-club—running past the loading docks—I got coughing and spit but didn't slow up. I could see people in front of the club—a lit-up dead warehouse—but no James—Branch and Jody and Nikki.

"You fuck—you're way late!"

"Where's the cash, wonderboy?"

"Where's James?"

"David—what the fuck's going on? Where the fuck is James?"

Nikki ran up and sleeved off my sweat—I pushed her off, said, "James . . . isn't inside?"

"—haven't seen him since you left—"

"—Is he in trouble? Where is—"

"—need cash now!"

I got caught in a cough, said, "He might be getting fucking snuffed!"

I turned around, got in the doorway, went to the bouncer—said, "I gotta find somebody"—he said, "Five minutes," and somebody followed me in—Nikki—and we looked around the walls of Square-people—checking faces—looking to catch James's face in the cigarette-light, or in the dance-floor backlash, went fast up to the

Other Side—dark dance-room upstairs—and looked over everybody in black and then jammed back down to the Big Floor—looking over heads and looking around people in the corner seats—and then he got in, James slipped in maybe ten yards away, and he caught us looking—he caught my eyes—and he stopped.

I nailed him.

I got from midfloor into his body—my face in his stomach—and got him down and waled on his chest, had him down by my knees, by a hand on his throat, and my fist came down, two more times under his ribs and he let out air and coughed and blood from my jumping him came out of his nose. By the throat—a bouncer pulled me up—I couldn't feel him, could only tell I was up and going up I cut loose on James's leg with mine—then another shot—kicking for—missing—a rib, a stomach, a face—and slipped and the bouncer headlocked my skull, crunched his hand into my head, crunched and held, walking me till I was through the hall and outside.

Outside, James was standing and bleeding.

"You fuck. You couldn't even wait."

He said, "Chill much, Davy, it was just *drugs.* I just wanted crystal and it was in his car. There's nothing to . . . bug on."

"You fucked me over. You know you fucked me over," and I coughed and James rubbed his eye and the side of his head.

"I'm sorry," he said.

"Fuck you are."

"I am. It went so fucking fast. We ditched the booth, got in his car—got high on one stupid little line each—drove around—barely wired—then he starts diddling himself, driving and diddling, then he parks the car, starts diddling me, then goes down on me and—"

"Doesn't—fuck with you—or anything?"

"No. Does me. Then reaches into his pocket—like he was gonna get the cash—and—gets out his teeth. His fucking *teeth*, Davy. Sticks them back in his mouth. I didn't—y'know—couldn't—tell. I was all like, Oh, this old thing isn't *too* bad, but, then, oh, the *teeth*. So I bailed out. Right over there. We were going maybe ten miles an hour and I bailed out. Fucker just took off."

He rubbed the back of his head and said, "I'm in pain, Davy," then he rubbed around his nose, around a crumpled up corner of a City-club flyer stuck up to cut the bleeding, then looked down his T-shirt collar, said, "There's a bruise coming up, right on a tit," then looked at me and said, "You gonna go off on me again?"

I looked back at the people outside of the City door. Jody sat on the steps with a couple club people and Branch stood up the street and smoked and Nikki stood by Branch and looked at me.

"You want to though?" James said.

I looked at James, then looked away. We stood by some garbage cans and I looked at one, kicked it. Dented it. The lid went rolling. Everybody looked over. The lid rolled and rolled and rolled, then finally clanked flat like a big fucking quarter.

At the end of summer I missed that night. It was *night and I was at a rest stop right before Kelso, Washington, standing in front of a candy machine digging in a pocket for change with one hand, looking at the video-tokens in my other hand from Sin City or Hart's, flipping them over, the side with the tits that said "Heads You Win" to the side with the chick's ass that said "Tails You Win" and back. Nikki was way around the bathrooms out of most of the rest-stop-light, holding our backpack, walking up and down a concrete path around some picnic tables in front of a big patch of trees, yelling low at me, "Davy, there's action here," and the pickup we'd scored a ride from was rumbling loud out of the rest area and back into I-5 night-traffic, driver-guy too nervous to take us anymore north, freaked he'd get caught hauling minors in his truck-bed, across state lines too. Nikki started walking back to me so I dropped a couple tokens into the machine and she said, "Those work there?" and I shrugged, hit the Snickers button, but nothing came out, and I hit cheese crackers and nothing and I dropped in more, a whole bunch, and Nikki, up in candy-machine-light, said, "Those don't work there!" and I said, "I know, but it gets rid of em," put in every one I had.*

"Davy, there's . . . action here."

We walked up to the picnic tables and stared into the dark trees and there were orange cherries from smokes lighting up and some coughs and clearing throats and I just stood there, still thinking about tokens, mind going off on when me and James'd skipped a park-deal Branch'd lined up for us, me and James going to the waterfront instead, whipping out all our tokens and skipping them across the Willamette, then sitting for a couple hours on a bench, James leaned up to my shoulder, head under my head, kissing my chin, and later, when we'd all met up again, we'd told Branch that the john he got us never showed. I'd said, "Must've found two boys cheaper," and James'd said, "Impossible," and Branch'd just said, "Shit," been pissed the rest of the night.

And in the rest-stop trees some of the glowing cherries went flying all of a sudden and got stamped out and Nikki, looking right at me, said, "Hey—don't—if you can't, that's cool—" and she pointed to the freeway, said, "I can get the next ride."

I rubbed my eyes, nodded. "You wanna do that? Just till we get somewhere. I mean a city. I'll do it then."

She reached up and rubbed the stuff from my eyes off my face and I reached over and picked the pack up off her shoulder, put it on mine, and we started walking to the freeway entrance, Nikki staying on the left, for traffic, so much of the summer coming on in my head that I had to get the headphones out of the backpack, drop behind Nikki some, let her start thumbing and I slipped the phones on, turned on Bleach, right at "About a Girl," right at "I need an easy friend," slow and low, so much of everything coming on that I had to sit, right in the shoulder, not far out of the rest stop, and just crank it.

Toilet Training
(The ABC's)

A couple days into this summer, it rained. Me and Nikki were still in Eugene, by the Rose Garden Park, and a ways into the night—by ten, ten-thirty or so, maybe—it'd stopped, and looked like it was going to stay clear for a while. We ditched our spot under the Washington-Jefferson Bridge, headed up the riverbank, past the bum camps, into the Rose Garden, and to the bathrooms right by the bikepath.

The mud squished loud and Nikki almost slipped but we made it through the grass, shortcutting to the bathroom lights. We toured around the johns—me, mostly, ahead—Nikki keeping back but keeping eyes open. I did a quick check on the boys' side, and all the stalls were empty, pretty much as we figured, as early as it was, but two of the middle stalls had empty Coors cans, and the last stall had a few stubbed out butts and a lot of new smoke.

I came out of the johns and Nikki was drinking at the water fountain right in front. I looked long around—down the bikepath, to the

trees off to the side, way over to the lights by the school-district building, back to the park, to the bushes and dark on the other side, by
the park's parking lot, then up the bikepath, and the bushes and trees
next to where we came from, and there wasn't anybody. Nikki looked
up, wiped her mouth, and said, "Let's bench it," said she didn't see
anybody either. My stomach bitched loud—I grabbed a drink of
water—and we squished over to a bench pretty far out of the parking-
lot-light, parked it, Nikki pulling my arm around her.

She pulled out a hunk of Snickers bar from her back pocket, broke
it in two and I took the hunk with the most nuts, too big, broke it
apart some more, gave her back some, but she said, "Take it." We
munched and my stomach still bitched so Nikki bitched back at it,
told it to shut up, thumped it, then—spotting something—got off my
arm and stomach and said, "There he is," pointed to a kid coming up
the bikepath, going into the boys'-side john—a kid we'd seen, four or
five nights ago, cruising a couple nights in a row.

"Maybe a cop," Nikki said.

"Too young," I said. And, "He's a kid. He's just like us."

"Maybe," she said. And then, "Check him out?" so I got up—but
the kid'd come out—was already off and out of sight, cruising the
outskirts. I turned around, popped buttons, peed in some roses by
the bench. Nikki said, "Prob'ly a cop."

"He's way young," I said.

"A dope cop," she said. "He's scoping for deals," and then, "or
maybe he's a dealer."

"He's just like us," I said, shaking my dick. There were other
voices—two older guys—coming up past the bikepath side trees and
when they got to the bathrooms, they stopped talking and looked
around, stood and waited till one of them—smoking—took a last couple of drags, stubbed out his cigarette—then they went in.

I was already buttoning up, set to jam, when Nikki said, "Shit!" and I turned around, saw the other kid cruising up fast out of nowhere and already into the boy's side. "He's takin' them," Nikki said.

"I fucking told you," I said.

"Fucker can't do both," she said.

"I'm going," I said, got out of the bushes, started up to the johns. I heard her say, "Watch out," real low, looked back, saw her climb up, park it on the back of the bench, start spitting down into the seat cracks.

I squished around and up to the john lights. When I got to the open john doors, I looked back again—seeing if I could see Nikki—and couldn't—she was hidden in all the dark. Car-lights came up, in the parking lot behind her, and a couple of cars came through, but nobody stopped, came in.

There was a splashy clank, clank—from the johns—and when I stepped in I saw the Coors empties rolling around and out from under a stall—the back, back stall—and then another one, fairly full, rolled after it, nailed the empties, spilled Coors, and made a quick puddle that spread big and squished loud when I moved up to the last stall.

There were shoes under the last stall—drowning in beer, but not moving—and when I looked around the stall wall the two guys standing—one holding a Coors, drinking—and the kid that beat me there—holding one dick, sucking the other—didn't move, didn't look back or around. The guy with the beer drank, kind of looked back, handing the can to the other guy, who didn't turn around at all, didn't drink, just put the beer on the kid's head, and with his other hand, pulled the other guy's dick out of the kid's mouth, put in his. The other guy wanted more, put his dick back in too, and the kid couldn't really handle, take, suck both, slipped off the pot, to his knees—squishing around in the beer puddle till he got so he could take them

both. My foot pinched a can—a cracky, small crunch from me peek-
ing around, checking out how the kid was doing it, how it was done—
but nobody turned, looked up, so I scooted back, stepped back over
the rolling empties, and out of the john.

There was smoke outside, right in my face—a guy by the water
fountain blew out a big wad of it, then soaked his butt in the water,
looking at me the whole time—but I squished around the cloud and
him, new lights from the parking lot coming up, and two cars coming
in slow, over by the school-district building, and a couple more little
bike lights coming down the bikepath. When I got to our bench in
the bushes, I checked back—and with all the other lights coming
in—the bathroom light didn't seem that bright anymore.

Nikki asked what's going on, and I didn't say anything, so she hit
my arm, said, "So what the fuck's goin' on?" and I didn't look at her,
just kept her eyes on the bathroom, just said, "He's no cop."

Kid was in for a while—ten minutes probably and then the two
guys came out, but not the kid. The two guys split a beer, wandered
behind the bathrooms, off down the bikepath, drank, walked,
chucked the empty, and the kid still hung inside.

New guys—maybe four, five, half a dozen—wandered, roamed in
the john-light, but nobody went in, nobody wanted to pay. One—the
one who'd blown smoke at my face—came back, smoked by the fountain again, was there for a while—like he was willing to pay, had
cash—drowned and flicked his butt, then went in.

"Jam," Nikki said—and I was already up the path—at the johns
even before his smoke could've blown away. Smoker-guy hadn't made
it back to the stalls yet—he was up front, turned around at the first

wall-pisser—didn't look up, and I went right beside him, stuck my head into the sink, turned the spout on, got a long drink.

He had his face kind of turned, and his fingers were moving over his dick, belt buckle jingling. I stopped my drink, turned my head to look at his face, but he kept most of his head down. I grabbed a paper towel from the other wall, started drying and warming my hands, looking down at the kid's shoes still sticking out, sticking in beer, empties around them, no pants around his ankles, and then I moved in, up behind wall-pisser guy, and said, "Man, need a hand with that? 'Cause for bucks I can maybe—" and then his face came around and up from his dick—smiling pretty big—and I said, "Oh man!" stutter shit—"Oh, shit, man—no way, no day"—and I jammed.

Nikki wasn't back at the bench, was wandering around the roses, behind the bushes, looking over to the parking-lot-light, checking for any new cars and cops. She said, "That was too fast."

"I didn't do him."

"Fuck!" She turned, spit quick in the roses.

I said, "It's Asshole. The Asshole."

"Oh, *fuck*. Sonofafuck," and she came over, back into my dark spot, started to say, "The dick that—" but I cut her close, said, "Yeah—right before the rain."

"What'd he do? Did he fuckin' try anything? What'd he try?" She was pulling at my arm, looking around me, up to the johns, then jumped on the bench to look around, see more. "He's still there, right?" she said. "Asshole's still in there?"

I said yeah—said they both were.

"Cool," she said. "Way fuckin' cool."

"Why cool?" I said.

She hopped down, told me to just watch the bathrooms—johns were coming up from somewhere, squishing around in the rain-grass, and a couple more were floating close to the fountain, but nobody was going in. And Nikki—up behind me—said, " 'Cause that sonofa-fuck that tore your shit's probably stiffin' that new kid right now is why." Her arms—fairly to really warm—came around my middle, and she talked up, low into my ear, "Dissin' the competition is why," she said, pulled her arms down low to my butt, and scooted me, started me moving, started us walking up the john path, said, "C'mon—let's get closer."

We went around, came up on the grass behind the johns, squish-ing over to and parking it on a picnic table off to the side, in the back of some bathroom-light. We listened close—Nikki said she heard the "Unh-humm" 's and "Oh yeah-yeah" 's of a deal being cut or going on already. One of the two guys that'd been walking around walked over to our table, sat on the other side, said, "Summer at last, maybe, humm?" and "Looks like the rain's gone at least," then asked for a light but we just heard him, didn't look at him, saw the other floater slip into the johns and come out way fast, head low, looking around, and Nikki laughed real low, said, "Oh yeah—it's going on in there."

A second after her last giggle, we heard "You *fuck!* You old fuck!"— and the Asshole was out—jangling his belt buckle and pants together, and walking fast—out of the john-light, off into the rest of the dark park. The kid came out—a couple seconds after him—yelling more, "You old fuck!" 's, and the guy at our table got up, took off, squishing fast away.

Nikki was cracking up and I kind of laughed—mostly just watching the kid. He spit a lot—shirting his mouth dry—then spit some more, then stomped over to the water fountain, got two drinks—not swallowing—turning—spitting out the mouthfuls. His last spit came close to us.

"Somethin' fuckin' funny?" he said. "You fuckin' think I'm funny?" and he started coming over. "You think that old fuck's funny?"

I shut up, Nikki giggled some more—one more time big.

He squished up closer to Nikki. "Hey babe," he said, "aren't you in the wrong fuckin' park?"

I scooted up closer, right next to Nikki, said, "She's with me." And then, "That all right?"

"You think I'm funny, too?" he said, getting into my space. "You dicks know that old fuck, maybe?"

"He's a sonofafuck," Nikki said.

The kid took a couple steps back—"You know him? You know that dickwad?"—looked at me—"He do you or somethin'? He fuck you over? Hey—you get fucked over, too?"

I looked over to Nikki—her face getting spotlighted by a string of car lights coming through—then looked back at the kid, said, "Yeah, I know." I said, "Fucker'd give you twenty-five for fuckin' you—big fifty if you let him . . . took his load . . ." Kid didn't move. Stayed, no squishing. "So then he gets you flat up," I said, "pants down—and he's got this . . . gotta monster fuckin' dick, right?—and he's goin' at it, and does it—blows it all in—and everything—then he jams. Just fuckin' takes off. No cash—total nothing. Right? Pretty much?"

He backed up more, wasn't looking at me or Nik, was looking off and squishing around, backing off. "Just head," he said, wiping his shoes in the grass. "It was head for a ten spot, and twenty for takin' it."

I looked at Nikki.

"Head's all?" she said—another car light catching her—only this time, the light stayed and she stared at it. "Cop," she said, and we looked over, saw the cop car stopped and searchlighting the park.

Me and Nikki got off the table—"C'mon," the kid said—"Follow me," and he said—"My place"—and we followed him, squished around the johns, down the bikeway, then off the path and down a bank, to a clear spot in the river bushes—the big light coming around, flashing everything above ground again. "This'll be cool for a couple seconds," he said, moving around, clearing some of his shit—shirts, a black jacket, tapes, a Raiders cap, couple *Penthouses*, Walkman, Pop-Tarts box—and crouching back against the big weeds. Other voices came down the river and I looked through the weeds, saw bums crawled up from their bum camps, looking over the bank for cops.

"Lazyass motherfuckers," the kid said. "These cops don't even get out of their fuckin' cars," he said. "Usually."

Nikki said, "Usually," then, "So—what's your name?"

He said Branch, and Nikki asked what the fuck kind of name was Branch.

"Californian," said Branch.

The bums were laughing and I looked past Nikki, watched them through the weeds crawling back into their space. The searchlight'd stopped and there was only some glare left from the closed mall across the river. Branch got up and whizzed into the weeds. I took and looked at a *Penthouse* and Nikki crawled up the bank to look over the bikepath.

"I think he's still there," she said, and then the big light came around again. Nikki came down, and Branch buttoned and got back with us. I squinted at the mag—used the big light when it came around—making out a few lines of a JO letter—hard-up guy puts peanut butter on his dick, gets dog to lick it till he comes—and Branch asked who we were, where the fuck we were headed.

"Dave and Nikki," said Nikki, looking at his tapes, and "We don't know where—do we, Dave?" and I said, "Anywhere but here," turned a page but it stuck.

"I'm going more north," he said. "Portland. I know people in Portland."

I looked up to Nikki, already staring at me. I put down the mag.

"What?" Branch said. "You guys thinking 'bout Portland?"

Nikki picked up his Raiders cap, said, "Thinking about it."

"You know that's *real*," Branch said—looking at the hat—"That ain't no fake. I'm from there. That ain't no fake."

Nikki put the cap on. The big light'd quit. She climbed back up, looked around, said the cop car'd left, said it was totally dark, and had to be eleven-thirty, and Branch said "Why eleven-thirty?" and Nikki said, " 'Cause the john lights go out at eleven-thirty." Then said, "Shit. I don't fuckin' believe it, no way," and then, "Get up, get up here," and me and Branch crawled up, looked over the cement to the bathrooms.

There was nobody around—except for one guy, right by the water fountain, smoking in whatever was left of park-light.

"He's back," said Branch.

"No shit," I said.

"Sonofafuck," Nikki said.

Branch came down and so did I. Branch said, "That's him, yeah that's him—the fuckin' balls. *Man*, what fucking balls."

I reached around for rocks, got a couple, then three fairly flat ones, stood up and whizzed one out through the river weeds, hearing it plop-plop-plop on the river, then I skipped another one upriver, waking the bums, a couple or more of them grumbling "fucks" 's."

"We gotta fuck him over," Branch said. "Take him out of this scene. You wanna fuck this guy over?"

"Roll him?" Nikki asked, up the bank, looking out.

"No—rip him," Branch said. "Just a mind-fuck."

"That'd be hard," I said. "I mean—he knows us all," and Nikki, looking down, right at me and Branch, said quick, "Asshole doesn't know *me*"—and Branch reached up, flicked Nikki—right on the Raiders brim—said fast, "Choice fuckin' hat, huhn?" and I skipped my last rock.

Me and Branch sat low on a bench behind a tree by the bikepath, facing the Willamette. Nikki stood behind us—on the path.

"He's still there, right?" Branch said.

"Uh-humm," she said.

I peeked around—watched her stuff a few loose pieces of hair back into the hat. Branch slugged me. *"Don't fucking stare,"* he said. "Don't let that dickwad see us." We were fairly close to the johns—and even though the john lights were out, a few path lights up the way still glowed. I turned back, stared at the river again, the closed-mall lights, heard Nikki moving the hat some more, screwing with and zipping up Branch's black jacket.

"Okay," she said, "check me out, I'm ready."

We turned around. I stared.

"Whoa," Branch said.

"You look like . . . you're maybe my little brother," I said.

"You gotta brother?" Branch said.

"No," I said.

"How's my hair?" Nikki asked.

"In-fucking-visible," Branch said.

She said " 'Kay—cool," kissed me fast, started to the johns.

"Keep your head low," I said low, and Branch said to her, "Scratch your dick."

We waited quite a while—watching the water—before looking back again. Asshole was leaning against the water fountain, just lighting up again, lots of smoke around the johns and Nikki walked around him, head low, hands in her pockets.

"Walks like she got a dick," Branch said, and, "Knows how to work it."

"Been watchin' me," I said, and Asshole walked around Nikki, looking at the Raiders hat, Nikki's sort of boy-butt.

She walked slow, started into the men's side, then stopped, leaned up against the wall by the open door, kept her head real low. Asshole stood up real straight, smoking and watching her.

"He's totally buyin' it," Branch said.

Nikki coughed. I said, "Good cough," and Branch said, "Hard, from the balls," then Nikki itched her crotch and then went in.

The guy reached around, got the water on, doused his cigarette, flicked it, and went in.

"Sold," Branch said.

"Let's get closer," I said.

We squished straight across the grass, sat up on the picnic table me and Nikki'd been on. Branch said he couldn't see good enough—I said me neither—so we got off, pulled the table around, till we were just about facing the doorway to the men's side. Car lights came up, I got up, looked around—a new guy was coming out of the roses. He came up, looked around us, and went to the bathrooms.

"*Occupado,* man," Branch said—nice and low—and I said "Big

time *occupado*," and the guy wandered back around and off. I looked at the rest of the park, cars came through the lot, but nobody else was coming.

Branch said, "Listen"—and I looked back—"He's cuttin' the deal. He's goin' for head again"—and I could hear Nikki saying all the right "Uh-hummm" 's and "Right" 's real deep. I moved off, walked closer to the doorway, Branch behind me, and we both looked slow around the corner.

Car-light made us shadows for a second—on the far wall in the john—our heads spotlighted under a big black patch of graffiti, but Nikki and the john—down in the last stall—must not've seen anything, weren't talking at all. We heard an empty rolling, and a clink—belt buckle coming undone, then a clank—belt buckle going down on concrete, then his "Good-good-yeah-good" 's with Nikki's low and deep "Uh-hums" 's, and we moved in closer, going from stall to stall—-then got into the next-to-last, got up against them.

I looked around, Branch looking around me—and there was a loud "Hmmm" from him, Asshole's monsterdick jamming into the dark under her hat—and his hand, going over her head—pushed and pulled—till it finally flicked the hat off, and her hair came down everywhere—all over him—and she laughed, laughing on his dick, and the guy's fingers stopped in her hair, and "A fish—" came out, "—a goddamn girl!" came out, bounced loud all over the stalls, and monsterdick died into nothing—right there—soft and gone, and Branch was laughing now, slapping me over, clanking me down into the empties and I tried to push up but my hands slipped on beer and I fell into the guy's pants-crotch—his balls and belt buckle hanging right over my face so I flicked his nuts and laughed and the guy looked down—yelled more "Goddamn" 's—pissed that I was on top of the clothes he was trying to pull up. He kicked empties around, kicked me off, pushed Nikki, grabbed up his clink-clanky clothes and got out—Branch pulled me up, Nikki pushed behind me—and we went off after him, outside, got to the edge of the grass, stopping and watching him squish off—going for the kind-of-lit bikepath, then turning, changing his mind, jamming over to the bright parking lot—and out of the park.

Nikki ran back in—came right back out with the hat—held it, stood flat against the wall and said—"Next."

We looked around the water fountain for a while, looking at the ground for big cigarette stubs. Branch said he'd been jonesing for one all night. Lights came up, cars rolled in and out of the parking lot, one—coming in by the school-district building—parked, and the driver-guy got out, started walking in.

Branch said, "This is stupid here, a total waste of time."

Nikki said, "Got one," stood up, held up a big stub.

I watched the guy head into the park through the roses.

"Nobody's got any money here," Branch said. "Nobody fucking pays."

"It's a small fucking town is why," Nikki said. "Branch—you gotta light?" and Branch said, "You guys should hitch with me. Portland's bigger—way bigger. Straights, breeders, Beamer-fags—everything," and Nikki said, "Maybe. That's maybe where we're headed," then—"Davy, what d'you think?" and I stopped looking at the bushes, got a quick drink from the fountain. I looked at Nikki and wiped my mouth. I said, "Yeah, cool, the big city."

"Sure?" Nikki said, and I said "Yeah," again, said, "We're not makin' shit here," and Nikki said to Branch again, "You gotta light or what?"

"Somewhere," Branch said, and they turned to go back to Branch's camp—Branch saying, "I got places," and "I know people," Nikki asking about the park scene up there—me staying back—still by the johns, hanging at the fountain, watching the new lights coming up, watching the new guy come in closer.

"What're you doin'?" Nikki said loud, turned around.

I put my hand on my stomach—it'd just gone off—and rubbed up and down. "I gotta dump," I said, and started into the john, and Branch said a loud, "Look out for assholes," and took them both back over the bank.

I kicked out one last empty left on the floor in the last stall, popped buttons, pulled my pants down, sat down on the cold pot. A car-light came up and a shadow came in. I held in my load. The guy came down, around the stalls, stood in front of me, crunching his crotch.

"How much for this thing?" he said.

"Nothin'," I said. "Free."

He unbuckled and unzipped. I tightened my butt to the pot.

He poked around in the dark in front of my face, poking my eye, hitting my nose, then touching dick to lips. I opened my mouth and let go. Everything blew out—plop-plop-plop—smell coming up everywhere.

"Christ!" he said, "You pig—you fucking pig!" and he pulled out, zipped up, jangled out—rolling, kicking, crunching the empties. Car-light came in—right after him—and I caught something on the wall—graffiti on the wall where the guy'd been standing—"Smile if your shit stinks."

I grabbed some paper, laughed low, wiped and flushed.

The Walkman clicked and switched sides and I opened my eyes in the couple seconds of quiet before "Scoff" came on and Nikki was still standing, staring down the road for lights, but the northbound was black and only one set of white-yellow lights were coming over the divider from the south side. Music started and I turned it down, pulled my legs up, got my chin on my chest, but kept my eyes open, didn't have to close them because both lanes were going black, and I watched the last of the southbound light go over and shine up, for a second, the two pink-polish smears on the side of Nikki's boot-toe.

Before Nikki wasn't much. Last summer my mom followed this guy, turned into a boyfriend, up from Ashland to Eugene and we stayed with him till they broke up and then we stayed in my grandma's trailer right outside Eugene, then my mom found a new guy and one night they went to Oklahoma and I ended up staying in the trailer with my grandma and some cousins. And also my dad lived in Corvallis but drove a truck all over with my stepmom so never really stayed in Oregon for one long time.

The trailer was outside town but there were a couple of city buses into town so I'd bus in for school but only went there a few times, till I met Nikki, right at spring, smoking in the soccer field where I was hanging, sitting, being by myself. She came over to me, sitting in front of some trees, stood above me and said, "You're, like, always out here," and I said, "How do you know?" and she said, " 'Cause I watch you," then I said, "But I'm not doin' anything." She was quiet a couple seconds, then said, "So what do you come out here for?" and I said, "I guess space," and she flicked her cigarette, stepped on it, then sat, right by me. She had black and silver-eyed Docs just like me, but smaller, and one smear of pink polish on one boot-side but I looked at her fingernails and they were blank. I pointed at the pink boot-smear and said, "You don't wear that." She looked at me and smiled and reached into her back pocket and pulled out a bottle of pink nail polish and held it up.

"It's my locker partner's," she said. "She put up a Natalie Merchant poster." She opened the lid, pulled up her boot and brushed another smear above the first, took a whiff from the smear, looked at me and I leaned in, sniffed, then we both leaned back and she capped the bottle tight, turned and threw it into the trees behind us, then bent forward again and blew on the new smear.

I said, "What do you listen to?" and she said, "Whatever my friends've got," and I said, "What's that, usually?" and she said, "Nothing, now. My friends moved, back East, both of them." She quit blowing, sat back, asked me what I was into and I said, "Everything but fuckin' Ten Thousand Maniacs," and she smiled again and we sat and didn't talk much more than that, both of us just there, listening to class buzzers going off. After a couple times, couple days, doing that we got to talking more, got to walking around downtown, into the park past downtown where we'd hang more, bench it and talk, lie in the big grass-patch in front of the water fountain and make out or go fuck on the riverbank and smoke till the last buses, neither of us wanting to head home. Both her homes were dead, she said, mom's and dad's, and she'd fight with everybody—mom, dad, stepmom—just to make noise, make sure they were alive, staying at her dad and stepmom's when she was fighting too much with her mom—and the other half of the time the other way around.

And when it'd start to get dark in the park, guys'd start driving through the parking lot and if we were sitting on the bench by the lot and I was up on the edge, sometimes they'd whistle and Nikki'd look up and say, "We could jam—another part of the park," but I'd say I was tired of walking, sitting was still cool. One time Nikki got up, going for smokes at a 7-Eleven, a little ways out of the park, and a car came around and the guy whistled, then parked, right in front of me. I looked around the park, heard him say, "Hi," low. I got up and his door lock popped. I took a step and he pushed the door open. I got in and he rolled up the windows and we diddled, I touched his, he blew mine. I thought it went pretty fast but Nikki caught me getting out and my face got hot and while the car was driving away Nikki said, "You get money or anything?" I shook my head and we got back on the bench but I sat on the seat and she said, "Hey, up," so I got back on the edge and she put her face up, smiling into mine. "I . . . just wanted to," I said, and she said, "I know. I knew," kissed me. "But you could get money, I bet, and we could maybe get outta here."

When I got in that night one of my cousins, real little, was asleep on my grandma, sleeping on the couch, cousin's head up by hers, his mouth open, drool on her glasses, crooked on her face, and two more cousins, almost my age, watched TV on the floor and they both looked up, said, "Hey," and my grandma looked up, glasses falling, and while she reached down to get them, holding up the cousin still sleeping, she said the phone company'd called me that day, wanting me to pay for a big phone bill left over from Ashland, and I bent and got the glasses before Grandma, gave them to her, watched her get them on straight, then said that my mom'd got me a Social Security number and we'd used that number to get a phone in Ashland because they wouldn't take hers because all her credit was real bad, and she'd told me a long time ago that they couldn't come after me for any of the bill because I was a minor and my little cousin coughed, hard, coughing himself awake, and my grandma looked at me and nodded and patted my little cousin's back.

When I woke up next morning, real early, I made my part of the bed and walked around my cousins and put a couple T-shirts in my backpack and felt around the bottom of the pack for bus change and left. And then that afternoon me and Nikki were making out, getting close to fucking on the riverbank, and an old guy came around the bush we were lying behind, watched us, pulled at his crotch and smoked. I watched him over Nikki's head then Nikki looked back and got up, looked at me and I got up. She moved around me and pushed on the bottom of my back and I went toward him. I looked down and undid my jeans. The guy came up closer and Nikki came around me, got between us for a couple seconds, then the guy pulled a ten from the smokes-pack in his shirt pocket and Nikki took it then got out of the way. He bent down, let the cigarette go out of his mouth, started to stub it out but Nikki reached down fast and got it, put it in her mouth. The guy blew out his last wad of smoke then went down on me and Nikki sat and smoked against the bush.

The last ride after a bunch of rides we caught on I-5 got

Nikki and me and Branch into Portland in early morning, dropped us
off at Washington Park, on the road up behind the tennis courts, and
a guy jogging came down the road, around us, breath showing because
it was still cold, not looking at us because he wasn't slither, Branch
said. Branch said that the part of Washington Park we were in wasn't
anything but Nikki said we wanted to see it anyway. Me and Nikki
went through some parking spaces, up to a low stone wall with stairs
going down and we climbed the wall, stood up on it, looked down,
then out. Under us was a hill, rose bushes all around it, making a big
square, and inside the square were rows of rose plants and behind
the plants, in front of us, were city buildings, and behind them, a
mountain.

"What's that?" I said.

"Hood," Branch said, and he turned my shoulders left, pointed to another mountain, left of Hood, further back behind the city and said, "That's Saint Helens."

"It's so huge," Nikki said.

"Which one?" I said.

"The park," Nikki said, looking back down. "All this right here."

"But nothin's up here," Branch said. "No slither. There's where's slither." He pointed down and left, to a little cement lake that was big and empty. The jogger we'd seen went around it. There was a road that went up beside the empty lake, up a hill, around, ended back at a big fountain with no water coming up, out, under the hill, under some swings, flagpole. "There's trails, up the hill, three levels of trails, trees on our side," Branch said. There was a house, real small, at the start of the road up the hill, across from the fountain, on our side. "That building," I said.

"That's a bathroom, dude, but that's not slither. Real action's the trails, okay, not these bathrooms," Branch said, and Nikki said, "Maybe it is," but Branch said, "Hey—it's not—it's in the middle of the whole fuckin' park and anybody can walk in and it's just too sketchy—" and Nikki said, "When were you here last?"

"Not real long ago," Branch said. "So, listen. Listen to me, all right," but Nikki'd gotten off the wall, was heading around the rose-bush outskirts and I looked at Branch.

"Man. Dave. I have been here a few times. I've been up and down here two times, Seattle to San Diego." I said okay, got down off the low wall.

Me and Branch followed Nikki down. When she got to a hedge right before the guys'-side door we ran, cut fast in front of her. The jogger, getting water from a drinking fountain next to the hedge, looked over, breathing hard. I got my hands on Nikki's shoulders, said, "This is different up here—don't be goin' off solo—we don't know here at all," and Nikki said, "*O-kay*, but someone's in there—I heard coughing and no pee or poop noise and look—" and she pointed around the hedge, to a car on a patch of road behind the hedge, and I said, "It's the jogger-guy's, probably," but the jogger stopped drinking, jogged away from the fountain, back up toward the tennis courts. I looked at Nikki then said, "Okay, but me first, for safeties," then Branch came down, stood behind Nikki and Nikki folded her arms and I went in. There was a guy at the end of some stalls without doors, standing, peeing into a tub, a piss-tub on the wall—water coming down out of holes in a pipe hanging right over the tub. He pulled his sweats up some, nodded, said something but he was holding sunglasses in his mouth so it was noise, not words. The door opened behind me and I looked back, said, "Nikki—he's pissing—and there's no piss-sound because—look—he's not hitting bowl-water or a wall-thing—it's a tub," and Nikki looked up over my shoulder and said, "Oh," and the guy said aloud, "Hey—c'mon," sunglasses falling out of his mouth into the piss-tub, and he pulled up his sweats some more, then Branch came up behind us and said, "See? Seattle to San Diego, all right? Seattle to—" but Nikki'd already backed out and Branch was following her, still saying "—San-fucking-Diego, I know the spots, the *right* spots," and the guy picked up his glasses and shook them and said, "Ray-Bans," and I said, "Shit, sorry," backed out.

We saw slither later, in the afternoon. Branch took us around the park, down some trails, and we parked it in some bushes between the trails, slept off and on till it started to get warm out. When I wasn't sleeping I was looking between leaves, watching cars, first not many, then later a lot, on a big street down under the hill, and Branch, up once with me, watching me looking, said, "That's Burnside. Goes straight through. Whole city." I asked if there was action anywhere on it and he shook his head, said, "No, it's just a street," and I said, "It's big. Too. You sure?" He said again, "It's just a street," and I leaned my head on Nikki's, closed my eyes till it was later, till Nikki pushed on me, pushed me awake, said she was seeing slither. She pointed down and I looked at Branch going down on an old guy in a patch of bushes between us and Burnside. Branch looked at us quick, then got going on him faster, hands and head, then stopped, held the dick and the guy put his head back, then down, and Branch let go of the dick, turned his head, spit on bush-leaves. Branch got up, and the guy got out money, two bills, gave them to Branch, zipped up while Branch walked up our way, wiping his mouth.

Nikki said to me, "How much was that?"

I shook my head. "Two fives?"

Coming up, Branch brushed off knee-dirt and we got up.

"Two tens," Nikki said, and I said fast, "No way," but she said, "Yeah, I bet so. You're like worth more here. Big city and all."

Up to us, Branch said that there was hardly any competition out, couple guys, not old, sitting by the big fountain under the hill, but he said they looked hooked, were just here being out together, weren't here selling it or looking to pay for it, and also there were a few guys on the hill, out to get sun, and a kid-kid, younger than us, walking, working other trails. "But this is ours," he said. "I got this side pretty much staked out for us. There's no cops and nobody pisses about payin'." I said, "Sounds cool," and Nikki put her hand in Branch's left front jeans pocket, dug around, and Branch said, "Hey—other one—" and she dug her hand in his right jeans pocket, pulled out two fives. I looked at her and she shoved them back down, said she had to pee, walked into the bushes.

" 'S up with that?" Branch said.

"Nothin'," I said. "I'm just worth the same is all."

Little bit later it started to get warmer and busier, quite a few cars coming in and Branch, still showing me around the trails, said we should split up for the guys that'd be walking up after they parked, Branch taking the trail down, me heading up, a kid—twelve, thirteen—coming down in front of me—the kid-kid Branch said he'd seen—and coming by me the little kid asked if I had a smoke, had a car, had a place we could go to, and I shook my head, kept shaking it, and then he saw Branch and cut down through the bushes and Branch looked at me, said up loud, "Fuckin' little shit—in our slither." I looked past Branch and the kid-kid crossed back to his part of the park and I said, "And anyway—Nikki's got the fuckin' smokes." Branch said low, "Little puke," back to me, walking down.

A while after that I was on the high trail going down on my first deal in Portland, Branch below me, low trail, getting done, and where I was on my knees I could see over trail-bushes and in between low-tree-branch leaves, and I could see Nikki on the swings on the hill, across Lewis and Clark Circle, not swinging, just twisting, kicking, then the guy put his hand on my head, arm in the way of seeing Nikki so I scooted my knees over some in the dirt, and could see the two guys sitting together on the big fountain, going, now, at the bottom of the hill, not looking at cars cruising by or at the kid-kid coming over to cruise them, too. They touched each other's arms and talked, laughed, and one of them leaned back into the other one's middle, then both of them got a hand down in the fountain water, splashed each other's face. The guy I was doing coughed and came and I spit and stood, and the guy got out his wallet, counted out eight bucks, started counting out two bucks more in change and over the change-noise I heard music, some bass-beats, from a car stereo, that'd maybe been there but weren't loud, now louder. I turned and looked up through leaves and a couple cars had parked in the lot, right above the high trail—one of their stereos blasting the dance-beat down—and I took all the guy'd given me so far—nine and some—and walked through the bushes, close to the edge of the lot, heard laughing then and some clapping, saw a kid my age dancing hard between two parked cars, older guys leaned against the cars, watching him, couple of them clapping. I moved a bush-branch to get a better look and the kid stopped dancing and leaned around into one car and stopped the music, said loud, "That's *too* happy," moved his arms around inside, screwed with the stereo, and something louder, less beat, came on, Temple of the Dog, "Hunger Strike," and one old guy asked loud, "Who *is* this?" and the kid said loud, "Temple of the Dog, 'Hungry,' " and another old guy said to the kid, "James, you *cannot* dance to this," and another old guy said, "Who's 'Temple of the—' *what*?" and the kid said to that guy, "*Dog*—and they're part Pearl Jam, part Soundgarden"—and said to another guy—"And Kent, you go like this—" started thrashing fast between the cars and everybody. One guy put his hand up to his face and shook his head and then the kid stopped moving, but still breathing hard, said, "Disco—is *not* the only fucking beat on this planet," then I got pushed in the back and Branch came around, said, "Ante up, dude." I gave him what I'd got and he pocketed it, said to follow him, because there was someone, a car he saw go by during his last deal, that he was sure he knew from his last run through Portland, parked down by the fountain and I looked back down and there was a car by the fountain and the two guys talking, laughing and splashing were gone. Branch looked out to the kid in the lot—back to dancing hard to Temple of the Dog—and shook his head, said, "Freak," cut back down to the trail and I turned, started down, but stopped a couple times quick and looked back, watched James thrash.

Rain

Rain

We slept up to high trees in the park at nights and it was warm but a few nights into Portland it rained and we got close together to a tree with tons of leaves over us but still got soaked, didn't sleep, started the day looking for dry space somewhere downtown, but close to the park, rain staying back till afternoon when we were all the way down around Fifteenth, in front of two big dead buildings, one with two shopping carts full of cans and glass-empties in front, and a bum sacked out on the sidewalk in between the carts. We went around the other building, and a door on the side was totally boarded, but we found a broken window in back, kind of high, flowertops stuck in the window-cracks, and we climbed into the building, Branch climbing in okay, Nikki's boot catching some of the flowertops, but my boot cracked more glass and when I fell in on the floor next to Nikki and Branch some girl's voice said, "Don't—don't— oh, please just don't make that any bigger because, like, the big riff-raffs'll fit in"—and when I looked up a girl our age was shaking her hands at us, one of them shaking a pocketknife, other one just up, open, shaking. Me and Nikki and Branch all looked at each other, and then the girl said loud, "Okay—*please*," and Branch laughed, then Nikki, and between some laughs Nikki said, "What the fuck're you?" and the girl's pocketknife hand came down some and she said, "What?"

Behind her, in other windows, some boarded, couple just cracked, were real little candles, not lit, and in wall-cracks and floor-cracks were more flowertops and there were also two bags on the floor, one with clothes, dresses, shirts, hats, spilling out and one filled with flowertops and plant-branches plus dirt, looked like, spilling out at the bottom of the bag.

"What the fuck is this?" Branch said.

The girl's hand dropped the knife more and she turned her head, looked at each of us, and Nikki squeezed water out of her hair, shook the water off her hands, looked around the place, said, "It'll work, for right now," and Branch shook his hair, said, "Warm too, dudes," bent his head, "Building on the other side must still have heat," reached back and pulled up, off his shirt, and I stomped water off my boots, started untying them, said, "Here's dry space, though," and Branch wrung out his shirt, and the girl waved the knife up high again, said loud, "*Hey*," and we stopped wringing and untying, looked at her and she said, "Hey," bent and put the knife in a crack in the floor by a flowertop. Then she sat in front of us, looked at me, Nikki, stopped and stared at Branch. Branch put his wadded wet shirt down. "Look," he said. "We're not gonna steal your shit or stomp on you or fuck you," and Nikki said, "We're just here for right now is all," got hold one of my boots and pulled, got it off, threw it on the floor, then said to her, "People been gettin' in here and givin' you shit—in this place?" The girl said, "No," put her hand out, touched Nikki's boot-toe, said,

"Just a couple times, a couple people poked their heads in, but they left, but that's the only bad, close to bad stuff. Mostly this place is non-evil, and super unthreatening and—warm," she looked over quick at Branch—holding his shirt up, last drops of water squeezed out— then leaned over, grabbed the shirt and got up, walked fast to the other side of the room, laid the shirt out flat on the floor under a window, said, "This side over here is so much nicer," she turned back, her hands moving around, said, "I mean, *warmer*." Then she pointed out the window, "The Chinese place puts out just huge vibes of heat, I think, and right here's where I crash," she looked at Branch's shirt, bent quick and brushed it with her hand, smoothed it out more, said, "You'll smell like ginger and ginseng—oh—and also old oil and boiled cabbage or whatever—but—it'll be dry faster." I had both boots off, on the floor, was wringing out one sock and the girl stopped talking, looked at me, smiled, and I stopped squeezing and Nikki, pulling off one of her boots, looked at me, started laughing, and I looked past her boot at Branch's head, shaking, mouth smiling and I held up a sock in each hand, high, and the girl came and got them, put them on the floor by Branch's shirt and Branch leaned out low, flicked the flowertop in the crack by the knife at me.

Later we were naked, in the other part of the place, us sitting around her, except Branch, standing at a window, watching rain, butt to us, all our clothes drying all over, candles going, food- and flower- and candle-smell everywhere. Some of the smell must've been getting big, and I must've made a face because the girl stopped shaking out Nikki's underwear, said, "I know, it's patchouli and vanilla, but these're all I had left, they wouldn't sell, believe me, the last people on the planet who want to buy patchouli-vanilla votive candles are

Deadheads at a Dead show." Nikki grabbed her underwear, put her legs out, got them on, smiled, said, "Hey, they're almost close to clean now," and I said, "Nik, check mine," and Nikki leaned back, grabbed and threw my underwear, said, "Check yourself." I got my hands out of my lap and felt my underwear, fairly dry, got them on. Nikki, feeling clothes, said the other stuff was still wet and the girl said "Got it—" pointed at each one of us, said, "Nik—David—Branch," and Nikki said, "Nik-*ki*," and I said, "Dav-*y*," and she pointed to herself, "Jod-*y*," smiled. Branch said he hated the Dead and I said, "Some of their shit's okay," and Nikki said, "How're the shows?"

"Well, I've never actually been—*inside*—*to*—one," Jody said, and Branch and me laughed but Nikki said, "Well you could fuckin' hear 'em couldn't you?" and Jody said, "Oh yeah, of course," she folded her knees, waved her hands, "Really—very—nice noise," she said. I asked where-all she saw them and she said here and Idaho. "Pocatello, there, and Portland Meadows, here, so actually I've only been to two, which is so not a lot, but it's a start and I'm staying to try to get to more, which is why I'm here, here since the May show, because I came out with some stupid friends who all just, like, chickenshitted back home to Idaho, flaked on our whole plan to follow them, Frisco was next, supposed to be next, and I missed that, I know, but there's probably still Oakland—" and Branch said loud from the window, "Fuck this Oregon piss weather." He looked back at us, me mostly, said, "We need to be workin'." Nikki said to me, "That guy from the park, couple days ago?" and Branch said, "Max," and Nikki said, "You need bucks for—'shrooms?" and Branch said, "Acid," then Nikki looked at him, said, "Well, so, what's the deal, what-all're you gettin', where're you gettin' it, and where're we supposed to get rid of it?"

Branch scratched back of his ass-crack, then turned around and picked up his underwear and felt them and sniffed them, said, "Like hippie piss," put them on, grabbed his jeans, said, "Max's got the A-sheets anytime, Pioneer Square and the park's where he hangs and also where we'll be slingin' it—there—plus I know some spots," he pulled up, buttoned the jeans, stopped and Jody said, "Still wet, I'll just bet." Branch looked at her, let the top button stay open, went back to the window. He said, "Fuck," hit a fist on wall-space by the window, fast breath blowing out two candles in the sill. "We need work and money and it's shit out there. We can't do a fuckin' thing in this," then Jody said she had some money, was saving some for when the Dead came back up, probably the fall, but that that was pretty far off, asked what we were going for, needed to make money for, and Nikki said, "Food," and I said, "Space," and Branch said, "Permanent space." Then he looked around, said, "It's about time for that for me," and me and him looked at each other a second, then he said, "Seventeen's time to settle, so what we're goin' for is permanent space, like this but real," and then all four of us nodded. Nikki asked Jody if she sold candles for cash around here and Jody said, "Oh no, not in the city, not here," then laughed a little, said, "Down here I suck dick," and Branch turned around, looked at her, and Nikki smiled, leaned in, up to Jody's face, said, "Hey, up here in Portland, where do girls go?" Jody got one of Nikki's hands in hers, said, "South-east Eighty-second, sweetie." She looked at Nikki's face. "I take the nine-thirty-nine bus down there and stay till, like, the one-twenty or two-fifty, because in the afternoon there's police and, like, *women.*" Nikki slapped Jody's hands, went on her back laughing. Branch rubbed on his jeans legs, smiled at me. Jody said, "What?" and folded her arms. "It's *just*, y'know, my mouth, it's not, like, *love.*" Nikki moved over to me, rubbed my legs, kissed my chin, said, "There's slither for me, in the city." I rubbed a wet hair-patch on her head and behind her Jody said, "This totally wonderful older earth-sister—who almost

OD'd at the Meadows show, not on A or 'shrooms, just bad bud, ex-boyfriends shooting big bad vibes, and maybe food poisoning, too—she told me, told me where, here, in the city. Eighty-second. The woman—Dee-Dee—she's my idol, if she's still, like, in the realm of the living *us*"—she looked at me—"What's slither?"

"Slither's slither," Nikki said, me and her kissing, "and I can do it, too," and Branch said, "Slither in the city," down to rubbing the bottoms of his jeans legs dry, then he bent up fast, said, "Sin City." He went over fast and got his shirt up, on. I pushed Nikki off some.

"Fuck. Sin City, Davy. There's Sin City. This viddie-place. It's in-the-city-slither and it's out of the rain and it's fuckin' packed, I'll bet, 'cause it's so fuckin' wet out." He threw me my shirt, said that when he first came through Portland last summer Max'd showed him through the arcades, and sitting down, getting his socks on fast, he said he must've got rain on the brain because he'd spaced remembering that we could work them.

I looked back and Nikki and Jody were going through Jody's clothes-bag, and Jody, holding up a dress, said, "This one's so close to clean you can't even smell that stain," but Nikki's head was close up to the bag and she held it open, said, "Fuck—*this* is cool," and Jody said, "Oh, yeah," and I said, "What?" and Nikki reached in, pulled out two handfuls of tampons. Branch said to me, "We need to know this slither anyway," tied up one boot and I pulled on one of mine, and I said, "Sin City?"

"Sin City, Hart's, couple others," he said. "And not just for when it rains."

A tampon hit my face and Nikki and Jody laughed, Nikki saying, "Lucky she don't save the used," and Branch, bent down to me tying, looked at Jody, said low to me, "Little granola-bitch is maybe good luck," tagged my ear with the tampon.

*   *   *

Me and Branch ran through the rain back up downtown, ducked under Nordstrom's front when it got heavy, and I asked Branch how close we were and he said, "It's totally close to Nordstrom," and then I asked if they had pinball too and he said, "Dude"—laughed—said, "Dude, it's not a viddie-*game*-place—it's, like, they've got viddie-*os*—" and I said fast, "Okay—yeah—I've seen a couple places—corner places in Eugene"—and Branch—still laughing a little—said, "Porn videos"—and I said, "Yeah, I got it"—and he said, "That you drop quarters and watch"—and I said, "Yeah," and he said, "You'll see, dude"—and I said, "Viddie-slither, it's viddie-slither," and he stopped laughing and looked at me and said, "Yeah. Okay. You got it," then the rain stopped. We kept walking until Third, stopped and looked at the big sign with lights that said SIN CITY, three kids standing under it, out of leftover drizzle. A car came up behind us when we started for the sign, then it slowed and I stopped, wiped hair out of my face, looked at it—old-guy driver—and Branch got my arm, said, "No Davy, no car shit—c'mon"—reached into his front pockets—said, "Singles?" and I patted my back pocket, wad of a few, and he said, "Good— gotta look like customers—invest at least a buck each—" then he turned back, looked up ahead, stopped us, said, "Little fuck."

Coming around one of the kids hanging out front was the kid-kid from the park, and Branch said, "Baby-slither—that kid-kid—always is in our shit," and I said, "Don't you gotta be older to get into—" and Branch said, "You haveta *look* like you *could* be eighteen," then he said the kid-kid'll get us all busted, got moving, fast ahead, but went around the door, past the guys our age, to the kid-kid and I said, "Hey," and Branch got Jody's knife from his front pocket, put it up quick to the kid-kid's face and I said, *"Branch!"* and the other guys hanging out under the SIN CITY sign moved over. I pulled at his shoulder but he put the knife up closer, just under the little kid's nose, and the kid turned his head and I got around Branch, pushed on both shoulders, and the Sin City doorbell jangled and Branch put the knife quick back down his front pocket, backed up off the kid. The old guy that'd come out of the place stopped behind Branch, looked past me at the kid-kid, coughed, jingled front-pocket change, crossed the street and the little kid pushed by me, crossed the street, followed the old guy, and Branch said to me, "That needs to stay outta our shit," yelled up to the little kid, "Gonna get us all busted," but the kid and the old guy were already around a corner. I said, "Come on," and Branch said lower, "Believe that shit, that little shit?" and I got right in front of him, said, "Come on, shut up, show me inside," then he nodded, rubbed his face up and down, looked at me, said, "Okay, Davy, be cool, in here," then we went in, got my first booth.

It was still clear, later, walking back, and close behind the building where we found Jody we could see a little bit of light in the window and Branch laughed a little, said he could almost smell the hippie-sweat from the candles going, up there, Dead Hotel, then we crawled up through the window and Jody came up fast to Branch before we hit the floor, yelled, "Where is it?" Getting up, Branch got the knife out, held it out by the blade, looked at the floor, and Nikki looked over Jody at me, then Jody yelled at Branch, "That's not what it's for." She went to the other part of the place, threw the knife into the back of her clothes-bag, and Branch said low, "You don't even know what we—" and she said, "Unh-hunh, yeah, well you snuck it out, so there was something—just—wrong—and that's not how I am—and that's, *that's* for protection—only—like, defense."

There was wrapper-noise on the other side of Jody, Nikki was un-wrapping a Snickers, few other on the floor by her and she sat, looked at me, moved her head for me to come over. Jody leaned against the windowsill with candles going.

Branch scooted up to the wall under another window, pulled his knees up to his chest, got his head down behind them and Jody said to him, "This space has to stay completely cool," started talking about the people she hung with at the shows and Branch kept his head down. I ate some Snickers but most of the bar was squishy and Nikki looked at me, melty chocolate on her teeth and top lip and she looked at her hands, wiped her mouth, then wiped melty chocolate off on her jeans, said she forgot this side of the place was warmer.

A ride, finally, outside the rest stop close to Kelso, and I was in the backseat while Nikki was up front, feeling the guy, maybe already hand-doing him while he drove us more north and Bleach'd played through seemed like ten times but probably just the two, so I picked up the backpack, went through it, feeling around the CDs and big videotape for cassettes, holding them up until headlights came up from a car in the southbound lane so I could see what the tape title was but everything was City-shit, mixes Branch'd scammed from DJ's, and the next time I reached in fast, poked, sliced some of a middle finger on Jody's knife, sticking up from the bag-bottom, and I let out some air but didn't say anything but Nikki looked back. I put my finger in my mouth, pulled the knife up, out some. She looked at me to put it back then said something in the driver-guy's ear and he said without turning, "Son, keep an eye out, would you, on the road. For things," then he looked at me in the mirror and I said, "Sure," Nikki's hands going faster and she looked at me again, jerked her head fast, eyes pointed at my window and I nodded and the guy looked at my window and I nodded and the guy looked forward and Nikki's head went down.

I rubbed my finger on my jeans leg, got hold of the window-knob, cranked the window down real slow, guy's eyes coming back to me in the mirror when it got open about a full inch and I said, "Fuck it's warm," and he looked back at the road. I wiped the blood off the knife-tip with my sleeve-bottom and held the knife by the handle, kept it low, kept the window at just an inch for a while, till once when Nikki got going fast and his head came back to the headrest some and his eyes went to slits for a second then I rolled the window down and chucked the knife, clunking it out to the road, bouncing into a road-bush and the guy's head turned a little, his eyes were at the mirror, he started to say something but I said loud, "Dude—you're swerving," and his eyes went back quick ahead then Nikki must've bit him because he said, "Hey—ouch," and Nikki, mouth full of dick, said, "Sorry—drive better," and he got his hands higher up the wheel, shot me a look in the mirror, said, "Close that," and I turned the knob a little, window coming back up, not much, and he said, "All the way," then I closed it. Nikki kept on him fast. I put the headphones, whole Walkman and tapes back in the bag, leaned back, watched the road, listened to the guy go, "You gonna take it, honey? Well okay, okay then. That's right. Here it is. There it is." Then Nikki sat up fast, cracked her window open fast, spit out to the road and while the guy zipped and drove she rolled it back, but not all the way, and the guy didn't look at me in the mirror and I could see the side of Nikki's face, smiling. I sucked on my finger, looked at it in next car-light, splotch of blood-crust on the small cut, then closed my eyes, leaned more to Nikki's side of the car, into more of the cool freeway wind coming from her window-crack.

And then later, crack of the next morning, another rest stop, north of Kelso but still south of Seattle, waiting on a curb in front of some empty parking spaces, I put my head on the backpack, yawned and asked Nikki why she wanted me to ditch the knife.

" 'Cause we shouldn't be carrying it. One of these rides might get freaked if they saw it. Plus—doesn't it—just feel like bad luck?"

All of that made sense, especially the last part, and I nodded on the pack, then she asked if I'd taken a swipe at Branch, with the knife.

I said, "No, I didn't touch him," moved my face into the pack, closed my eyes.

"Because—I know he didn't do anything to you," she said.

I felt both her hands come over one of mine.

"But—to James?"

I shook my head, slow, grinding it into the big videotape, and the little cassettes, then I stopped and looked at her. She took a big breath but didn't take her hands off, moved them all the way up to my shoulders, already figuring out, I'm pretty sure, that I couldn't tell her, maybe could never tell her any more than what I said—"Branch is—a freak."

City Living

A few mornings after we got Jody we had just enough to get the acid sheets from Max plus share a couple medium mochas at the Metro on Broadway before me and Branch headed up to the park and before Nikki and Jody headed down to Southeast Eighty-second. Under the COFFEEPEOPLE sign on the counter was a big chunk of cake, black, chocolate, on a plate on a stand, the kid that'd sold us our mochas on a stool, behind the counter, reading but looking up, at us, once in a while. Branch blew off steam over the cup between me and him and said low, "You could get him 'cause he *is* scammin'," and me and Nikki looked at the kid quick but he looked down fast back to his *Oregonian*. Branch said, "That tip glass's fairly full, other side of the counter, Davy. You could be talkin' him up on his side and I could pick out those singles in the glass."

I took a fast drink before the steam came back.

"You were lookin' at him," Branch said, and I shook my head, got my hands around the cup, blew a ring in the coffee and Nikki said, "I didn't catch that."

"I'm checkin' out that cake-chunk," I said. "Big, for all of us, maybe," then Nikki said, "Chocolate, nuts, like breakfast Snickers," and Jody leaned in, said that food in the city costs way too much, said we could get a whole cake—day old—Eleventh and Jefferson Safeway—for the price of that piece and Branch looked at her, said, "Hey, we can get that piece for nothin'," got up, said, "I mean, *I* can," walked over to COFFEEPEOPLE, put his arm up on the counter, leaned against it, started talking to the kid, *Oregonian* going down.

Jody said, "That's slither, isn't it?"

I said to Nikki, "I wasn't scammin'," and Nikki said, "I know, whatever," pushed the rest of her and Jody's mocha in front of Jody, said, "Here," and Jody said, "You've only had one sip," started to push it back but Nikki kept her hand up to the cup—Jody said, "Caring is *sharing*"—Nikki looked back at her hard, said, "So *let* me, bitch," and Jody bit her bottom lip, shook her head, drank the rest. Nikki looked at an open paper's comics page and I watched Branch talking and then Jody said she had to pee and right after she got up Nikki pushed the paper over, looked over at Branch, still talking, then looked back at the bathrooms, girls' door just closing, said low, "Knew she had to go, the way she was shaking her leg like she does," pulled something shiny out of her back pocket. Then she got in close on the table and I leaned in too. She opened her hands some and inside was a flat, shiny silver card that said FONECARD in raised letters, someone's name and a bunch of numbers underneath. I said, "Where'd—"

"Me and Jody, yesterday morning, pits and tits, Nordstrom girls' room, Jody was in a stall on the pot and this woman was changing her kid on the baby-table. Davy, she had her wallet out up by some shitty diapers, then left, left them and *it,* forgot the wallet 'cause the baby was cryin' *so* loud." She looked back around and behind— Branch was still talking, Jody was still gone. Nikki said, "No cash, but cards, chucked it all before Jody got out of the stall but I saved this one, this card, it was—"

"Shiny."

"*Yeah*—we could—I could or you maybe—if we ever had to—in case it gets weird here—"

"Weird?"

"For safety, in case it starts getting wrong—"

"Nothin's wrong—"

"Branch—maybe—" she looked around again, said, "You never said if he got weird, with the knife—"

"That wasn't anything—okay?" I said fast. "You weren't there." Over Nikki's head was Jody, out of the bathroom door, brushing her hands on the front of her dress.

"It wasn't anything?"

I looked at her—"Nothing. Total nothing." Over Nikki's shoulder came Branch, chunk of cake on a plate in one hand, piece of paper in his other, Jody coming up behind him. Nikki put her hands flat, pushed the card under into mine but I stopped it and she said low, "Just hold it," and I said low, "It's cool here," and she said low and fast, "Just in case," and I got my whole hand around it, reached back, scratched hard right above my butt, dropped the card in my back pocket. Branch put the plate down in front of me, sat by me, said, "*And* his fuckin' phone number," put the piece of paper down, tapped a finger on it.

Jody got back by Nikki, said, "Then, like, officially, that *was* slither," and Nikki said yeah, put a hand on one of hers.

I picked nuts out of the top of the cake-chunk, said, "You gonna use the number?" to Branch and Branch looked at me, scrunched his eyes and nose, "For what?" He looked over at the kid, up, helping people waiting in front of the counter. "He's got no money, Davy," Branch said. "He's almost just like us." He tagged my arm with a few fingers. "He's got a job, we got a job." He wrinkled up the piece of paper, chucked it under the table, and Nikki said to Jody, "Practice slither's what that was," and Branch got a gulp of my and his mocha, said, yeah, in the cup, and I got a few fingerfuls of cake, then Jody reached in, got some and Nikki reached over, picked and downed my nut-pile.

Later, Nikki and Jody gone to Eighty-second, me and Branch on swings in the park, swinging high, looking at cars coming in, Branch said something while I was up and he was down and I said loud, "What's what?" and he said louder, "I said we need to relax," and I yelled down, "How's that?" and he said, "The City—the club, the City," and I said up, "What's that?" and he said it was a dance-club for anybody—under eighteen, over eighteen—anything—gay, straight, bi, then he said, "It's Friday—you know it's Friday, right?" and I said, "No, I didn't know it was Friday." A line of three cars came in the start of the hill and I slowed swinging, looked at them close and Branch said, " 'Cause we all need to take a night to chill, least a night," and I said, "Yeah, especially—" and Branch stopped—feet out, down—done swinging, looking at me.

I kept looking at the cars that were coming around, nodded to the middle one in the three and I said, "Is that him?"

The middle car stopped just after the big fountain and Branch said, "Max, yeah, that's him," then, "What'd you say?" and I said, "Especially . . . everybody," and he smiled, faked elbowing my head, got up, then me, and we went down the hill.

*   *   *

Max gave us four big plastic Ziplocs, three with a full sheet in each, Simpsons—a mom, a Bart, and one the whole family—the other one another sheet, but already cut up in squares, chunks of everybody's faces, then Max flicked the rest of his cigarette out his car window between me and Branch, leaned in, over it. Branch put the bags with whole sheets under his shirt, flat, up to his chest, rolled up the bag with the cut-hits, stuck it down his pants-front, dropped his shirt over everything. Max looked up at me, said, "When you're slinging these cut ones, let your buyer do the reaching in, get their hit, then you close it, Davy," he moved a hand over Branch's pants-front—the cut-hits wad—and I said, "I know, your hands, it can go through your hands," then I looked at Branch, pointed at the rolled-up bag, said, "We had that shit in Eugene, A's not just up here," and Max said, "Absolutely right, Davy," got his hands in on the wheel. Max started the car and revved it a couple times, said to stay out of the Square today because bike cops were there, then said, "Later," drove up, out of the park on the road behind the tennis courts. Branch started walking us up the hill across from the swings and I said, "This way to the zoo?" and he said yeah, but we weren't actually going to be slinging at the zoo, but by the zoo-train, little train that picked up kids right over the trail we'd be at, said that people looking for A just know to go there, and heading into some trees I asked how come Max didn't do the slinging himself, and Branch laughed, pushed some bush-tops out of our way, said, "Because it'd look real stupid, some thirty-year-old freak hangin' out by the fuckin' kiddie-train. We just look like we're waitin' for our little brothers or somethin', and see, that's why he needs us," and I reached in front of him, felt up his front pants-wad, said, "Yeah, that's why he needs us."

Branch stopped a second, pointed down, said, "No, *that's* why we got this extra bag for nothin'." He walked back in front of me, and after a few seconds got fairly far ahead of me, up the brush, and I got the Fonecard out of my back pocket, ran it between a couple of my front teeth, popped out a nut from the cake at the Metro.

A kid about my age with his shirt off and a jacket with a big *L* on it, tied around his middle, reached into the Ziploc bag of hits I was holding and got two squares stuck on the end of one finger, then fingered around and got two more hits stuck on the end of another finger then pulled his hand out, said, *"Mark,"* and the kid behind him, same age, no shirt, same jacket, stood up from leaning against a car, walked up to us, getting out his wallet, opening it up, and the kid that'd reached in the bag held up one of the fingers with two squares. Branch said, "Six," and the kid getting into his wallet nodded, got out a five and a single, took his hits from the kid in front of him, then Branch took the money and I closed, zipped the bag, shook what was left, not much. The kid that'd paid put his hits in his wallet, said to the other kid, "Where're you stowin' yours?" right when the kid by me put his hits on his tongue, pulled his finger out of his mouth. Then the kid that'd taken the hits said, "Here," reached into his pocket, got keys, turned around and threw them at his friend and his friend caught them, said, "Man, Brian, you're gonna be fryin' before any of the party's even goin' on," walked around the car, got in the driver's side. The kid in front of me said, "Hopefully," tightened up his jacket and I said, "What's the *L*?" and he brushed at it, said, "Lincoln, Lincoln High," pointed over his shoulder, just out of the zoo parking lot, empty, except for them, late afternoon, and he started back to the other car-door, said, "Where d'you guys go?" and looked back at me and Branch when he got in, head out the window. Branch said, "Over there," pointed the other way, toward the rest of the park. The car started, the zoo-train whistle went off, Branch said we should move on, and they drove off, and the zoo-train, empty, came around tracks in trees above the lot. I looked down, and through tree-spaces I could see some of a mountain and I said, "Saint Helens," and Branch said, "Wrong—dude—Hood," and I said, "Bullfuck—half of it's, like, gone, so it's Saint Helens," and Branch smiled, said, "Good, right, we're good," and I looked further down to the trails we'd been on under the parking lot and train tracks, asked him which way now. He cut from the parking lot back down to the trails, said loud, "Plaid Pantry on Vista." I rolled up the Ziploc bag, stuck it down my pants-front, cut down behind Branch, said, "To deal out the rest?" and he said, "No— Davy—dumb fuck—for *burritos*—I'm fuckin' hungry." Then he slowed up till I was walking with him and he said, "We'll get shit for Nik and Jody, too, they'll be back, and dude, we'll surprise them with a shitload of—burritos, nachos—and we'll drop change on a Burnside bum to get us booze—and we'll just take a night off—" And I ran my hand over my pants-front wad, said, "Get into this?" and he said, "Hey, yeah—one, or maybe a couple hits each—sure, 'cause we don't want to be cuttin' into profits," flicked my front wad fast with a couple fingers.

The sun was starting to go down and the cars were still coming up when we got back into the lower part of the park, cutting through to get to Vista, and there was noise, one guy, talking loud, but echoing all over, and crossing down the slither-trails, I got ahead of Branch, slowed down, patting his chest, keeping flat the full sheets in his shirt, and he said, "Hold up, sounds like a cop-radio, maybe a walkie-talkie," but I was already down further. I slowed and looked through some brush at a car coming around Lewis and Clark Circle, a kid's head sticking out the sunroof, his hands holding a bullhorn, and he talked into it, talked up our way to the bushes, said, "Go *home*, Kent, I see you, get your big ass *out* of the azaleas and go home"—and the kid put the bullhorn down, looked down into the sunroof, then got the bullhorn up again, laughing into it, said, "Kent, you have already missed the first ten totally important minutes of *Oprah!*" Branch, up by me, said, "That's no cop—who the fuck is—" and the car slowed and I saw the kid better, said, "That's that kid, that kid that was thrashing, James," and he said, "Who?" then a guy, older, came out of the bushes below us, pointing his finger at the kid in the car, driving by with a bullhorn. The car got faster and the kid's head jerked some but he was still laughing, said between laughs, while the car was going around the hill-corner, "Naughty Kent—*go home!*" and the old guy under us got his hands on his sides, shook his head, a kid coming out of the bushes behind him, zipping jeans. Branch shook his head too, snapped his fingers, said, "The wad you got, Davy, here, alright, just so it's all in one stow-spot," and I reached in my pants, laughing low, gave him my bag, said, "That James kid—" and Branch said, "Freak, Davy," and stowed the cut hits on himself.

We took two hits each a while after food, right about dark, then walked around downtown, then hung in the Square, all of us sitting on the high steps around the feet of the statue-guy holding the umbrella until a MAX train came up the Yamhill side of the Square, stopped, and Branch looked in the front MAX-car, at a clock, said that it was ten up, City was open, so we headed up to northwest downtown. Branch walked fast by Nordstrom and Nikki grabbed, held my arm going by some kids popping skateboards in front of the Galleria, and Jody jumped at the lights hanging over the Mark Spencer's doors, and then, getting patted down by the City's doorguy, after Branch and Jody'd already gone in, I started coming on, got my arm tight on Nikki's, and kept looking at the top of my hand where the doorguy'd stamped, but not seeing anything, no stamp-mark, then Nikki pushed over me, said she was liking the noise going on inside, gave the guy her five, told me to get in.

Light came in big from the dance-room—flashed down the entrance-hall, lit up Beavis and Butthead on a wall right in front of me, sitting, smiling, Beavis with a boner, sticking up from his shorts, Butthead reaching for it—and I walked with a hand up to the wall, fingers flat over Butthead's "Heh-heh-heh-heh," music-boom making the wall pound under my tips, and at the end of the hall were tons of people dancing, on the floor, on a stage, and on a counter across from a mirror-wall, guys with guys and girls with girls, mixed up in groups and some solo people, all my age, and a few older guys, sitting under the counter or standing in corners out of the dance-light. Jody waved down at me from up on the dance-stage, then twirled around, and Branch, past the dance-floor, waved at me to get with him in front of a corner of video games and a pinball machine, then shook his head, said loud, "Quarters, dude," and I dug around in my pocket with my other hand and Nikki said loud behind me, "Davy, your hand, cool," and I looked at my wall-hand—and in some dark between club lights it said FAG in glowy green letters—and Nikki said, "You okay, you on?"

I said, "Getting there," looked at the change I'd pulled up, shook it, picked at the hand-pile, all viddie-tokens, then laughed, looked up from the tokens at Nikki, said, "Yeah, okay, *there*," stood and laughed more, not being able to stop for a little while, till Jody jumped down, helped Nikki get me up onstage, dancing.

James

The day after A we didn't do much. At coffee at the Metro Branch said, "Let's just hang, everybody," and Nikki, holding her head over the coffee-steam, said, "Okay," and Jody said, "Too vegged to slither," so we got lids and left. We got up to the park but hung in the open, on the hill under the tennis courts, sitting on big rock chunks in the middle of the rows of rosebushes, Branch cutting A-hits on a square rock with a checkerboard top, wiping a scissors-blade on his jeans after cutting two or three hits, then wiping his fingers on his jeans after flicking the hits into a Ziploc. He saw me watching him wipe, said, "Dude, it's not about doin' A in the AM."

Nikki, back leaned up to Jody's back, said, "I hate after A," passed her cup around to Jody.

"A can be better," Jody said, sipping slow. "This was okay, this was close to fun, I've had better, though, it's just that A can be made, mixed with so much—*anything*—strychnine, rat poison—*god*—Nu-traSweet—"

"Shut up," Nikki said, got the coffee cup back.

"The only good after's really X," Branch said. "Day after X is always cool."

I rubbed my face, looked down to the entrance part of the park, cars coming up.

"M and A're bad afters," Branch said, looking close at the scissors-blades.

"Meth," Nikki said, blowing into the cup.

"Mushrooms," Branch said, starting to cut a new sheet.

"M could mean meth," Nikki said.

"Crank's meth," Branch said.

A car, then another parked by the big fountain, one guy got out, walked into bushes, the other guy got out, leaned up to his car, lit a smoke, looked around, then walked into the bushes.

"Or M could be MDMA," Nikki said. "M could be that," and she held the cup up—back for Jody—but Jody slapped her hand on her and Nikki's rock and said, "Then 'A' could be plain MDA 'cause, like, it's got an A and no M, and 'M' should be MDMA 'cause, like—you know—the extra M."

"Meth's got a bad after," I said.

"All the M's are bad after," Jody said.

"We can call 'em all shit," Nikki said.

Branch put the scissors down hard on the top of his rock. "God. Fuck. Shut up. Call 'em what they are. A is for A. A's always A. X is X. Meth is meth and 'shrooms're 'shrooms and that's fuckin' it."

A guy on a bike came up after two more cars. The zoo-train whistle went off. I picked up the coffee cup in front of me, on my rock, cold, then Branch looked at me and I shook the cup, said it was cold, popped the lid, dumped it out.

Jody said, "What if we had crack?"

I got up, said to Nikki, "Gotta pee," started walking and Branch scratched his head with one of the scissors-blades, said to Jody, "There's no crack up here, this ain't no fuckin' park in California."

I peed in the piss-tub in the bathroom, buttoned, got out and rubbed my head and face, walked down around a car coming up, driver looking at me, to the big fountain, sat on the edge and rubbed my face some more, and there was a noise. I quit rubbing but kept my eyes closed in my hands till I heard it again. I got up, crossed the street, went into the bushes, across from the fountain, looked around, heard the sound, took the low trail down. The trail bent around and after it bent I could see a kid sitting on the ground, back to a tree, backpack on a plant, his face in his hands, crying low. I stopped almost in front of him and he looked up.

I said, "Thrasher-kid."

He rubbed his eyes with his sleeve, said, " 'Thrasher-kid'?" and I got closer, said, "Bullhorn-guy, thrasher kid, you've been around here, I saw you dancin' and yellin'."

He coughed, sniffed and spit. "You saw me?" he said.

"Couple times," I said.

He nodded. "Is it that you—live here?" he said.

I looked around, guy on the trail above us looked at us. I looked at the kid. He had big red eyes and a real small smile. "Not anymore," I said. He coughed hard, looked down. I said, "We got kind of a place, some space in a building, boarded-up, off Burnside."

He sleeved his eyes again, smiled a little more, said, "Well, I am so fucking embarrassed," put out a hand, "Crying here, in front of Trump," and I shook his hand, said, "What're you meaning?" then he took his hand back and just waved it, said, "I mean nothing," and shook his head then I bent down in front of him, said, "So how come you're not dancin' or yellin'?"

He laughed till he coughed, got some breath, then said he got left, by a guy, just now, lobby of the Westin Benson, didn't know where to head, so ran to the park looking for space in some trees or bushes to dance and yell and also to scream. I asked how he got into the Westin Benson and he said, "Douglas," and I asked him if that was the guy I saw driving him around and he nodded, started crying some more. He took a couple big breaths then said, "He's not rich at all. He's just a fucking retail retard. Douglas does display windows for Nordstrom's—Washington, San Francisco, here. We hooked up in Seattle. We were going to San Francisco. And he was looking at an apartment, Northwest Twenty-third, here. Not rich or anything, but I could've been a cool dependent." He took in some more air, said, "He gave me fifty, sent me shopping, bright and early today, for CDs, said he was finally giving up some disco, getting into grunge, then when I came back to the Benson they said he'd checked out and he left this at the desk," and he pointed to his backpack, tagged the strap. I asked him what was in there and he said, "Underwear, some dollars, some change, CDs, tapes, old Soundgarden, Temple of the Dog, Nir-vana—*Bleach*—and *new* Alice in Chains, and *new* stupid, fucking stupid Pet Shop Boys because, well, it just seemed the nice thing to do with his money."

I asked him if he had enough to get back to Seattle and he shook his head, then I said when I'd seen him once there were other, older guys around him and he said, "Those're some of Douglas's friends here and I am not getting sugardaddied by any of Dickless Douglas's troll-buddies. Omigod—can't you see I'm so obviously on my way to incredible independence?" then he screamed, big sound, but no words, just noise echoing up the trails and I looked around behind

me and up the trails old guys turned around and two old-guy heads
came around a tree. I asked the kid if his name was James and he
said, "Yeah," and he asked me my name and I said, "David," then,
"Davy," then I said, "You were way louder yesterday," and he said,
"That bullhorn, you mean, Davy? Prop from a Polo display. I play
better with cooler toys." Then he looked up at me, maybe a lot of sun
real bright behind me because he squinted and he said, "You said—
you had space?"

I nodded, tagged the strap on his backpack.

"You don't live *here*," he said. "But you work here?"

I nodded. He stopped squinting. I said low, "We slither."

"Slither?" James said. "Slither. Yeah, slither. In Seattle, in Volunteer Park, that's what I did." He smiled some more again. "Davy, I
was you. More north."

When I got back to the rocks and roses under the tennis courts,
Nikki and Jody had moved off their rocks, were walking around the
roses, backs to me, bending and reading the nameplates in front of
each bush, but Branch was still cutting hits on his checker-top rock.
I stood, waited, watched them till James caught up, came up behind
me, said, "Woo—it almost looks like a real city up here, Davy," then
Nikki and Jody turned around and Branch looked up. Jody said, "Hi,"
real loud. Nikki and Branch looked at me. Jody waved, looking at
James, said, "I said, 'Hi,'" and James pushed me over some, got
around me, jumped down into the rosegarden square, said, "Hey,"
loud, back, ran over to Jody, pointing at her, said, "Juniper-hugging
Jody," and Jody said, "Yeah—I guess—but who—" but James was
pointing at the rosebush nameplate her and Nikki'd been looking at,
said, "Don't even bother trying to pronounce half of these, it's like

flower-Latin," and I said to Nikki and Branch, still looking at me, "This is James."

Jody said, "What?" and I said, louder, "James," and James said, next to her, "James," then Jody asked James if I'd called her "Juniper Jody" and James said no, but that I'd said she dug flowers.

I said, "This guy's been here, I've—" I looked just at Branch—"you and me saw him, couple times," and Branch nodded, went back to cutting. "He, he's kind of, pretty much, stuck here," I said, Jody and James talking, Branch cutting, so it was just to Nikki, only one left still looking at me. "This guy hooked him up," I said, "In Seattle, and brought him here, then took off. He—he got snuffed—and stuck." Branch was nodding, still cutting, while I was talking, then I got down, James and Jody stopped talking, and I got in front of Branch and said to his head-top, "Can—he?"

Branch stopped cutting, put the scissors on the rock-top, wiped his hands on his jeans, turned his head, said loud behind him to James, "Can you deal?"

James said, "Oh, yeah, I'm totally, mentally cool, now, with it, I've been ditched by way better than dumbass *Doug*-las," and Branch said fast, "No, dude, I mean, can you *deal*. Acid," and James said fast back, "Right, oh, duh, yes. I haven't but I've seen it, all over, Volunteer Park, you walk by whoever and say it, *doses, doses, doses.*"

Branch looked at me. I said, "That's how we do it here," and Branch said, "If the freak can earn his shit," then James said, "I can do that here," looked out, down at cars coming in the park, then yelled, "Go *home*, Kent!" and Branch, back to cutting, shook his head and Jody said to James, "Who's that—who's Kent?" but Nikki, eyes still on me, smiled.

* * *

James knew dealing and park-slither but didn't know booth-slither so that night me and Branch took him through Sin City and it was crowded—Branch said because it was Saturday and yesterday must've been a payday—and in with the noise of quarters dropping and viddie-machines going was low talking, from a few guys standing together, up to the aisle-walls, all booths filled—all doors closed and red OCCU-PIED lights on.

Branch said to me and James, "Split up, we'll all take a row of these, 'cause somethin'll open," and over Branch, the guys up to the wall laughed, talked a little louder, then Branch walked past them, around the corner to another row of booths. I looked at James and pointed at myself then pointed to the booth-row on the other side and he nodded and I started walking, then James grabbed my arm real fast, said, "This is *easy,* Davy—and absolutely no chance of get-ting stickers in your snatch," and I laughed and the wall-guys shut up, looked at us then started talking again, and James said, *"Ssshh,"* to them, "I can't hear myself slither," and I rubbed his arm, went around to my row of booths.

Later, at the City, not on anything, me and Branch sitting under the dance-stage, Nikki, Jody and James above us, grinding into each other to the music and passing a cigarette back and forth to each other, I said to Branch, "You really cool with James?"

Branch had his head low but nodded, and his hands were going down the top front of his jeans. He pulled up a corner of a Ziploc. "Knew if I shoved this perfect down here the doorguy wouldn't catch it."

I said, "Where you gonna—?" then nodded up to all the people on the dance-stage, and Branch said, "No, there," nodded over to some kids by the pinball machine, couple kid-kids at the video-games, then he folded the corner back down under a top button, looked at James—thrashing in the middle—said, "He's kind of fuckin' obnoxious but, y'know, good earning power."

Nikki, her turn with the smoke, looked at me, took a big puff, and waved the orange cherry in circles over James and Jody's head, her light-circles mixing in with club-light and James and Jody looked up and James said loud, "Nicotine tracers."

Branch said to me, watching them, "Davy, didn't wanna get your hopes up or nothin' but, dude, we got a lead on a place," and I started to look at him but he elbowed my arm, said, "Dude, don't even look like this is important, okay? You gotta keep this quiet till I hear more from Max. But he's got a friend that owns a building—whole fuckin' building—on Twenty-third and Flanders. It's gettin' redone but when it's done, we could get the basement. Whole fucking basement. *Real* space."

I nodded but didn't say anything. Jody got the smoke fast from Nikki and took a long puff, cherry lighting up big, then she coughed big, spit the cigarette out and Nikki reached over James, tagged Jody's chin, said, "That was a *clove*! I had to kiss a dyke-chick for that! That tasted *good*!"

Branch said, "We'd do rent, all that, and sling A, 'shrooms, whatever shit for Max, right, too, but it'd be—" and I said fast, "Real space," and Branch said, "Hundred percent," then he said, "But no fuckin' word on this 'cause it's not here yet."

I said, "Right," then Branch tagged my arm, said, "Gotta make movin'-in money," got up, told me to cough loud or something if door-people came cruising by him, then went over to the kid-kids at the videos. I looked out past the people on the downstairs dance-floor, watched Branch talking to the video-kids and felt around, inside a back pocket, felt the Fonecard. A couple seconds later Branch came by me, said, "Hey—junior high's a bitch, too," kept walking around the dance-floor to the bathrooms, patting his jeans-front acid-wad down, two video-kids going there, after him, couple seconds later. I looked at the door and the doorguys were still stamping hands and I looked up at the stage, caught Nikki looking at me and I pointed outside and she pushed James and Jody together into just a two-grind and Nikki jumped down off the stage and I started for the exit.

Outside, little ways from the club, I was standing over 405, watching cars. Nikki caught up to me, breathing hard, asking what was wrong, why'd I pull her out, weren't things going okay and I said things were cool, going fine, asked if she was really cool with James, and she said, "What?" Then she got some air, said, "Does it fuckin' look like I'm trippin' on James?" and I said that I just wanted to make sure, and she said, "Davy, he's cute and funny and you been smilin'—all fuckin' day—since gettin' him—okay on that?" and I nodded, pulled out the Fonecard, held it up. I said, "This—maybe we should just—" and she got her hand on half of it and twisted and I held on tight, started twisting the other half and we kept on till it split, then broke, and she chucked her half over the guard-rail and I threw mine. She said, "That what you were thinkin'?" and I said, "Mmm-hmm," then James came running up through Burnside traffic.

James yelled, "Two little leather predykes're eyeing our flower girl close, alright? Jody's not safe solo grinding," and then, up to us, he said, "Also Nine Inch Nails is on—blasting the *Big* Floor," then stomped a foot hard in the street and pointed both hands back to the club.

Me and Nikki hardly fucked at all, in Portland, before James, maybe once, in the woods, Branch down getting burritos, don't now why it wasn't more, we were too busy, I guess, doing Portland shit, but after James we did it more, did it in the Dead Hotel, and once, really late and kind of loud, a boot came flying at us, nailed my knee just as Branch sleep-shouted, "Keep it low, don't get us fuckin' kicked out," and his head rolled back over into his dark corner, then Jody's voice came up from another corner, trying to whisper, "It's sw-eet," but it came out loud and echoed around and Branch said, "Fuckin' wake up everybody," but when I looked over to James's sleep-space he was already up, sitting, watching. I looked back down to Nikki's eyes and started to say something, ask something, but she caught it, snuffed the question before I had my mouth even halfway open, moved some hair off the side of my face, pushed her pussy all the way up my dick, pussy-hair to ball-hair, and we finished fucking and I think that was her answer to what was probably a pretty fucking stupid question anyway.

The first time he watched us I'm fairly sure he just watched, there wasn't any sound or movement from his space, but another time after we'd started and he was watching, I caught some movement and a little sound. I slowed down on top of Nikki and looked at the crash-corners close and long, making sure that the other two were totally out. She put her hands, warm from holding my nuts, up to the sides of my face and I looked at her but her eyes were back and looking at James, and that time, I did ask, I kissed right under her ear and said, "Is that—too much—what he's doin'?" Her hands came off my face and went on the floor and she wiggled and got out from under me, walked over me and around on tiptoes to Jody's corner, picked up one of her candles, pretty well burnt down, and flicked a lighter on it and walked slowly back with it lit with a hand around the fire and she set it down by me, in front of where she'd been laying before we'd started fucking, then bent down and moved and wiggled back under me. Flat on her back, she looked at the candle again, reached out, moved it more, further from her head to the center of the floor, candle-glow lighting up a little of Nikki's smile and a lot of James's beating off.

Up Three, Four Streets from the Big Bart Wall's the Big Nike Wall—Says NIKE AIR, Says BUILT FOR SPEED, Says JUST DO IT.

I was pissing around the corner from Bart Simpson and I'd scratched my leg up near a nut when Nikki said, "Don't scratch! You just make 'em spread more, is all." I said, "It's just an itch, it's not bugs," quit pissing, said, "Here," turned, pushed out the nut, and said, "Have a ball."

Branch—next to Nikki, in the dark, in the lot—said to save it, so I did, put it, all my business away, and buttoned. James and Jody laughed. Nikki came up, kneed me, just in the knee, and Branch said, "Piss break over," kept us moving.

It was late into June and Branch'd said Max'd set something up for us—me, James, and Branch—somewhere in Chinatown—and we were in a lot around the corner from Bart and the other Simpsons painted on the side of that building, the building on Burnside just before it turns up into the bridge, and when we crossed the lot, the car lights from cars heading up the bridge would spotlight Homer's fat stomach, go up to the baby sucking the sucker-toy, then light up one of Bart's big, white eyes—big, white pupil maybe ten yards up from us, lighting up, going dark, blinking.

We kept on till the Chevron station, then stopped, waited for a break in the car flow, then ran, Branch way ahead, fastest, first one to hit the lions in front of China Street.

James just missed the break—car coming fast in front of him—and had to wait while we stood under the China Street arch—no other car break close so he put a hand up, crossed and some cars stopped but one didn't, so James waited a second in the middle of Burnside till it went then ran, made it. Branch—sitting on the lion with his arms up—said to James, "Where to, wonder boy?" and James said, "If it's where you said, then, there," and he pointed straight ahead, "Across from Greyhound, that's where," got his arm down, got some air too, "So fuck you I know this town too," and Branch laughed, said, "Knows his fuckin' geography—boy gets a big fat A," jumped off the lion, kept us moving, and James, staying back some, said low to me, "Boy don't want A, boy needs X."

In a second—we were off Burnside, and that was the end of all the lights for a while, because past the lions was total black, with no cars moving, no Simpsons, no big eyes.

We got around the Greyhound station, then the Amtrak station, to the building that used to have the coin-op in the corner but now was X'd out by boards, a bum on top of another bum in the doorway.

We walked around the bums, up some stairs—two floors—and Branch ran ahead, then James, and they found a door in the hall. Branch knocked and said, "Hey, it's Branch. It's us."

The door opened some and long hair fell out, then an eye and half a woman's face. She said, "Lose the girlfriends please," and Branch looked down the hall and Nikki looked at Jody, touched her arm, and they went back down the stairs, Nikki going by me, not looking at me, not punching my arm.

We got inside and there was a low hum from two corner-standing bright lights.

The woman got my arm. There was a man between the lights, screwing with a video-cam, a couch, and another man right by the couch, in front of a fan, putting out a cigarette and waving smoke away. James stuck a finger in one of my back belt loops and held. The woman pointed to us, pointed us to a little bathroom in the corner, told us to shower fast and we went in. James let go of me, and we got undressed and showered one at a time. I was last—Branch and James'd already gone out—and I showered fast but dried slow, smelling myself where there used to be smell, but none now, and I wrapped the towel, went out.

The hum was louder. Both lights'd been shoved to the other side of the room, pointing light to the couch where Branch and James were making out, and the woman crouched low, out of the light, watching, saying things to the vid-cam guy and snapping her fingers every other second or so, telling him where to point the cam. The guy came around, got near them, got in real close, and I got into the light some, then the woman looked at me, waved me back, waving me back to wait, so I stood in the black in front of the fan—the fan going back and forth, blowing all over—and watched Branch and James kiss and touch each other until the woman snapped and pointed at me and said, "You need to be getting hard," and so I let the towel drop, played with my business, flopped my dick around. By then James was going down on Branch, wet hair flopping up and all over Branch's stomach, balls, maybe tickling, but Branch didn't show it, leaned back, made some noise, kind of laughed.

The woman started to wave me in, but I wasn't hard yet. I spit on my fingers, rubbed my balls, scratched around, and backed away more, out of any of the light, and into the line of the fan. I closed my eyes, kind of tried to get into the wind, pumped my dick harder, kind of moved around, in and out of the line of the fan, more into the line of light, fingering under my balls, watching the couch action, even though the big hum was right in my ear, obnoxious, seemed huge and more than a hum—a machine-whir—a big machine-whir that wouldn't quit, until a guy's voice—the guy right behind me, not the vid-cam guy—said, "We're wasting time, it's not happening, he's not hard, it's not coming up," and I backed up, not even half a step, my foot hitting something—the light—tripping the hum, my dick—all my business—out of my hands, the light hitting the floor, and me right behind—floored—down, with the lights, next to the vid-cam man. I looked up—facing right at the couch scene—and James's head went off Branch's dick, and then both of them were looking at my mess—James looking under his wet hair, Branch looking over his hard-on. A finger came in front of my face—the woman's—snapping and pointing up, then over to the door, and her face—right in mine—said, "Get up. Get dressed and get out," and the vid-cam man and the other guy started getting me up, pulling up all the equipment, and she said, "Get out—go for a walk, goddammit," and I got up for the bathroom, heard, "Come back here ready and I mean ready, please—" and she nailed my butt with the towel.

Nikki and Jody were leaned up, waiting in the hall, and after I dressed and got out I heard Nikki's "What's going on?"

"Nothing," I said, pushing off a cigarette from Jody, going for the stairs.

Jody said after me, "Are they cool in there?" and I said, "Yeah, they're fine," and Jody said, "They're fine but you're, like, out here, Davy," and I took the stairs and Nikki said, "What've they got you doin'?" and I said, *"I'm not doin' shit right now!"* and Nikki came up right behind me, followed me downstairs, met me at the bums.

"What's goin' on?" she said. "Where're you goin'?"

"I'm walking, that's where I'm goin'." I went faster, back the way James brought us—past the tracks, the buses—Nikki catching up again at the lions, the China arches, saying, "Davy—what'd they do? Did they do somethin'? Something to you? What the fuck is goin' on?"

"Nothing is goin' on." I'd stopped us—there were tons of car lights on Burnside—so we didn't cross. *"Nothing* is going on," I said, and then, "That's what the fuckin' problem is." She pulled me around because I was facing the street, pulled out my hands because they'd been stuck in my pockets, and screwed around with my jeans—unbuttoned them and buttoned them again—because I'd done them wrong.

"Keep losin' it?" she said.

I looked over to the street, watched the car lights, looking for a break. "Can't even get the fuckin' thing started," I said.

"Was it scratching the bugs? Was that it?"

I jerked all the way around—"I don't have bugs!"—found a break in the lights, and went fast across. I crossed through the Chevron, heading back for the big Bart wall, watching his eye get lit up, go dark, from the cars whizzing by, till I heard cars honk, caught Nikki out of the corner of my eye, blocking traffic but crossing. In a second she was coming out of all the Chevron-light, over to the wall.

She came over and kissed me. She pulled on my arm, pulled me around the corner, out against the building, against Homer's stomach, under Marge's smile and the little kid's sucker-toy, and under the parts of Bart, a few yards under his eye, and in the line of the car lights that hummed up the bridge.

She kissed me more, didn't let my hands go, played with my fingers. "It's the lights in there," she said. "The lights is what you're not used to. That's what's fucking you up, that plus maybe you never doing it with James before," she said and I looked away, at the Chevron sign. "In there's prob'ly not like when you and me first did it—at the river, on the rocks, boats goin' by—y'know—all *intimate,*" and I looked back at her and she let my hands loose, kept me up with her mouth on my mouth, and moved her tongue around between my teeth and then I got into it, fingers first, feeling under her shirt, her hands rubbing me, cars whirring up the bridge. "You just gotta relax yourself," she said and her fingers undid my jeans, popping the first button, and double-lights came up—a truck, jamming fast up the bridge—and I squinted one eye to block it out, heard it honk, someone yell, and Nikki licked my ear, laughed a little in it, pulled us more out of the dark part, pulled my top buttons apart, popping the bottom ones open, winding her fingers down—she wound them around my dick, rubbed and scratched a nut, both nuts, and itched me—and I started getting big between her fingers—another set of double-headlights from another truck came up—but they didn't bug me, and I didn't have to squint an eye.

"But y'know," she said, "I could be wrong and it could totally just be the bugs," but I didn't say anything, and she stopped winding and scratching, looked at her fingernails, bit the end off one, then a couple of others, then stuck them back down and scratched, scratched low and slow, the rough stuff getting me hard-hard, bouncy against my balls, and a red light must've gone green because a bunch of headlights—bam-bam-bam—whizzed up, headlight after headlight, and then Nikki went down on me.

I didn't have to squint my eyes when a long, car-light line whirred up, but I must've jerked closed my eyes a second because Nikki looked up, said, "Cars don't bug you," and a rush of three or so cars zipped up—vwoom-vwoom-vwoosh—but Nikki was back to doing me, and the vwooshing just got so loud that it was nothing, and there was an underneath sound, something, a vibe on my dick—Nikki— humming. Buzzing a song up and down on my dick. "You know this?" she said, "You know this song?" and then she said low, "Depeche— 'Just Can't Get Enough,'" and I said, "But at the club we go—" and she said, "'Just Can't Get It Up,'" and then I started to laugh a little and so did the vibe on my dick, so did Nikki—hum and laugh some, and suck and suck and hum and laugh more—till I was close, two or three times close.

But it didn't get liquid. She stopped and buttoned me up and backed us back into the dark, kissed me a lot, rubbed me, kept it ready. She hummed all the way out of the dark, through Chevron, crossing the cars, and the lion and the arch, and buses and tracks and the bum on top of the other bum right up to the door.

Nikki turned the knob and the woman opened it and I was inside, and someone in a corner by a light said I was right on time, said everything was ready and said my face said I was ready. The woman didn't touch me anywhere, or point, or tell me anything.

I stood in the middle of the everything and took my clothes off. Branch and James were in towels in a corner. Branch smoked and didn't look at me, but James did. He hit Branch in the arm and they both looked at me.

I got closer to the couch but didn't sit. There was an itch but I didn't scratch it. For a couple seconds, I stood in front of everything, watching them watching me, and then I went solo, just going off on myself, using and watching both of my hands, then, a couple seconds later, I looked up, just at James, and got one hand off my dick. I started beating slower with one hand, kept eyes on James and got the other hand up, out, opened and then I smiled. Someone—a guy behind a light—said, "Good, good"—and James smiled back, big, at me, came to the couch and sat and held my legs and I touched and rubbed a side of his face, then a couple seconds later, moved my hand, held his chin, beat faster, then my legs went tight inside his hands and he stretched his neck, closed his eyes, opened his mouth and caught all of my shit on his tongue.

The woman said, "Great scene, perfect start," and I closed my eyes, held James's chin tight, leaned down and got my lips on his and the woman said loud, "Branch, get in," and Branch came up fast, rubbed my shoulder, moved me over, and moved James's lips apart with his dickhead.

Nick at Night

It was dark when we got out and Jody came up to us fast, asking how it went, what-all'd we do, would they do one with a chick, too, and Nikki said to me, "You didn't come back out, so it must've went good," and I nodded and Branch said he needed to drink, could get us into the back door of the Brig, and Jody said, "Yea, public drinking," but Branch got an arm partway up and around me and James, looked at Jody and Nikki—dropping, walking behind us—said, "Hey, today's been a guy thing, can we keep it that way?" Then Branch said to me, "What is it, Thursday, right?"

Nikki, behind me fairly far, said, "Thursday."

Branch said, "Dollar drink night, okay, there, some cheap drinks here for the hardest-working dicks in showbiz," got his arm all the way up to my shoulders and James's, pointed up Burnside with his other hand, said back to Nikki and Jody, "Later—the DH—some-time," and I heard Jody say to Nikki, "Hey, those viddie-tokens work in that Laundromat, behind the Embers, so there's, like, laundry," and I got my head around, and Nikki was shaking hers, looking down, and I started to say, " 'Night," to Nikki, but Branch said fast, "Break," ran us across Burnside to Ankeny, kept us moving till the bar.

Branch talked to a guy at the back door of the Brig, and got us in, got us served, then talked to and left with a DJ he'd done at the park.

James counted funds, our cuts from the day, said we had enough to get fairly blasted, jammed to the bar-line and I looked around, drank some of his drink. I got James's hand and got us in a corner in some chairs under the DJ booth and James looked at the dance-floor and said, "You see park people?" and I watched the dance-floor, looking close at three or four guys, nodded.

"Our clientele," James said. "And them," he said, looking at a guy kissing a girl in a corner by the door, and while he was kissing her he was looking at me and squinting some but the music switched, got faster and lights went everywhere and I couldn't see him watching me, heard James put a shot glass on the table.

"What's this?"

"One fifty-two."

"One fifty-*one*," I said.

"Whatever," James said. "It's whatever Douglas drinks, *drank,* held me at gunpoint to drink."

I looked at the glass. "One or two," I said.

"What?"

"Ounces," I said, "Is it a one-ouncer or a two-ouncer, 'cause these're huge fuckin' shots."

"Oh, hold on," he said. He pulled the glass up, put his lips around it, stuck his head up, swallowed, put the empty on the table. "Ones," he said. "These here are one'rs."

I got mine up, said, "Douglas," drank half, rubbed my face, and James pushed my glass back to me, said, "To him being gone," and I drank the rest, then said, "And you bein' here," and he looked at me, said, "Uh-oh, sloppy drunk," then he leaned in close.

"It was cool today, Davy, everything, but I mean, sometime, though it *will* be better," and I nodded, raised my shot glass, then looked around him, behind, into the dance-floor backflash, caught the guy that was watching me, but the girl was gone, and he was looking nowhere now.

James turned around, said, "That guy," looked at me.

"His girlfriend jammed," I said. "But he's scoping us—I think."

"We know him," James said, still looking at me. "Do you remember? Recognize him?"

I said, "I've seen him."

"Nordstrom's, Davy," he said. "Last week, we were trying to work up a little slither in the third-floor men's room and then—*him*," he burped and wiped his mouth.

I said, "Now he's here," finished the last drops of my shot, then my eyes went closed a second and I put my hand around the shot glass and James said, "The one-fifty-something?" and I said yeah, and James got off his chair but his boot caught a leg and he started to go down but I caught him, said, "Let me, okay?"

I mazed the dance-floor, tripped on a light, got to the guy, got right in front of him. Music was loud and I talked loud. "You're Nordstrom," I said.

He looked around me, pulled up a beer bottle and drank some. "What's that?" he said.

"You're Nordstrom security."

"Yeah."

"You threw me out," I said. "You threw me and a friend of mine out"—I turned, pointed at James and he waved—"that friend, there—

out of the third-floor bathrooms is where it was—not real long ago.
A week ago. Right?"

The guy quit looking around me, behind me, looked at me. "Yeah?
Yeah. That was probably you."

"You 'member what for?"

"What's that?" he said, and I said, "You remember why you snuffed
us out?"

"Yes," he said.

"You remember what for," I said, "but you're here. A place like
this."

He drank some beer, didn't say anything, and I said louder than
the music, "You're here in this place and you're mostly doin' the same
thing here that me and my friend were doin' there, *right?*"

He grinned up from the bottle-top, said, "No," said, "My girlfriend
just took off."

And I said, "So then—so why—so what the fuck are you still
doin' here?"

He held up his bottle. "Dollar drinks," he said. I put my hand on
his leg and rubbed some and he pulled it off, said, "Look, I'm not into
you—or this—okay?"

I walked away, back to James.

"What up?" James said.

I shook my head, said, "He says he's just here for booze."

James started checking out funds again, put down about twenty
bucks on the table, then said, "Davy, Thursdays're dollar drinks everywhere, *all* the bars."

I looked at the cash, said, "So that's for—"

"What's the point of being rich movie stars if we can't buy a friend
a drink?"

*   *   *

Me and James got to the dance-floor, James got us under the lights, in the Brig's dance-pit, then James gave some money to a bar-guy and sent Nordstrom a shot, and we danced for a while, and James gave another barguy some more money and sent the guy another shot and me and James got close and the guy didn't get up so me and James got closer together, closer to Nordstrom-guy, James watching him, till the guy'd drunk his last shot, then James looked at him long, and moved down big on my leg.

The guy fingered his empty, watched us grind a few seconds, then took his finger off the glass, walked around us, away from the dance-floor, sat on a stool in a corner, in front of a video-poker machine, pulled some singles out of his pants pocket, stuck one in the machine and started playing.

"Fuck," I said.

"Snuffed," James said, pulling his crotch off my leg. We moved apart more and danced slower, me with my back to Nordstrom-guy. A guy in a T-shirt that said BRIG walked around the dance-floor, looked at everyone dancing, talked into a headphone and I looked down, told James that club security was cruising but he kept his head up, eyes on Nordstrom.

I said, "Dude," and James said, "Is he gone?" and I looked back up and the security-guy had moved, was leaning on the bar-counter, talking to two guys with no shirts. I said, "Yeah, he's gone, but you gotta be cool in here—" and James said, "Davy, Nordstrom's not leaving and it can't be only the cheap drinks keeping him here—" and I said, "James, quit staring at him—okay?—he could get club security on us here—" but James said, "Davy, I'm telling you we can somehow snuff this asshole—" and I said fast, "Me and Nikki never had no problem takin' out asshole guys like that"—and James slowed way down, almost stopped dancing—and looked at me.

"That's it," he said, and I said, "No man, I didn't mean me and her were—better—or—" and James, smiling, said, "No—that's what we need, Davy, that's what *he* needs—just a little female influence to—to—get him over the hetero-hump—" and I nodded, said, "Oh, oh," —and James looked back over my shoulder and I said—"What? What's he doin'?"—and James said, "Flattening dollar bills on his pants-leg and also looking at your ass."

Over James's shoulder, the Brig security-guy was pulling down his headphones and touching a tit of one of the shirtless-guys and James asked me if I could run to the DH, get Nikki, and get back in less than ten and I said, "Less than five," and he nodded, said he'd just dance solo, in the floor-crowd for five minutes, then be at the exit door to let me and Nikki in and I said, "What if Nordstrom jams?" and James shook his head, "He's just ironed, like, forty singles," and behind James's head the Brig security-guy leaned over, kissed the tit of the shirtless-guy he'd been stroking and I said, "I'm out." I moved back through the dance-crowd, broke up two girls dancing close, said, "Sorry," fast, got to the exit door, got it open enough to get through, stepped out and saw Nikki sitting on the big Brig steps under the door, her hand out, passing a cigarette to a drag-dude sitting next to her and I said, "Nik," and both their heads turned back and I got a leg back fast, held the door an inch open with my boot-toe.

Nikki said, "Hey, Davy," and the drag-dude, taking a puff, said, "Hey, child," squinted an eye through the smoke coming up from a mouth-corner, said, "And you are a child." I said, "What're you doin' here?" and the drag-dude gave the cigarette back to Nikki, said, "She's waitin' and makin' sure your sorry, drunk-butt can make it to wherever-the-hell you're callin' home tonight"—and Nikki, smoking,

said, "The DH"—and the drag-dude waved a hand, said, "Wherever"—and Nikki pointed the cigarette at me, said, "Jody's doin' the
wash so I'm doin' the babysittin' "—and the door opened more, pushing my boot away and I turned and James, coming out partway, said,
"Davy—what're you—" then saw Nikki and said loud, "You—Nik—
you're *needed!*" and I looked back but Nikki wasn't up.

She brushed dirt off her boot-smears, then looked at me and said,
"I want to hear *you* say it," and the drag-dude laughed and James
pushed my shoulder hard, before I could talk, but I said fast, "We
need you—we got a snuff and we—I—" and Nikki said, "Okay—
good—don't get sticky—" gave the cigarette to the drag-dude and got
up, brushed off her butt, and James reached out, pulled her into the
club and behind her the drag-dude said, "Woman's work is just
never—" and I got in, pulled the door closed. I stopped us, inside,
said, "Just a sec," because the Brig security-guy was turned our way
but had his arm around both shirtless-guys, was pushing them both
toward an "Employees Only" door behind the bar—so James started
telling Nikki about Nordstrom-guy and Nikki stopped him, said, "Just
point—who and how"—then the shirtless-guys pushed the Employees door open and the security-guy turned, back to us, and followed
them in, and I said fast, "Okay, cool,"—turned, but Nikki'd already
moved around me, was taking space on the dance-floor and was looking over at Nordstrom-guy, and James's boot-toe tapped my boot-heel
and he said, "She's already working magic without you—" so I jumped
down fast to the floor, got with Nikki. She pulled me into a grind
with one hand, ran the other hand through her hair and put her head
back and over the top of her chin, Nordstrom-guy, watching us,
stopped feeding a dollar into the poker machine, pushed it into his
back pocket, got up, came to the edge of the dance-floor and leaned
against the wall, and I leaned down and licked Nikki's neck, said

into her ear, "That guy's the guy that kicked me and James out of Nordstrom"—then her head came up and I touched her cheek, got my arm tight around her back, said, "So—thanks," and a barguy came behind Nikki—handed two drinks to Nordstrom and he took both, raised one to me and Nikki and I looked behind me and James was leaned back against some wall-mirror, smiling, fingers up and crossed.

Outside, later, I stood by a car till Nikki, inside, pushed the back door, said, "Get in." I looked fast across Stark, saw James on the sidewalk outside the Brig, sharing the drink he'd snuck with the drag-dude, and I smiled and they looked over and James held up the glass.

"C'mon," Nikki said, and I got in, Nikki in the middle, Nordstrom-guy way over, and Nordstrom said, "Watch is all, he's only watching, okay, maybe some touching, but mainly watching."

Nikki undid him, got him out, said it was cool, I liked to watch, and she said she'd caught the guy watching me dance, too, and Nordstrom said, "Uhn-uh, no, just maybe his butt, that's it," and she smiled at me then moved her hair around and went down on him, and I watched her mouth and his dick, then watched her hand come up his shirt, go up his neck and push his head back, till he was looking up the back windshield, making some noise. He must've been close because he tried to look down, and Nikki said, "Keep your head back."

"What?"

"Keep your head back." She slowed down on his piece, rubbed his neck, said, "Don't look down," and he moved his head back again, said, "Don't look down," and Nikki said, "Shut your eyes," and he said, "I can't see anything," and Nikki moved off and I moved on, her mouth going up Nordstrom-guy's shirt, mine on Nordstrom-guy's piece, and he said, "It smells in here," and Nikki said, "It's me, I'm a dirty girl," and I laughed a little on his dick, then kept going, and he said, "He's not touching me, is he?" and she moved up, put her mouth on his neck, and said somewhere higher, "He's not touching you," and I heard them kiss, a while, back and forth, and heard her say, "He's not even here," and then, just about then, it got liquid.

Out of Albany

Nikki reached into my front pocket, pulling out a smoke from her pack of cigarettes, but I grabbed it fast out of her fingers, rolled down my window and chucked the smoke and the whole pack out of the car and she hit my shoulder hard, kicked my knee, pushed me over to the door with her butt while I rolled the window back up. Branch, other side of Nikki, said, "Fuckin' chill it," not looking at us from watching the road out his window. We were in the backseat of a car, almost to Albany, an hour or so out of Portland, couple hours into night, friend of Max's driving, James and Jody up front, talking to the driver-guy and screwing with the stereo. It was a couple nights after Branch and me and James'd done the viddie, hit the Brig, and Nikki had a cough and talked bad, and when she quit hitting on me, got her butt back in the middle of us, she coughed four times hard, then swallowed and folded her arms up close to her chest and said, "Fucker, it ain't bad enough to trash my smokes," and I said, "That's what got you sick," and she said, "Not those—Davy—

those were light one-hundreds"—and I said, "Then that drag-dude's smokes—" and she said, "Camels, straights, no filters—okay, a little harsh—so maybe—" then coughed, three more times, and I said, "Save your fuckin' throat," and she said, "I should've stayed back 'cause you don't need me for down here," and I said, "I can watch you here," and she said, "You'll get my shit," and I told her to shut up and save her shit and she started to say something back, got caught in a cough, and Branch said, "We're here," and the car stopped.

I said, "Where's this?" and Branch said, "Just into Albany," and when we got out something smelled everywhere and James and me asked at the same time what it was and the driver-guy said, "A big paper mill real near," and just over the roof of the house we'd parked in front of there were lights blinking, topping off some smokestacks, pumping out steam. Branch said, "Hey—here," to me, and driver-guy popped the trunk and Branch said we had a lot to unload, some 'shrooms but a bunch of A—sheets of Mighty Morphins and Mortal Kombat—that nobody, not us, not Max, could sell anywhere around Portland.

Unloading the bags, James said, "Power Rangers on A is wrong— who wants to fry on expired 'toons?" and I said, "James, Morphins ain't 'toons, it's, like, live, man," and James said, "Pardon?" and I got a couple handfuls of Ziplocs and so did driver-guy and he said, "It'll sell here, Albany's the black hole for fry that doesn't move anywhere else," and Nikki put her face in her sleeve and sneezed, then coughed, quite a few more times, hard. I gave the bags in my hands to Jody to carry, went around the car, got an arm around Nikki. She pushed me off a little but I said loud up to driver-guy, "Hey—what's around here?" and he pointed off behind me, said, "Graveyard—past the tires there," and I walked me and Nikki out toward a tireyard, heading for some tombstones planted on a hill not much more up, and I said to

Nikki, "We'll mellow somewhere," but didn't get too far before Branch said a loud, "Hey—" nodded his head fast at the house, some guys—couple about as old as driver-guy, plus a few guys our age, wearing Albany High shirts and baseball caps—coming out to the porch, saying, "Hey," to the driver-guy, getting into the house. Branch said, "Here to work, jerk," and James looked at me and Nikki over the A-load he was holding and rolled his eyes up.

I stood in a corner of the kitchen holding one Ziploc with three sheets of Mighty Morphins—two red guys, one yellow—and two Mortal Kombats in it and a door in the front room came open, and more guys in Albany High shirts and the guys' girlfriends—already all over—piled in, the guys' hands up fast for high fives. A bottle came up—a fifth of something brown—and started to go through the hands, make the rounds, till one guy said to the others, "Ditch it, man—don't you know drinking and frying makes your dick fall off?"

Nikki—behind me on the counter—tapped my shoulders with her boots and I pulled her arms around and into my neck, hair, and cold nose in my ear, and she said, "We're done here, right?" and kicked my shoulders a little harder, said, "Davy—are we there yet?"

I said, "I heard Branch say the 'shrooms're gone. Sold out." I shook the Ziploc. "But this stuff."

Nikki coughed, pulled her boots back.

"Lemme see," I said. I put the Ziploc in her hand, got out of the kitchen and got around the sort of line into the deal room, an Albany High guy's girlfriend pushing me, looking pissed, the boyfriend saying, "Fuck the cuts, faggot."

"It's cool—" I said, got out of their way, got on my toes, looking up, said, "I'm outta Portland—" looking over some girls' hair and some guys' baseball caps to see the head of the line, deal table in front of everything, looking up for driver-guy—because he'd been dealing— and James—because he'd been cutting hits and cashing—but they were gone. Two older guys—driver-guy's friends—were at the deal table, cutting and cashing. I heard Nikki cough hard from the kitchen—three rough rumbles in a row—turned around and caught Branch running with scissors. He had a drink in one hand—brown— maybe Coke and rum—scissors in the other and he came up behind me, pushed around to the table, put the scissors in the hands of one of driver-guy's friends, who ditched the straightedge he was holding— had been using—under the table, and started cutting the sheets into proper hits.

I said, "Where'd he go—the guy that got us here—where'd he go?" and I said, "And James?"

Branch pulled a wad of little Ziplocs out of his pocket, gave them to the other friend of driver-guy, said to me loud, "Hold on." He came around, had the drink up, over everybody, in my face, and I took it, drank some, and I said, "And Jody"—spit an ice cube back—"Where's Jody, too? Where the fuck is everybody?"

Branch came over, leaned in and took a drink, but the glass stayed with me. "They dropped," he said, walking us out of the acid-line, just into the kitchen. He said it again, louder, looking over to Nikki. "James and Jody dropped. But—like less than a hit—not even half a hit—they're on half a hit each, at most. Plus Jody took a cap and— yeah—I think James probably got the stem."

Nikki nodded her head—started to say something but coughed. I walked my drink to her, but she didn't drink. I said to Branch, "Her cold's worse, man."

"Shouldn'ta made the trip," Branch said.

Nikki cleared her throat.

"And driver-guy," I said. "Where's Max's buddy?"

"He's in town—took off for town is where he said—one of these blond things is his girlfriend and she's twenty-one and he said they're gonna do the bar thing, be back here early AM, and we should just be cool and hang." Nikki coughed, Branch said lower, "Just hang here—that's the deal."

Nikki dropped the bag I'd given her on the floor, then looked over me. I said, "Looks like Albany for the night," and her boot-bottom nailed the back of my head, and Branch said, "Fuckin' *ouch*," and she said to me, "You brought me, now you can't get me out," then coughed more, big and throaty, and while she was coughing snot-drip came out her nose and I got a hand up under her nose and got it, rubbed my hand on my jeans, then she put out her hand because she was ready for the glass.

I pulled Branch's black jacket out of the seat, handed it back to Nikki, got out and closed the back door of the car. I took Nikki's glass, got her into the coat and walked us past the car, into the tire-yard, toward the graveyard. A round of coughs came—long—just as we came up from the tireyard to the first flowers at the front head-stones. Nikki took and killed the rum, made noise in her throat, swallowed a snot-wad, said that was it, she was definitely done for a while, and I dumped the ice, set the glass on the tip of a tombstone.

She said, "Davy—you don't gotta—" but I pulled us down—shutting her up—got us on another grave-top, looked back around, past the dead tires and the car to the house. Guys in Albany High shirts and baseball hats and some girls went in and out of the house, and I could see Branch talking to some Albany High guy, then hands out, taking the guy's fifth-bottle, not much left in the fifth but I heard

Branch say, "Thanks"—and nobody followed us. I got Nikki close, arms around her arms, leaned us back against the tombstone, closed my eyes and put my face tight into her hair, nose to her neck, ear to ear, listening to her try to breathe. I said, "Check out the sky—no fucking rain in sight," and Nikki looked up and I kissed her neck. Paper-mill smell came, a huge fart breezing in, and Nikki, head still up, said, "Cloud," and she said the sky-lights were getting covered for a second or two but I didn't quit the kiss, even with the stink and blacked-out stars.

There was a laugh, but no cough from Nikki and loud laughing close by, coming closer, but nothing from Nikki, just breathing. I pulled my eyes up through Nikki's hair and caught Branch coming out of the house-light, walking up through the tireyard, holding a fifth-bottle in each hand. Albany High guys came out behind him, got in a couple of cars, and took off, but the driver-guy's car stayed.

Branch got to the first tombstone and I said, "Dude—the glass," and he picked up our empty, filled it with stuff from his bottle, came up, passed the glass to me and I drank, passed it to Nikki, looked behind him and there were four people on the porch but nobody was moving around in the house. And then driver-guy's friends came around from the back of the house and sat on the front steps and talked and laughed, smoked and counted cash.

Branch sat next to Nikki, said, "Fuck—this place reeks."

"Mmm-hmm," said Nikki.

"Driver-dude's still out?" I said.

Branch drank off one of his bottles, said, "Unh-hunh," nodding, and a big "Fuck!" echoed up from the tires, and coming out of one, getting up, and walking, then walking on his toes on the edge of another tire was James—he slipped—came down on his balls, yelled, "Double-fuck!" and laughed, then grabbed some stuff off the ground and stumbled up to us. He had a Big Gulp and a box of Pop-Tarts and a thing of cream cheese and a plastic knife and he gave the Big Gulp to Branch, and Branch dumped some, filled the new space with stuff from his bottle and James got open the Pop-Tart bags and broke open the cream cheese and put the cream cheese in between two Pop-Tarts and sat on my side of the gravestone—butt mostly in the grass—and after his laughing'd died some, he took a bite and said, "This place is Oregon's colon," then to Nikki, "He should *not* have made you come here."

"I told him," Nikki said. "But he's guiltin' out 'cause he thinks he owes me for doin' Nordstrom," and I said, "I'm makin' sure you don't get sicker, is all," then James said, "But it's way cool, you're sick with us," kissed her head.

"You're a fry-baby," Nikki said, laughing some, and then James started laughing again, loud, then louder and faster, and he coughed and spit out some Pop-Tart and cheese and Branch reached over, handed James the Big Gulp. James drank on the straw and Nikki said, "Where's Jody—is she cool?"

"She's cool," James said, still laughing low. "She's on the football field with a jock harvesting dandelions." He passed the Gulp, but I said no, gave it back, then Nikki finished our glass, gave it to me, said that was all, she was fine, and I got up, chucked it way far, waiting for the crash but it must've made bushes. Nikki said to James, "You sure Jody's cool?"

"Oh yeah," James said, not laughing, drinking. "The jock—he's high and stupid—Jody—she's safe and coming down. She's just up the road, no big walk," and I said fast to Nikki, "You want me to get her?" and Branch said, "Hold on," pointed to the house-light, and a girl was talking to the driver-guy's friends, on the porch, and they pointed her up to us.

Jody came up, dandelion behind an ear, stopped and kicked a tire and she shook her head, then stood with her hands on her hips, said, "This place is, like, Idaho's soul. I mean, not to be evil or anything, but here's why I left there," and she was pointing out, way over the paper-mill smokestacks.

"Where's your jock?" James said.

"Puking on the forty," Jody said. "I hate this place." James gave her the Gulp but she looked down and took a Pop-Tart, got cheese on it with a knife, ate some, then asked where the driver-guy was, and said, "Oh, well, shit," after Branch said that the driver-guy'd taken off into town with his girlfriend. "Fuck that," she said. "I am not staying here," she said and got another Pop-Tart, turned, walked down.

"You're not hitchin'," Nikki said, loud, lots of snot.

"See me in Portland," Jody said, almost to the tires. Nikki got my elbow with her arm and I got up—Branch too.

"C'mon," I said, and Branch asked Jody what the deal was—Jody just said, "I am not here anymore"—and we told her it wasn't cool at all, not safe to hitch alone. She turned at the tires, came back up— talking and laughing, walking and laughing into James and he laughed loud and fast some more and she went through the Pop-Tart box, pulled the plastic cream-cheese knife and wiped the white on the grass, stuck the knife in her pocket and walked off.

We watched her walk for a few seconds, then me and Branch sat down. Branch tagged James's arm—James was still laughing loud and fast and trying to take drinks off the rum and Gulp.

Nikki—body balled-up, head down, close to asleep again against the headstone—said something low—asked what was going on, where was Jody going—and I put my hand under her chin and pushed on her chin and she stopped talking, coughed, and looked down and I said, "It's okay—it's cool. She's going the wrong way. I-Five's the other way." James laughed big, spitting stuff out and I said, "She's still frying, that's all."

Branch hit James on the head and then on the back of his head, then hit James's arms again and said, "Fuck the acid-laughing!" and James quieted down some and Branch quit hitting him and James took long Gulp drinks. I pulled Nikki's arms, but she wouldn't get up, stayed scrunched, already a couple seconds into sleep. Branch took James's cup, drank the last of the Gulp, chucked it, laughed loud, and James hit Branch's head, then the back of it, said, "Fuck the laughing!" I got up and bent down, got my arms around Nikki, picked her up and started down, going from the graveyard to the tireyard, just as James and Branch started on bottle-shots.

I sat down on a big flat tire, in sight of everything—the house, the car, the dealers, Jody walking nowhere, the straight-shotters at the tombstone—and listened to Nikki sleeping, cool breathing, no noises going off in her throat sounds. Nikki scrunched up in me and I leaned back, down on the black whitewall, stretching across and covering up the hole.

Drive-Thru

Drive-Thru

She slept through the night, mostly quiet till morning, till I heard the car start. I shook Nikki off my shoulder, got up, and pushed Jody—on the ground, head against the tire—with my boot, and yelled up to Branch and James, flat on tombstones up the hill. We were all tired and quiet, nobody talking getting in, or when we got going, everybody crashing on each other, nobody catching that the driver-guy was going more south till Branch, up front, got full awake, said, "Dude, we're southbound," then driver-guy said he'd got a taste of great bud last night plus a lead on where to get more, great deal, Rose Garden Park, Eugene.

Nikki got awake—little later, closer to Eugene—got off Jody and rubbed my knee and her eyes, and looked up over James's head—middle of the front seat, leaned up on Branch's shoulder—then at me. I nodded at the driver-guy, said to Nikki, "Some quick shit in Eugene," then James's head went up and he asked loud where we were, where we were heading and Branch told him, then the driver-guy turned his head back some, said, "We're gonna need some gas funding there also," then, "If we could—get that—taken care of," and me, Branch and James nodded—James saying—"Woo—new territory"—then he turned, looked at me, said, "Shit, sorry, old stompin' grounds."

Nikki coughed, put her face in my shoulder.

I said loud, up to the front, "I'll get it," and James said, "Whatever," turned back around, cranked on the tunes and I said to Nikki's head, "I got you here, I'll get you out," kissed her head then some of her face sticking up.

"Don't," she said. "You'll get my shit," and she coughed again.

Little later, some guy, Wes or Whit, finished me up fast and I got liquid in his mouth in a car in a garage in a house in south Eugene, fairly far from the Rose Garden Park, and the guy's boyfriend said, "Whit, spit in this," threw a towel back from the front seat and I caught it, gave it to Whit, wiped my fingers on my jeans because the towel was already sticky because the boyfriend in the front seat'd beat off and come in it already, and Whit pinched around the towel, found a dry spot, spit, corner-toweled his mouth, handed the towel up to the boyfriend and took the water bottle the boyfriend was handing back, drank a big mouthful, then opened the car door and spit down on the concrete. Whit got out of the car, got into the front seat, driver's side, gave the bottle back to his boyfriend and he screwed the lid on, put it in the glove compartment. Looking back at me the boyfriend said, "I'd offer you some but it's not Evian, it's antiseptic. We always reuse the bottles."

Whit asked him what time it was and the boyfriend asked back what time Whit's shift started and Whit said three-thirty, and the

boyfriend said Whit had more than an hour left, and then the boyfriend asked Whit if he was still going to show him that doctor's house
that was going up, somewhere around Spring Boulevard, and Whit
said, "Yeah," and they kissed and I buttoned up and my stomach went
off, kind of loud, I guess, because Whit said, "Buy you lunch, Davy?"
and I said sure, and the other guy said, "Will your friends wait for
you?" and I said yeah, said they'd be busy in the park for a while—
"They're gettin' dope and I'm supposed to be gettin' gas money," I said
and Whit said to his boyfriend, "Kev—Taco botch," and the boyfriend,
Kev, said to me, "Davy—Taco Bell drive-thru okay?" and I said yes,
okay, thanks. I buckled up and Whit started the car and Kev clicked
a button and the garage door went up and afternoon light came in
and we backed out.

In the car in a Taco Bell lot about Twenty-ninth and Willamette
I sat holding almost half a burrito in one hand, a little less than half
a large 7UP in the other hand, and I watched three skidders cruise
in front of us, skateboarding through the lot, up the street, and they
stalled, played around till there was a sort of break in the cars, then
they went fast across Willamette, stopped and cruised around a while,
skidded and popped a bunch of speed bumps and curbs right across
from us, in a 7-Eleven lot and hippie-bakery lot and in a Deadhead
fruit stand parking lot.

In the front seat Whit had maybe two burrito bites left and he
took one, said to Kev, "I guess Russ and Fineman and Dr. Mulvahill—
you've never met Mulvahill, I don't think—I guess they've all got an
interest in that whole lot on Spring Boulevard—actually their section's called Spring Knoll, it's like at the end, a cul-de-sac—but Russ's
girlfriend holds the title to the lot because his divorce hasn't finalized

and so his wife can't claim it as mutual property, or assets or whatever, and I guess he wanted to hold off building on it, but, you know,
they had to start up before the rains." Whit took his last bite, wiped
his mouth, put on sunglasses and Kev held up their drink and Whit
sucked the straw, kissed Kev quick, started the car and I wrapped up
my shit—the half burrito, a full load of chips—stuck them in a paper
bag, put the bag on the floor, on a floor-pile of papers and pictures
of cars, and drank my drink and Whit pulled the car out into Willamette, and I looked out the back window, watched for the skidders
and caught them cruising way up Willamette, done with parking lots.

We came around and onto the bottom part of Thirtieth, twisting
around the running trail and the bike trail and the skateboard pit,
passing runners, bikers, more skidders and I shifted around,
scrunched up, kept my head low. Whit looked at me in the front
mirror and said, "My driving that bad?" and Kev looked back, rubbed
Whit's shoulder, and I said he was driving okay, that I thought I saw
someone I knew was all, and he smiled in the mirror and Kev looked
away and after a red light on Hilyard, Whit gunned the car way up
Thirtieth, steep, and in a couple seconds, turned right, gunning us
up steeper, high onto Spring Boulevard.

Kev pointed, said, "That's hot," opened his window some, pointed
out, and Whit slowed the car some, looked over and I looked out, at
a big blue house with no cars in front of it, and Whit said, "Yeah—
Russ says it's on the market for close to half a mil," and Kev said, "In
Eugene? No conceivable way. In Eugene?" and Whit said, "It's got a
bowling alley," and he looked in the mirror at me and said, "And a
very big garage," and Kev looked around, made a small smile, and we
were moving again, going up higher, quite a few huge houses on both
street-sides. My stomach messed around so I drank more 7UP. Kev
said, "Sorry about the garage, Davy," pointed at the house again, said

something about the house to Whit, then said to me—his eyes still looking out the window—"It's not the most romantic of places, we know, but it's a safety thing—for us—"

"—It's enclosed," Whit said.

"It's easy access and easy escape," Kev said, "in case someone—not like you at all—but someone—else—were to pull out a knife or whatever, not that you would, David."

"We never take strangers in the house," Whit said, and then Whit's boyfriend said Whit got the idea when he worked split shift E-ward this one time. Kev said, "Whit, was it two or three?"—and Whit said, "Three," and Kev said, "These *three* kids did themselves in, a suicide pact, in a car, in a garage, inhaling fumes, so I suppose that's where the idea came from." The car leveled out, followed a long line of big houses, and I looked out the window, over the road, caught some clear ground, blank space, and I could see almost all of south Eugene and Whit said, "It's a safety thing," then rolled down his window, pointed out, across Kev and said, "Oh, this view is absolutely priceless."

"Absolutely rocks," Kev said, and Whit, still looking across Kev, hit something, nailed a bump, and my nose hit the window because I was still looking and I moved back, got over in the seat more, kept eyes ahead.

The street got high again, the car went up and I slid, over and back to my window. A couple houses came up. Kev said to Whit, "The brickwork is really fabulous here," and Whit said back, "But it's really mixed, it's like—what is that—that really cheesy, sixties layered stuff and Spanish style, a bad mix, very Mexican-border, it's really Californian," and Whit pointed out again, said, "Actually, yeah, this one's better, it's not as bricky, and that one there's too much brick-work—like so much that they didn't even know what to do with it—

this one's better, the chimney and the carport—that's where the brick is, and really ought to be," and Whit pointed up, to a corner, said, "The place is up here, right around there," and Kev looked up ahead, said, "Our five-year plan needs something here as its goal, something on this block, with brick, well-done brick."

We turned right and I looked for a sign around the corner of the street.

"It's got its own name," Whit said, "Spring Knoll, it's not official, they haven't put anything up yet, but it has been named," and we got into the cul-de-sac, hit some bumps and gravel, and my stomach turned around and I sucked on my straw but the drink was dry.

Whit said, "That's it," and Kev said, "It's huge—Whit, it is huge," and I looked around—there were only four houses total, two on each side, pretty big, taking up a lot of space, but Whit and his boyfriend were still looking ahead, and I looked ahead and didn't see anything. We drove higher, slower, to the end of the cul-de-sac and there still wasn't anything—we'd hit the end of a dead-end street.

"Seventeen K," Whit said, and stopped the car, and we all looked out the window. There was some gravel going out off the street to some cement, big slabs, fairly big slabs, with wooden sticks sticking out, and I leaned out my window more and Whit got out, then Kev and then I got out of the car, followed them a little way down the gravel and stopped. There were more sticks stuck in the ground, no cement yet, but the sticks were way apart, squared out really wide, and Whit and Kev walked a little more, stopped and stood just about in the middle of a huge stick-square and Whit looked at Kev, touched his shoulder, got him close, and said, "No—wait—seventeen thousand *five hundred* square feet, that's what it is, that's the total," and Whit kissed his boyfriend, and in the middle of the kiss Kev said, "That's like a Nordstrom."

My stomach went off—big—and turned and burned and came up—really fast—and I puked 7UP and beans and hot sauce on the gravel, outside the sticks, and then again, more, splatting the ground, painting the gravel, and then I coughed and coughed and spit and wiped my mouth and looked around, and the car-guys were still standing in the middle of the big stick square. Whit looked at me. Kev looked at me, put his head down, rubbed his head, looked away, looked at the view, looked at the city.

A couple seconds later we got back in the car, Kev in the driver's side, asking for the keys, Whit giving him the keys, reaching back, giving me the bottle with the fake water. I took a hit, and Kev started the car. I swished the stuff around and spit on the ground, closed the car door and gave Whit back his bottle, then asked if I could please get my money now.

Later afternoon, back in the backseat of the driver-guy's car, going north, Branch had his head down, smelling the big bag of bud, and he brought it up some, up to his window, and James looked over Jody in the front, said, "Branch, baby, don't be flashing traffic," and Jody, not turning, looking at the road through the window, said the stuff was reeking out the car but it was a good reek, and I got my face close to the side of Nikki's, her eyes staring ahead at the road and I said real low, "We maybe have a place."

She stayed looking ahead.

"Friend of Max, not this guy, he's settin' us up—"

She nodded.

"But Branch—he only told me—so don't tell—"

She nodded again, coughed a little one.

"Oh, yeah—guess you can't—but—so—get better, okay?"

The back stereos came on real loud, and Branch dropped the bud-bag, said, "Fuck," then James turned around, said, "Shit, sorry, just found those knobs," turned back and I said to Nikki, " 'Cause it's a whole basement," and she said, "Oh, cool," but James caught Nikki's "cool" and said loud, back speakers going down, "It's Everclear—Portland grown—gonna be big—you likin' it?"

Nikki said, "Yeah, it thrashes," rubbed my knee and I rubbed up her arm, said, "Save your fuckin' throat."

Non-Foods

When we got back, we slept. It was night and we all got in our spots and I heard Nikki cough two times at the start of her sleeping, small ones, throat-clearers, then didn't hear anything else till Nikki said loud, "You got a shitload of cinnamon here, Davy," and I opened my eyes and she was holding a Coffeepeople to-go cup out to me and I looked around her and everybody was gone and daylight was just coming on.

"Somebody fucked with the cinnamon lid," she said, took a drink from the drink-hole, "Loosened it up so a ton of it came out but I stirred it in but you can still taste it," and she held the cup back out and I drank some, but it was mostly mocha, said, "It's all right," asked if it was very crowded, this early, at the Metro, and she said, "Davy, it's almost dark." I sat up, fast, looked out the windows again, said, "Late night," and she said, "You slept through, whole day," and I rubbed my eyes, looked down at my chest, saw drool running down past a rib, and Nikki said, " 'Cause you watched me the whole damn trip, that's why you crashed and burned." I drank more, and then said, "You sound better," and she said she was better, moved over, pulled up and flipped open some newspaper next to her and I asked where everybody was and she said, "At P-Square," and I said, "Just hangin'?" and she said, "Just hangin', all day, all we did," then she pulled up Jody's knife, said, "Drink that and get up."

I took a big sip, she put the knife, point down, in the middle of a newspaper-page, started slicing a square and I leaned over, looked down, saw she had the Food Section, was cutting around a coupon.

"What's that for—"

"Safeway—" she said, " 'cause we're done hangin', you're done sleepin', and we're goin' shoppin'—" and I said, "You up to that?" and she pulled out a coupon, set it flat on the floor, said, "Davy—it's just the Safeway on Tenth—Branch says we need some 'non-perishables'—" and I said, "Yeah, but you feel—?" and she said, "Fuckin' *better*—" and I took a drink, said, "Okay"—then coughed, hard.

"See—*you* got my sick," she said, but I shook my head, till I was done coughing, then said, "Got to be the cinnamon."

It was dark by the time me and Nikki got to the Safeway lot on Tenth and Jefferson and everybody was leaned on a truck by the store-doors. James—looking at me—said, "It lives"—and Branch said to Nikki, "You get pit-stick?" and Nikki, up to Branch, at the truck, looked through her coupon-stack, stopped at one, said, "Seventy-five off Soft & Dri"—and James laughed and Branch said, "Too pretty"— and Jody said, "Pretty is okay," and Branch said too bad we didn't have enough cash to get two pit-sticks, so the girls could smell pretty and the guys could smell like guys, and we started up to the doors and Nikki gave Branch her coupons, said she'd be right in, she had to pee. She walked back, got between the truck and another car and

I followed her, said I'd cover her, and Jody, following Branch into Safeway, said, "We're *real* shoppers—she should be able to use the bathroom," and Branch said, "Doesn't matter, *they're* Nazis downtown," and I got in front of Nikki, and she got her pants down and squatted, and James held back too, leaned against a car across from us, watched for people.

I said back to Nikki, "There's no coupon for smokes in that stack, right?" and Nikki said, "No!" and James laughed and I turned, looked down at Nikki, said, " 'Cause just 'cause your throat's cool now, no reason to smoke right off—" and James—laughing louder, walking over, said, "Davy—get off her back!" I stepped back because the pee was running down to my boots and James pushed my shoulder, said, "Guard her, don't preach to her, Reverend Slither," and Nikki shook her butt, looked up, said to me, "Would you ask Branch if we got enough for TP?" and James pushed me again, harder, so I went into Safeway, left them in the lot.

A couple minutes later I was standing next to Branch in the soap and pit-stick aisle and he was going through the Soft & Dri's, popping the tops, sniffing and holding them out to me, one at a time, asking, "Does this smell like snatch?" but before I'd say anything he'd sniff the stick again, say, "Yeah, too much," put the top back on, put the thing back on the shelf. "Dude, there's gotta be one that doesn't reek like chick," he said. "Like neutral, nothing." He reached up, got one with a white lid, got it off, sniffed, held it out and I sniffed and there was no smell and Branch looked at the label, said, " 'Soft & Dri Unscented,' cool, remember this, the brand for *both*," then Jody came down the aisle, said, "Davy, I need you for two seconds, okay?" got my arm, got us out of the aisle, fast past a bunch more till we were in front of some flowers in a refrigerator. She pointed to three big purple ones in a vase and I said, "Pretty, yeah," and she said, "Well, of course, they're lilacs, Davy, but can you get them down your pants?" and I looked behind us, down the milk and cheese section, then over Jody's shoulder to the checkouts and I said, "You seen James and Nikki?"

"I saw them come in, but—" she looked around—said, "But—no—not real recently—" then looked back at the lilacs, said, "So—do you think?" and I said that Branch'd said there were cameras in the ceiling here, so not to try to scam anything, we'd get caught and Jody, looking up, said, "But lilacs put out great smell and the DH needs . . . something." She looked down and I got her hand, said, "Yeah, okay, this way," took us down the milk aisle, past the back of a few more, then up one, stopped us in front of some cardboard car fresheners, between the motor oil and car wax. She looked at them, took down a green tree-shaped one that said OREGON SPRING and sniffed it.

"They're not, like, pretty, or anything," I said. "But they got smell."

Jody said, "Oh, this fucking stinks," put the tree back on the wire holder, looked at me and said, "No. No way. I mean, I'm sorry, Davy, but at least DH BO is, like, *real.*"

Branch went by the end of the aisle, carrying a red plastic basket of stuff in one hand, holding, looking down at his coupons in the other, and I said loud, "Branch—hey—" got up to him and asked if he'd seen James or Nikki and he shook his head, looked down at a four-pack of MD TP in his basket, and said, "Some old chick just told me they had this on sale two days ago so I could've saved almost a dollar instead of just forty-five cents from their fuckin' *in-store* coupon hangin' up next to it, so I'm gonna make a stink at checkout, get the fuckin' difference, bet shit on that, 'cause we can't help it we were outta town, couldn't make their fuckin' sale," and I nodded, said,

"Cool, Branch," turned, said I was going to do a quick look for James and Nikki.

I went up to the checkouts, looked over them to the magazine racks, didn't see anybody, looked down at the cigarette-case by the bread, didn't see them, so I started across the front of the store, stopped and looked down each aisle, most empty, not many people shopping, stopped at the candy aisle, crowded with some little kids and an old guy, talking, holding the candy they were picking up and I looked past all of them, didn't see James or Nikki but heard Nikki laughing loud, next aisle, over the kid-noise. I backed up, looked around some big bags of stacked-up Reese's Pieces, saw James hand Nikki a red bottle that said "Vidal Sassoon Mousse," close his eyes, lean back onto some shampoo bottles that fell, then he smiled and Nikki shook the red bottle, put the spout up to her mouth, pushed it on her bottom lip and sucked and giggled, then James looked over, saw me, tapped the bottom of the red bottle. Nikki looked up, pushed too hard and white foam sprayed on the side of her face and she said, "Shit," and wiped at her face, and James, smiling at me, said, "Well, you won't let her smoke!" He got the wad of white she'd wiped off her face onto his fingers and rubbed it into her hair and she took another hit, just fumes, then said to me, "It's okay, Davy, I got a coupon for this," laughed and James laughed, turned, got the shampoo bottles straight on the shelf, but one, then two, fell, hit the floor. I rubbed my head, walked down, picked the bottles up, put them on the shelf, then took Nikki's red bottle, already up to her mouth for another hit, and her and James both looked at me and I shook the bottle, got the spout up to my mouth, pushed it down and got some fumes and swallowed them down, then shook my head, the hit coming on, then a "Hey" came loud, down the aisle and we looked over and Branch was there, in front of the bags of Reese's, holding his basket full of stuff and Jody, beside him, held up one big purple lilac with a white ribbon around it and she said to me, "Branch said we could afford one, this time, sometime, more," and Branch said fast, to all of us, "Yeah—and we ought to be able to afford better fuckin' drugs than *that.*"

Nikki laughed—coughed once—then kept laughing.

5X

We were waiting for Branch, back at the DH, a few nights after Safeway, all of us sitting around the floor, holding Big Gulps, cherry Coke, no ice, James looking up to a window every few seconds at the night street, sitting back, saying, "*It* better not get here before *he* does." James'd just got back on his butt when Branch came crawling through the hole in the other window and Nikki laughed loud, said, "He beat it, now shut it," and James said, "Girl, you bug, when you're not incapacitated," and Branch got up, said, "Hey—nobody—no sudden moves." Branch pulled a square wad of paper out of his back pocket, unfolded it slow and said, "Bring 'em here," and we went up to him, fast, holding our cups out, and Jody, coming up slow, said, "Oh, should I be doing candles?"—and James, Nikki and me said, "No," and Branch said to Jody, "Get your knife, though." Jody looked around, got her knife and Branch put the unfolded paper on the floor, then Jody handed him her knife and Branch crouched and cut the white powder pile in the middle of the paper into five little piles. Branch held the paper up, scraped a pile into each of our cups with the knifeblade and we finger-stirred the stuff into the Coke. Branch said drink fast because it was bitter shit, and James, looking back at the window, said drink fast because the cab was here.

We finished drinking, chucked our cups on the floor, cup-bottoms spinning into each other and I must've looked at the cups a couple seconds too long because Nikki—in front of me, behind the line to climb out of the window—looked at me, smiling, and I said, "No, I ain't on yet."

We got out of the DH, into a cab parked across the street, cab-guy looking at us, asked Branch, first in the back, for cash up front, and Branch handed him a ten, said, "Pittock Mansion," then a wad of ones—four, maybe five—said, "Go slow," and the rest of us got in the back, pushing up against Branch till he was flat to his window. The cab got going and James leaned over Nikki and said to me, "Branch must be on 'cause he's not freaking on the money thing," and Branch said, "Hey, it's a national fuckin' holiday, okay?" Cab-guy got a little of his window open, said to the mirror, "Mind this?" and James sniffed Nikki's pits and Jody said, "Blech—stinky boys," and I got my head up some, got into the fairly cool air coming in. Then, little while after getting moving, we stayed quiet a while, everybody looking out, watching nightlights and Burnside people, and then, going by the big blue Volvo sign and car shop under it—JULY FOURTH SUPER SALE in big letters in the windows—Jody said, "See, actually, I heard X was supposed to be slow," and Nikki got Jody's hands in hers, looked at her face, said, "You're on," and Branch leaned over me, said, "Hey— look at mine," and Jody leaned over James, Nikki and me, looked at Branch, nodded, then Nikki got her face into James's and James said, "Woo—fixed and dilated," and Nikki said fast, "Yeah, you too," and James kissed her mouth quick, said, "Uhm—nope—still ain't love," and Nikki kicked his knees and James yelled, then laughed, then Nikki put her face in mine and I kissed her long. Jody said, "Big fat sweet vibe," and James said, "Thanks, Max," leaned on Nikki's back, fingered my hair, then Nikki's, and Branch, back to watching Burnside, said, "Yeah, thanks, Max," then loud, "Hey, besides, getting good shit and grooving on fireworks and everything, there's another whole reason to be celebrating," and the car stopped hard at a light and cab-guy said, "Yeah, sorry," and Branch looked at the cab-guy in the mirror and all of us were looking at Branch.

"Tell you on the hill," Branch said.

James and Jody said, "What?" but Branch looked back out. Nikki moved her face into my neck, got some teeth on my ear.

We stopped way up Burnside—almost to the zoo—on the side of the road—all the doors already open, James and Jody out first, fast up a side road through trees. When Branch, me and Nikki got out they were already standing against the gate and they saw us and smiled and climbed over it and walked fast up more of the road. Nikki looked at me and Branch and smiled then turned and took off and Branch said to me, "Walk," so we stayed slow, and I said, "I think I'm on a comedown," and then we got to the gate, climbed over and when I went over change jingled out of my jeans pocket and I bent to get it and it was all mostly viddie-tokens, and Branch said, "You told Nik," then I looked up from picking the stuff up and nodded.

He said, "Figured that," bent and got a couple tokens.

I got them all in my hand, stood up, said, "Nobody else, though," and he said, "Cool, that's cool," got one of the tokens between two fingers and whizzed it into the trees off the trail. I said, "Hey"—real fast—"shouldn't we be stowin' those for—"

"Sometimes," he said fast, getting the other tokens ready to whiz, "You just gotta fuck it," flicked it way up the path.

We split the rest of the real change and tokens, flicked and whizzed all of them into trees, up the road, while we walked. The road got steep and in the fairly bright night cloud-light I could see peel-out holes in the gravel and I kicked around them with a boot, til the road got real steep, and we had to bend forward some, the more we went up.

"Branch, man," I said. "Comin' up here, comin' *here,* Portland—"

"I told you it would be."

Two booms came on, same time almost, up the hill, then two big patches of white lights came up in the sky way over the trees.

"Dumbass," Branch said, "You hittin' again?—You comin' on again?" and I said, "Fuck, yeah," started walking faster, then Branch tagged my arm, hard, said, "Run, fag," so we both booked up the hill.

More noise and fireworks came on and we slowed up to watch at the start of the top of the hill and when the sky-light got big I looked around where we were and the trees and bushes'd gave way and there was an empty parking lot on one side, and a huge lawn on the other side, and in the middle, the mansion—two skateboarders doing flips on the porch—plus Nikki behind them—leaned forward on some window-doors looking into the place.

I ran up Pittock's porch-steps and around the 'boarders up to where Nikki was looking in—all the gray brick and black glass getting covered in color from a couple more hits of fireworks. I looked over Nikki's shoulder, inside, and Nikki moved back, leaned up against a metal plate with names and dates stuck in the Pittock wall. Inside Pittock were stairs and signs and doors closed and a hallway roped off and some big bangs went off and I looked back, tons of small lights whiting up the sky, brighting out all the city and river and airport lights under the hill, under us. The skaters on the porch stopped their boards and yelled, "Whoa," and Jody, way over, off the lawn, bent up from some flowers, yelled, "Yeah," and James, standing on a bench, end of the lawn, edge of the hill, yelled, "Woo," and Branch, still standing in the gravel, said loud, "Yeah, that kinda rocked." The big sky-light went down, smaller ones, not as much bang, coming up, and James turned around, yelled at me and Nikki, "They did a Madonna flick here," he pointed at Pittock, "in there," and Nikki yelled, "What flick?" and a skater-dude yelled, "The one that sucked," high-fived the other skater and James jumped off the bench, said loud, "Huh! The *one,*" started humming, and I got going down the porch-steps, across the lawn, Nikki right behind me, and Branch started moving toward the bench too. The skaters dropped their boards, sat on them where we'd been at.

At the bench, Nikki asked James what the fuck he was humming, said she'd heard it but couldn't nail it and James said, "From the club—superdisco—kind of old—" sang loud—" 'Disco me to ecstasy Babyford, Babyford, chikki chikki ahh ahh,' " and Branch said, "Thought you didn't like disco too much," and James said, "I like a little—just that part of that tune—chikki chikki ahh ahh," then a huge handful of flowers came up over Nikki's shoulder and Jody said, "Omigod—look at these," brought them down lower and shook them, said, "Look at these fucking colors I'm holding here, like—five, six, eight— eight colors in my hand"—she looked over Branch—"and I haven't even got to the roses yet," then she looked at Nikki and me and smiled big, said, "I'm peaking."

"Good," James said. "Go peak over there," then Jody nodded, ran off to some bushes behind Branch. "We got space," James said.

Nikki looked at me, then Branch, said she told everybody while me and Branch were still coming up the hill.

Branch said, "Hey—cool—now—'cause it's for sure," and I looked quick at Branch, nodding, more fireworks-light coming on. Branch said, "Saw Max in the park—he said it's totally for sure, real soon, couple weeks at most," and James yelled, "Woo for basements," and Jody, standing up, way behind Branch, rubbing her face, getting plant-dirt on a cheek, yelled, "You know—you can *grow* shit in basements!"

The bangs stopped and the night-sky got dark, stayed dark. James said to Branch, "Where's it at, where's the building?" and I got up on the bench real fast, looked out at the city, pointed toward some lights, off by Jody's side of the lawn and Branch said, "That ain't close," got on the bench by me, pointed to other lights, more in the middle of the city light-spread, said, "You had us in Heathman, Davy, Jesus-fuck," then James got up, pointed just at the lights under me, said, "Branch—total boob—*here's* the Heathman, okay?" then pointed back where Branch'd had his finger at, said, "*That's* the Benson, mapless freak," and behind all of us, Jody yelled, "Basement of the Benson? Omigod!"

Branch yelled back that we weren't getting the fucking basement of the Benson, or the Heathman or the Marriott, then Nikki sat down, felt my ankle, said, "But we're gettin' out of the Dead Hotel, that's what's cool, that's what counts," and me, James and Branch all nodded and sat down. Jody came back, got with us, next to Nikki. Branch leaned his head back, folded his arms, and Jody licked her hands, wiped dirt off her face.

I was in the middle of Nikki and James and got an arm around both and they scooted close, Nikki's head on my neck, James's head and hands on my chest. There were some real small bangs down in the city but no more lights came up and fireworks-smoke clouds still stayed over the trees. There was laughing right behind us and then the skateboarders came up beside Branch's side of the bench, holding their boards, flicking the wheels, looking at the light-spread, then one of them looked at all of us and said, "What're you s'posed to be?" and Branch got his arms unfolded and looked at the kid a long time, till the kid shook his head then him and his friend left. Branch got his arms back folded, closed his eyes, put his head back and smiled and James hum-sang into my chest, "Chikki chikki ahh ahh, chikki chikki ahh ahh."

Seattle's too big and you can tell it's too big from not very far away. Portland's different, was different, coming in, it's flatter, and everything, buildings, lights, are under you and I-5 goes down into it, fast, with a lot of turns, but the ride into Seattle is all up and straight because Seattle's high and everything's above you and when our ride let us out, late at night, right in front of the Kingdome, I said to Nikki, "There's no fucking way—is there? This's too fuckin' big—isn't it? He's gone and he's gonna stay gone." Two huge whistles went off from a train coming into the Amtrak station, real close, and I yelled, "Am I right?" but Nikki already had her head going, shaking, shook it a while, until all the train noise was gone.

We stayed in Amtrak a while but got kicked out for not having tickets so we took turns sleeping, staying awake in the bed of a truck with no alarm-light in the front, parked across from the Kingdome, until first light and Nikki shook me up, reminded me that our ride had said to head up toward Capital Hill to get to Volunteer Park. And we walked *and hitched and asked directions but everything—all the moving, so fast, getting out of Oregon, into Seattle—caught up with both of us, not very much later that morning, in a place that wasn't a park but a baseball field, somewhere in Capital Hill, off Broadway, where we grabbed a stall in the men's side of the johns, locked the door and I took the floor and Nikki took the seat, let her feet rest on my head so she could stretch out totally.*

We slept that way a while, could've even been a few hours, before I got awake, Nikki's feet down, hanging in front of my face, boot-toe twitching giving me little kicks in an eye. I swiped at one, hit the pink side-smears, and when she grumbled and pulled them into her I saw two dicks, hard and twitching, sticking in our stall-walls. One of the guys coughed and the other one was whispering, "Hey, you in there, hey, you in there?" One dick, the bigger one, twitching through a hole on Nikki's side of the stall, pulled back little by little out of the hole until it was out, then a second later it came back through, wet.

I scooted back, balled up more in my stall-side corner. A dribble of dick-spit dropped off the tip of the big one, into one of Nikki's eyes, then both her eyes came open fast. She said, "Fucking yuck," looked over at me, at the dick above me, then brought her hands up and flicked the dickheads hard with her fingernails and the big-dick guy whispered hard, "Hey—!" and the other guy didn't say anything but both of them pulled out. There was flushing-noise, then footsteps, then Nikki laughed, scooted around, stared at me, laughed more, and I guess I was still partly asleep or still fairly tired because I couldn't.

Foo Fighting

Just past mid-July, it got hotter, even early, and one morning after Nikki and Jody'd already caught Tri-Met to Eighty-second, me, Branch and James were going through Yamhill Market, getting food, and passing the newspaper and magazine stand, James said, "Wish we could just whip these off," pulling on his shirt, and Branch, looking at the front of an *Oregonian* laying on the counter, looked up over to James, then James said, "I know," looked down the top of his T, felt over the little lump sticking out further down, said, "Twelve goddamn ounces of fucking dried cranberries," and Branch got us moving through the market again, said to James, "Don't know why you snagged that shit—" and James said fast, "I was reaching for raisins—or trail mix or prunes—because all we eat is puke and I was thinking fiber and everybody likes raisins—"

"Jody'll eat 'em," I said, right as we were going by the candy counter and Branch stopped us, let other market-people walk around us. I patted my two shirt lumps, said, "I got fiber—peanuts and them protein bars," and Branch nodded, looked back quick at the candy counter, then at us again, said, "Orange slices or Gummy Bears?" and James, putting his shirt further into his pants, fixing his lump from falling, said, "Let's ask ourselves if we *really* need either of those particular food groups," then Branch said, "Bears, then, fuckhead," looked at James, pointed up to the fish counter and James said fast, "Uhm—no—no bass next to my nipples," and Branch tagged his dried-cranberries-lump, said back, "No, there's jerky—real meat jerky—around the corner, there, in these open things you can just reach in for," started to walk to the candy counter, said, "Remember—wait for a little crowd, then snag, get the shit with cheese if they got it," then a bunch more people came walking through and Branch said low around them, "Davy, you're full up, you watch, you cover," and I turned back around to follow James but he was already going around the fish counter. I looked at Branch looking slow over jars of jelly beans and Gummy Bears, saw him get the lid off and reach in the Gummy Bears when the countergirl started scooping out a jar of chocolate balls for an old guy and a little girl at the cash register. I walked over to the fish counter and looked down past the ice and big fish but James wasn't at the jerky jars. I walked fast down more of the market, got around a corner and James was coming through a small crowd of people around some guys sitting at a table. James was holding a CD and he saw me, walked faster, held the CD up, said, "Woo—it's Foo!" when he got to me. I said, "What—what's what?"—looked at the CD cover—over a picture of a toy-gun it said "Foo Fighters"—and he said, "Foo Fighters," pointed back, "That is them, Nirvana leftovers, well, one, anyway," and I took and looked at the CD more, said, "How much was—"

"Free," James said and I got us walking back around and he said there'd been some chicks at the end of the fish counter holding Foo

Fighters CDs, talking about the band being here, giving out some promo-copies, and James said he also heard they were doing a show at Roseland, up Sixth, and he said it'd be cool to go or even just hang early, see them set up if the show was way expensive.

We came around the front of the fish counter and I looked over some ice to the candy counter but Branch was gone, said, "Shit," and James said, "God, *great*," tapped a CD corner real light on his leg, said, "Tells me to watch out and he gets snagged," then we went fast through the candy-counter crowd, by the newspaper stand looking at heads and faces, then we stopped at the Taylor Street corner of the market, looked at each other and I said, "Fuck," and James said, "Davy—maybe the bathroom," and I nodded, looked down the Second Street side of the market and Branch was running, hands full of CDs, up to us. He said, "Run," kept going by us, so we followed him, up Taylor, out of the market, holding our shirt-lumps, James shoving his CD into one of my back pockets. James looked back while we ran, said he saw some of the band chasing us and I looked but the guys he'd been talking about'd stopped on the corner of Third, then James, looking ahead, said, "Branch's cutting up here," so we turned on Fifth, followed Branch around the Saks part of Pioneer Place, then he stopped, up further, holding his hips, breathing hard in front of Newberry's.

James, getting breath, said to Branch, "I can't believe it," then James bent some, straightened his cranberries-lump, said, "You robbed Foo—didn't you?"

"Ozone'll take 'em," he said, holding up the stack of CDs, about ten. He sleeved some face-sweat, said, "We can resell 'em at Ozone, right, Davy? Like maybe four but prob'ly what, three bucks each here and"—he pointed at the CD James was pulling out of my pocket—"there, got one, just one, James?"

James emptied his shirt, held the cranberries-bag but had fingers tight on the CD, said to Branch, "You only sell music for total money-emergency—not just—to get rid of them," and Branch said, "Keep one—whatever—but just one." I got the little food bags out of my shirt, wiped face-sweat off with my shirt-bottom, and James said, "Branch, these guys are playing at Roseland, we could attempt," but Branch was already turned, shaking his head, straightening out his armload of food and CDs and he said, "Can't really waste the funds," then fast to both of us, "Let's hit Ozone now 'cause those guys could call up all the stores and report these or somethin'," and we walked fast with him up the street. Then James said, "We could watch them setting up, Branch, before the gig, possibly catch a tuning-up, get an autograph," and Branch, still walking, said, "No, dude—we can't waste the fuckin' time either—now we're goin' Ozone, then park, and that's what today is, that's all."

James looked down, kept walking but came around the other side of me, cranberries-bag crinkling from his fingers holding tight and he banged his CD real light on his leg and I looked down, couple streets later and there was a crack in the cover so I told him to quit. James held up, looked at the cover, going through a crosswalk, letting Branch get ahead—and the crack was over the toy-gun barrel—wasn't long, but had two bumps—and I said it looked like a pulled-out W and James said, "No, it's Branch's sad sorry ass."

Branch got twenty-five at Ozone and coming out he said to me, "When I had to give them an address I put down something that'd be right in the middle of the Market," and he went ahead some and James said to me, "Twenty-five'd get us right up to feel Foo-sweat," but Branch heard, stopped, said, "Hey—it's our future—it's rent, food, shit." Branch kept us stopped, stood in front of James. After a couple seconds James said, "Right," looked at me, said, "Right," again then Branch got out of the way.

We ditched our food and shirts at the DH, got to the park and later it got hotter, especially at the top trail, the one I was cruising, and a guy in shorts was following me down but I caught a noise by a bush and stopped, looked around, and James stuck his head up from the bush, said low, "Chikki chikki chikki," and the guy following me went by, looking back at James and James said loud, *"Ahh Ahh!"*

I said, "You blew that for me," and James, getting out of the bush-leaves, said, "Well if I you want, I will, but, Davy, it's not like today's exactly *dead*," and I looked back up the trail and there was another guy in shorts, stopped at a tree, looking down at us, up behind him a few feet, another guy, in jeans, no shirt, some stomach hanging over his belt.

"Let's jam," James said, picking at two bush-leaves in his belly button. He flicked out one, looked at me, said, "Stalk grunge-stars at Roseland."

I looked down the other trails. "Where is he?" I said.

"He's talking to a car at the fountain."

I picked the other bush-leaf out of his belly button but James got my hand before I could flick it, pulled it up his chest, then pushed it flat over his heart.

"The bruise is totally gone, Davy," he said. "It's not even tender anymore, here."

I let go of the leaf and it went down and I got my other hand up around the back of his neck and I felt the skin under the short hairs and James said, "The lump back there, yeah, that's down too."

He smiled and I looked down. The leaf was on my boot-top and I kicked it off and said, "You're tryin' to—guilt me out. To get me to go with you."

James nodded. "You're not gonna go off on me again, like last Friday, at the City, are you?"

I looked up and said, "No."

He said, "Well, then, I have to make the most of this time, don't I?" and then he let go of my hand but I kept it there and got my other one off his neck, onto his chest and used both hands and rubbed in some sweat that'd come up on the skin over his heart. "Roseland," I said, "That place is on Sixth?"

James nodded and we started walking down the trail then I got ahead of him, cut off the trail, kicking bushes and breaking off low tree branches and James said if the band was tuning up they might be tuning to a few Nirvana covers and I asked James if he ever met them or maybe saw them anywhere around Seattle and he said he'd never met any of them, but had a friend who saw them at Pike Street Market, once, signing CDs, then Branch's voice came up loud echoing through the bushes and we looked back at the trail but he wasn't there but he was calling our names louder and faster and James stopped in the middle of stepping over a tree—split and down in front of us—looked around me, said, "He was at the fountain, but now he's closer." Then I turned around and Branch was standing on the trail wiping off chest-sweat. He yelled, "Hey—I been fuckin' callin' you!"

I didn't move. James got his foot down on the other side of the split tree.

Branch quit wiping himself, moved his head a little, said, "You *did* fuckin' hear me. You totally heard me," then looked up the trail, shook his head, then started walking toward us, going over the breaks me and James'd made in the bushes. "I got a deal lined up," he said, watching the ground, pushing back stuff hanging, "All three of us, and the guy's waitin'"—and James, stepping up closer behind me, said over Branch, "Why three?" and Branch kept going, talking and walking, getting closer to us but heading for James, "—and we really totally don't have time for whatever fuckin' bullshit thing—" and James, right beside me, said, "Why does this guy need all *three* of us?"—and Branch, in front of James, took one more step so they were face to face, chest to chest, said louder, "—this stupid fucking bullshit thing you *think* you're going to!"

I got up behind James and looked at Branch.

James didn't move, said, "Okay, but why all three of—"

"Because some fucking asshole's gotta hold the fucking camera while the dude's fucking you and Davy."

I looked down and Branch's hands were in fists but he kept them low, while we just stood, couple seconds, till a car-horn echoed up through the bushes and James took a step around Branch, and I stepped up and Branch looked at me then I went around Branch's other side, following James back to the trail, and I looked back, head down, and Branch's fists were undone, one hand scratching a pit. When James got on the trail, started down, Branch said loud, "Blue Beamer, by the fountain," and James nodded while walking.

The guy's place was in northwest Portland and after the deal he dropped us off at a Plaid Pantry on Northwest Twenty-third and it was getting close to dark and I'd said in the car that we needed to get dropped at the DH but Branch said he was hungry and we were close to the building-basement we'd be renting, said we might as well get burritos, go take a look at the place and that Nikki and Jody, if they were worried, could just wait.

In front of Plaid Pantry's microwave, watching seconds count down, Branch said, "Maybe all the workmen'll be gone and we can get fairly close." The countdown hit double-zeros, the dinger went off and Branch popped the door open, got his burrito on a paper plate, said, "Not like last time we looked, middle of the day, tons of people around." He got a hot-sauce packet, bit it open, squeezed it on and behind him James put his burrito in the machine, started it up. Branch got a spoonful of sour cream, put some on top of the sauce and I held up my plate and he dropped the rest on my burrito, then threw the spoon back in the container, went up to pay. I watched James watching the microwave time, then when it was done James put the burrito on a plate, held it up in front of all the burrito and hot dog stuff and spooned out sour cream, relish, ketchup, mustard, then more sour cream, then Branch, at the door, yelled, "Hey—," then James grabbed a handful of hot sauces and we left, James squeezing all the packets on his burrito pile while we walked to Northwest Flanders.

We ate on the steps of an apartment building almost straight across from the building we were going to be in, couple workguys on scaffolding passing down paint cans to a couple guys underneath. Branch, middle of a big bite, pointed to one of the guys on the ground, at his legs, said, "There, by him, that window's gonna have to be blacked out all the time 'cause it faces the street, but that other window, around the other side, faces the alley so we won't have to black out that one, so, I mean, there's a view."

I looked at the guy Branch was pointing to, to the window behind the guy's boots, sticking up some out of the ground, and I said, "It's pretty small."

James, other side of me, looked around my shoulder, over Branch's head. I looked at his plate and there were no bites missing out of his burrito-pile.

Branch wiped his mouth, swallowed big, said, "Yeah, it's small, yeah, but Davy, Max said his friend said we could still be seen from the street here, so we cover it. Listen, we're gonna do what this guy says." He pushed a burrito-chunk around in some hot sauce on his plate. "I mean, we're gettin' space and—and it's real—and it's, y'know, permanent, but it's still not *ours.*"

I said, "Dude, you're right," and Branch ate the bite he'd been dipping. I looked back at James, looking at the other buildings on Flanders, some streetlights already coming on, lighting up the fronts of the buildings, then I looked at his plate again and said, "James, eat."

Branch and me got our last bites and he folded up his plate and I handed him mine and he took both, went over to a plastic Sani-Pac can by a sidewalk-tree, said, "Max said by August, prob'ly, the start of next month," got the lid up, threw the plates in, then looked at James, said, "You done or what?"

James shrugged.

"Well there's too much shit on it," Branch said. "Davy, look at that shit."

I looked at the plate again, then at James, and James looked up at me, gave me the plate. "It looks like a Mexican woman's pad," James said, and I got up, trashed his plate, Branch and me laughing a little, and I looked back at James but he had his head on his knees, arms wrapped around them.

In the park, the next day, walking the trails with my shirt off, shoved in my jeans, I met Branch when he was coming up the high trail and I was going down and he said to me, "You watchin' him?" and looked down the trail to James, talking to a car by the big fountain. I told Branch I'd been watching James all day and Branch asked if he'd been working that car a while and I said, "Maybe twenty minutes or a half-hour."

James was standing on the driver's side, head down, talking into the window, his hands up on the roof.

"You guys didn't make no noise last night," Branch said, flicked the shirt-wad in my pants-front. "None of the usual, y'know, none of you guys."

I nodded. James's hands tapped the car top.

"He stayed in his corner, whole night, huhn, like last Friday?"

I said, "Yeah," then Branch, getting closer, said, "So he's kinda bugged, okay, I was right, so just watch him, like you are, like you did, at the City, that was good, takin' him down, showin' him we've got him, 'cause you know he knows we're fuckin' good for him."

James's hands went off the roof and he came fast around the car, got in the other side and the car started and I ran down the trail, and the car went fast around the fountain, down the hill.

Branch yelled, "Hey—hey" behind me, and I looked around and he had his arms out wide. He said, "Babysit him, Davy, but—shit—back the fuck off when he's makin' money."

After James took off I hung out by the bottom trail, let Branch work the top, did a deal, then a couple more, looking around between the guys' legs or through their arms when their hands were on my head, watching the big fountain and the road around it for James or the car he took off in. One guy had his hand twisted so I could almost see his watch and I slowed down sucking him and looked at the time;

it said close to three and I dropped my mouth, let his dick out, ran off the trail, looked around the fountain, then wiped my mouth and sat on the fountain-edge. People came down the trails and went into the bushes and I looked at cars pulling up, the people inside, but nobody was James and after a while Branch was in front of me, asking if I was done for the day, and if I was ready to give up funds so I took out what I had in my pockets, gave it to him, and, counting, Branch said, "He's gonna show—where's he gonna go?" Then Branch said he was going to make a quick trip to get food, said, "You wanna—?" then stopped, said, "Right," turned and went down the hill.

Couple minutes after Branch left I had my knees up and my head down in them and someone sat up next to me on the fountain-edge and I looked up and James was pulling his knees in. He said, "Your face is all red," and I said I'd had my head in my knees and he said, "You thought I jammed," smiled.

I said, "I didn't know is all." I looked around him, at parts of the park behind him, said, "Maybe, after yesterday," and then, "Where'd your deal go?"

James said, "Just dropped me at the entrance," and I asked him what all he did and he said, "Nothing," then asked him how much he got and he said, "Nothing," held up the Foo Fighters CD laying on the other side of him.

"I just wanted to hear this," he said. "No slither. I snagged it at the DH then we just cruised around—and what's-his-Lexus has a very awesome sound-system, totally perfect sound, no static, no skips, like being right there in front at Roseland, waiting for Dave Grohl to stage-dive."

I said, "You did this before," looked back at him. "You left like this before."

"What—? Last Friday—? That guy at Sin City? You nailing me *at* the City?" he said, put the CD down, ran a finger over the Branch butt-crack. "That was different. That was drugs. And, anyway, I'm back, again."

"You keep—fuckin' doin' this," I said.

He got the finger off the crack, onto my cheek, said, "You didn't go off on me this time."

I got up, his finger fell, and I said, "You—testin' me?"

"I just wanted to hear my tunes, Davy."

"Cool," I said, "Whatever," rubbed and flicked off some neck-sweat under my chin, said, "Tell Branch—that the guy—tell Branch that you couldn't get the guy to pay."

James stretched his legs out, looked at his boots.

"Okay?" I said.

James said, "Yes," then slapped his boots and said, "There was air, too, you know. This guy's car also had air-conditioning."

Picture This

A couple afternoons later all of us were in the Metro getting ice mochas and Branch held up an ad in the back of *Willamette Week* for a new big adult-viddie arcade in southeast Portland and pointed at it and said we needed to be checking out new spots, and everybody nodded and James, mouth full of a couple of ice cubes, said, "Woo for fucking up routine," spit an ice cube at my cup but I moved it quick so it didn't hit, splash. So later, start of the night, somewhere southeast, I was waiting with Jody and Nikki because Branch'd said the new viddie-place looked yuppie, classy, and probably iffy about groups of guys so I stayed, sat under a basketball hoop on a playground across from a Safeway while Nikki smoked and Jody scoped the Safeway cop who was cruising the storefront end-to-end, door-to-door.

"I thought this was supposed to be, like, a cool neighborhood," Jody said, "but they have a cop. A real cop-creature cruising Safeway with sidearms. *Not* a rent-a-cop."

Nikki faked a shot above me. "Well, see," she said, "that's basically why it's supposed to be a cool neighborhood—cops in shops"—and the cigarette fell out of her mouth—and Nikki said, "Shit," and Jody said, "James is coming," was running this way, said something must've gone wrong. I got up. Nikki stepped out the cigarette. I looked past Jody—James was coming up, slowing down through the Safeway lot— and we got out of the playground, got to him, and he grabbed Nikki, out of breath, said, "We want you guys."

"Everybody?" Jody said.

Nikki said, "Is it breeder action?"

"No"—James coughed, caught some more air—"no action. No deals." James smiled right at me, said, "We just need you guys," and we started moving, nobody asking anything else, saying anymore, till we were clear, and out through Safeway, right in sight of the vid-shop and James got my shoulder, dropped back with me, said, "Okay—be really cool," said, "We'll be in the last booth on the left," told me that when we got inside, I needed to hold up at the counter and cash some ones, get tokens, just tokens because the booths only took tokens, and James'd run out and Branch was broke. We went in and James, Jody and Nikki walked to the end of the hall.

Counterguy was a girl, on the phone. I changed some ones in a machine in front of the hall, scoped the halls, and it was mostly low to no action—saw one guy come around, go in a booth, then a girl and a guy came out of a booth, kind of laughing, and they came by me, left. Saw the halls were different than the vid-place halls down-town—these were bigger—and saw the booths were way different— spread out, and the booth the couple'd come out of was open and the walls weren't graffiti'd and the floor was fairly clear and the vid screen looked huge, and I guess I was slow because Nikki came back, up to the counter, caught me looking around, said I was stalling, grabbed a wad of tokens out of my hand, grabbed my hand, pulled me down to the last booth on the left—me saying—"Stallin' for what?"

I was the last one in the last booth on the left and inside was no vid-screen-light, just hall-light, and when I got in, I pulled the door, made total black.

"Been like five minutes," Jody said, sounded way over, far side of the booth.

"Coinage," Branch said, somewhere in the middle of everybody, and I could feel Nikki moving around me, see her kind of push into James because he was by the screen and the channel buttons, and I heard a couple tokens clank in, then the screen-light came on, and I reached around, locked the door. The viddie flashed big—big people—and the screen was clean, not like the downtowner screens—no spooge stains and spots—it was real clear there, and the sound didn't blast, it was everywhere, maybe stereo, but not loud, the sound was down, clear and real.

Viddie music played and the viddie people moaned—two girls licking up a guy in a pool, dildo on a diving board, and Nikki said—"So."

"Wrong channel," Branch said, pushing over, pushing James off the buttons, clicking channels fast himself. "You fucked with the channel," he said, hard to James, and James said, "Wasn't it forty-seven?"

Vid-screen numbers flashed forty-seven—a black girl on a floor, getting felt and fingered by another girl, white, with big white nails.

"Fuck," Branch said.

More numbers flashed under the channel numbers—sixty, fifty-nine—the token-time countdown.

"We've been here too long," Jody said. "There's too many of us and we're going to get snuffed."

Nikki moved by Branch, dropped in a couple more tokens and the token countdown went away.

"Twenty-seven"—James said—"Try twenty-seven."

Branch clicked fast down, heads and lips, arms and boots, clits and dicks flying till screen number said twenty-seven.

Army guy going solo, shooting white on a green hat.

"So," Nikki said.

"*Wrong,*" Branch said, flicking.

"Maybe seven—" James said.

"Why'd you fuck with it?" Jody said, and "Whatever it is is probably completely snuffed by now."

Branch'd clicked to twenty—clicked down through to sixteen—then clicked quick back—up one—stopped at seventeen, stepped back.

Three guys on each other on a couch in a room somewhere, wet hair.

"Here we are," Branch said.

Token countdown came on and Nikki dug in, gave Branch the last of her tokens, and he slapped them in and she stepped back next to me and I moved back, behind everybody, felt around, found corner-space and kind of leaned into it.

On the screen I kissed James and jacked Branch's dick and he pushed my head low and the picture zoomed on me blowing Branch for quite a few seconds, then the picture pulled back, showing James blowing me, Branch screwing with my hair.

I looked up off the screen and James was looking at me, and he stared—quite a few seconds—like he was way close to saying something, then he looked back down and watched, like everybody else.

"This dick is famous," Branch said, "official star-fuck," and Jody said, "Oh, it's basically a local thing," and Branch said, "Whatever," and I said, kind of loud, "We can jam just about anytime."

"No—" Jody—and then Nikki—said.

The vid'd switched to the start of the fucking—me on my back on the floor, Branch's dick rubbing my crack, James's face right above my face, kissing pretty hard, and above the right-before-fucking noises the TV Branch and the TV me were making, I heard Branch, by the channel buttons, laugh a little, say that it looked like James was giving me mouth-to-mouth.

I moved up some, right behind Nikki, and said low, "We can jam."

"No," Nikki said, eyes on the screen, and I looked and Branch had my legs up higher—was done playing around—had pointed his dick at my hole.

Branch said, "Is my dickhead that big?" and James said, "No," but I said, "Yeah," and nobody moved so I moved up more, closer to Nikki's face-side and said low, "Let's get a smoke, okay?" but Nikki said, "No," watched the vid, and I reached out, into Nikki's jacket, fingered out a smoke, but didn't light it, didn't smoke, then Branch pushed his dick in and Jody went, "Ouch," and James went, "He was lubed," and Nikki didn't say anything, didn't move, and Branch went, "Is my dickhead that big?" and looked back at me. I saw the token countdown flash but nobody said anything, and I fingered and jingled the tokens in my pocket, dropped the un- smoked smoke. I touched and played with Nikki's hair a little bit, looking at the side of her face, watching her watch me getting fucked.

"Tokens," James said, but the viddie went out, probably a minute before it got liquid. And Branch said "Tokens," but nobody but me had any left and I didn't pull mine out—Branch said, "David—*coin-*

age," Jody said, "You got 'em 'cause I heard 'em," and James tapped my pocket, made a jingle, said, "I want to see this—this is trippy," then Nikki turned around—looked me hard in the dark, stuck her hand out, said, "Davy, you know it's bad luck to stop a viddie-nasty before the spooge scene," and I grabbed in my pocket, got out my tokens, gave her the rest of the wad, then moved back, leaned into the corner and closed my eyes, right when the clink, clink, clink, clinking fake quarters went down.

That night on my back on the floor in the DH, Nikki was rubbing my arm and started going lower but I got her hand when she got under a nipple.

She said, "What?"

I moved my head slow side-to-side.

She coughed, then again, rubbed her nose on my shoulder, said, "Cold's back," and I looked at her, smiled, said, "Uhn-uh," and she got up some, head and hands on my chest, face in my face, asked why the viddie was bugging me and I shrugged.

"But it's buggin', though, right?"

I nodded, reached up and rubbed her fingers. Branch, snoring under the window, said in a loud sleep-talk, "Star pecker," then laughed a little, rolled over, went back to snoring and Jody, other side of Branch, pulled a shirt off the floor over the back of her head and James, across from them, in his corner, got his head up on an elbow, watched me and Nikki.

"It shouldn't be weird," Nikki said low. " 'Cause I've seen you before. But—is it—just weird—seein' yourself?"

I shrugged again and James got up, walked slow around everybody, sat down by my head. He said, "It *was* fairly weird, Davy."

I looked up and his eyes were down on mine.

"But also—fun and freaky," he said. "And cool. Davy, it's—it's all of *this*"—he moved his hand around the DH—"and all of *us*"—he pulled his hand back and tapped his chest—"completely *caught*—on tape. For-fucking-*ever*."

I looked at his chin and eyes, only parts of his face that were catching night-lights. Nikki hit my shoulder, said, "Well, duh, Davy, yeah, cool slither can happen," and I nodded and Nikki reached over, pulled up some of the blanket over James and James got flat by me then Nikki said, "Spoon it," and I turned on my side and she turned on her side, tits in my back, got an arm around me, fingers on a nipple, and James got on his side and I got an arm around him, some fingers on his nipple and Nikki said real low in my ear, "See, it can totally happen, sometimes."

In the morning Jody got up first and stood in front of the window-light looking at me, Nikki, and James—James's butt still on my knee, Nikki's tits still in my back—and Jody said, "Oh, we need a picture of this," and Nikki moved her head under my arm, got her head up, said we needed a camera, then James got his head up, rubbed his eyes, said he'd seen a photo-booth downtown, said you could get pictures, three or four for a buck and Jody said, "Oh, that's it, that has to be done," then Branch, head up under the window, said, "No, not possible," scratched his hair. "That booth's busted," he said, looked around the DH. "It's at Newberry's and it's out of order. Almost always is out of order," he said, then got up.

It was Thursday, still hot, and Branch said a day just to hang and by afternoon we were all on the steps at Pioneer Square, Branch by me, but one up, Nikki and Jody on the same step as me, James stretched out one step down. There were a lot of people in the pit, mostly in bunches—threes mainly, but some fours and fives, plus a solo guy stretched out on the flat bricks above the fountain, shaking his head in some of the fountain spray.

I said, "That's the cool place to be in the city," looked up at Branch and he said, "What're these guys supposed to be?"—stared into the pit.

I looked down and fixed on the bunch Branch was fixing on, four guys, no shirts, three of them wearing Raiders caps like Branch's, turned backwards like Branch's, the other guy's head in a scarf.

Nikki looked down, said, "Those're gang-bangers."

Branch said, "No way," scratched his cap, said there weren't any bangers in Portland. He said, "Davy, I'm toastin' already," got his hat off then got his shirt up and off, then put his hat back on backwards.

Nikki said she'd read there were bangers at Irving Park.

Branch said there were a few, maybe, out there, but no real big banger hookups, and James said, "Oregon wanna-bes, right?" and Jody looked at Branch, then James, then she said, "People—don't rain on the nice."

I looked in the pit and two of the three guys in Raiders hats were looking up at us and talking and then the third guy in a Raiders hat looked up.

I said, "We're bein' loud or somethin'."

Branch shook his head, said, "Public space."

"It's your hat," Nikki said.

Branch leaned back on the step, rubbed his chest, said, "Public space."

"It's your stupid fucking hat," James said.

Down behind Jody, all the bangers were looking up and two pointed.

Branch leaned up, put his elbows on his knees and put his head down and spit slow between his legs on a step and said the guys in the pit were nothing to worry about because they weren't even real, said they were Oregon wanna-bes, Portland try-too-hards, and Jody said to Branch, "Maybe if you'd just turn your hat around, brim in front, you'd kill the bad vibe."

Branch spit again and the pit bangers were moving around, getting close to the side steps, and Jody said again that Branch should turn his hat around and Branch looked up, square-down to the bangers, and James said don't act like a fucking Californian and I said, "Branch, fucking just do it."

Branch turned his hat around the normal way—front in front—and one of the bangers in a Raiders hat slapped the shoulder of another guy in a Raiders hat and the guy in the scarf laughed and another guy, no hat, no scarf, plain head, walked into the Square and got with the bangers and the bangers stopped looking at us and they talked with the new guy, and then the whole bunch walked away, over by the fountain, and the solo guy stretched out on the flat brick above the fountain rubbed water off his hair and face. The bangers talked in front of the waterfall for a while, then they walked up the side steps right across from us and walked up Ninth.

Nikki and Jody looked at Branch and James looked at me.

Branch said, "Let's go—let's go check out our space."

We got up Flanders and the scaffolding around the building was empty and Branch said that the workdudes must be on break so we got further up the street, Nikki getting closer faster, on her knees at the basement window when the rest of us got there.

Nikki said, "They cleared it out, those boxes, that shit's gone," and she wiped her sleeve on the glass.

James pushed Nikki over some, looked in, said, "There's a beater chair and a big shred of sunlight."

Nikki got a hand up over her eyes, got her eyes tighter on the glass, said, "They're doin' up bathroom space—Davy—there's a toilet and a tub."

James looked back at me, said, "Apparently *not* the same thing," smiled.

"James, that's a ton of sunlight," Jody said loud, her head up from around the corner of the building, other widow.

Branch, up behind me, got his hand on my shoulder, said, "Davy, check out Jody's window," rubbed my shoulder, said, "I'll watch the street for the workdudes." I looked around, slapped his back, went around to the other side of the place and got on my knees next to Jody.

By the time the workers got back we were all on the steps of another building across from our building, burrito-plates on our knees, everybody cutting, taking bites with forks except James, holding his burrito over his plate and my knee, trying to drip hot sauce, sour cream, relish and ketchup on me. He took a big bite and I elbowed the bottom of his burrito, got meat chunks up his nose, and he got a finger on a nostril, shot some back on my knee and Branch said, "Don't waste the grub," but I got my knee up and Nikki looked at the chunk, then flicked it onto a corner of Branch's burrito-plate and

Branch said, "Fuckin'—*thanks*," kept eating. Then Jody said, "How'd we all, like, end up here?"

Nikki, mouth full, sour cream spot on the side of her face, said, " 'Here?'—Where?—What?"

James said, "Oh, Plaid Pantry's terrace tables were all taken. Remember?"—waved his hand over the steps.

"No," Jody said, "What I mean is *what* did it, you know what I mean when I mean *what*?"

All of us looked around our plates at Jody, except for James, wiping the white off Nikki.

"The home thing," Jody said. "Me, I just left."

"Oh," said Nikki.

"Kicked out," said James.

"Left," I said.

"Left," Nikki said.

"Left," Branch said, and all of us looked around our plates at Branch, except for James, shaking his head. "Okay, booted," Branch said. "But I was about to leave anyways."

Jody farted, Nikki tagged her arm, James scooted over and Jody said, "Okay, what's the 'why'? Me—I left for the Dead and because it was *Idaho*."

"Oh," Nikki said.

"Ma's boyfriend fucked me," James said, folding his plate. "And she caught us, and I told her I asked him to, so she kept him."

"My mom's a bitch," Nikki said. "So's my stepmom. And my dad, too."

James had his plate folded into an airplane and he threw it but it fell on the bottom step.

I said, "It was crowded and I was looking for space."

Branch said, "Wailin' on my little brother," laughed, got up, went by all of us, got all of our plates on top of his, went down the steps, put the plates in the blue Sani-Pac can, still laughing some, and James pointed a finger at the plane on the bottom step, got his throat clear, said, "Missed one—Twig."

Branch, reaching for the plate-plane, stopped and looked at James.

"Prob'ly," Nikki said, looking at James, "his bro got wailed on for sayin' shit just like that."

Branch nodded, said, "Fuckin' right," smiled, chucked the plate in the can.

Riding MAX

That night was still hot so we rode MAX because it had air and Branch said Max'd said cops were clearing out Stark Street, the Square, the park blocks and the park, at night, because of a church thing coming up at Civic Stadium. All of us were spread out, on MAX, coming back from going almost to Gresham, and Nikki, laying out on two MAX seats, reading an *Oregonian,* flicked down a corner of her page and said to me—head on the window in the seat across from her—"Says it's going through the weekend, that Billy Graham thing," and Branch, behind her, leaned up reading the page she wasn't, said, "Whoa, snuffed," and James, end of Nikki's seat, holding her boots, getting more air fanned on his face from Jody, right next to him, waving the comics and crossword section, said, "They won't snuff us too bad."

Branch said, "Not them, somethin' else, here," pointed at something in the paper and Nikki said, "Guess I'm done," threw it over her shoulder and Branch picked through it, said to me that he'd seen that some cop'd got knifed, by a kid he'd picked up, Southwest and Eleventh and James got his hands off Nikki's boots, said, "Wait—" and Jody said, "That's boy-slither space—" and Nikki, kicking at James's hands, said, "They get the kid?" and Branch, flattening out a page, read more, said, "Yeah," laughed, "Found him sitting in front of the City," and James said, "Ha—closed weeknights, dumbass," then Branch, still reading, laughed again, harder.

Two girls, little older than us, sitting in the next car, turned and looked at James, then all of us, then looked back out their windows.

"Cop was off-duty and in the E-ward," Branch said, "and was makin' up how he got knifed but everybody figured out he was lyin', so he finally says that he was rolled and they snag the kid." Branch looked up, smiling, flicked the paper-page closed, said, "End o' story," and Nikki got her boots down, said to James, "You guys ever do a cop?" and James looked at her, said, "You know, they don't pin their badges on their dicks, so I really don't know," and I looked at Branch and said, "How do you roll somebody?"

MAX stopped, some kids, younger than us, got in fast and the two girls, up, pushed around them to get out, and the kids looked over at some seats by us, and Branch, looking at them, said loud to me, "You need a knife," and the kids turned, sat in another car and MAX started again.

"You get in the car, knife hid," Branch said, "tell the guy you need half the money right then, and when he gets out his wallet, get the knife out, grab the wallet and get out, but if they don't give it up, slice him."

Jody'd stopped fanning James, had her paper-section flat on her legs and she looked at Branch.

"But that's stupid, I know, 'cause look what happens," Branch said to Jody, and then to me he said, "Or some guys could be packin' in the glove compartment, plus, you can only do that a couple times before you get known, word gets around, nobody stops for you, so you're—unemployed."

I nodded, said, "I wasn't thinkin' we should—try it—I was just—" and Jody said to Branch, "And I know you weren't even considering using my—" and Branch said loud, "I know"—to both of us, and the kids in the next car stopped talking, looked over a second, and Branch said low, "It's probably cooler outside now," looked out his window.

The kids talked again, James leaned back, smiled at me, and Jody, still looking at Branch, said, "Nikki, Branch has got a newsprint-spot under his eye there," and Nikki, smiling at Jody, reached back, moved her hand around but Branch, already up, moved and sat two seats behind her.

Clean

It got to be Saturday night, pretty far into dark, warm, but not hot out anymore, and we were standing and sitting on some part of some stairs cut into a hill in Washington Park across from the trails and Branch'd just called for the alcohol but James'd just passed the forty to me and I swigged long, burped, splattered some, swigged more, passed it back to James and he drank like I drank, passed it over to me again and I drank again and Branch, sitting a couple steps below James, said, "Whatever, asswipe." I gave the bottle to James and he dripped a couple drops into Branch's hair and Branch got up, tagged James hard in the stomach. I took the beer, held it. Branch looked at me, looked at James, shook his head, said, "Fuckin' *whatever,*" sat down a couple more steps, next to Jody and Nikki, and Jody said, "People, vibe check," and Nikki said, "Don't be fags."

Noise came up, crowd noise from lights down at Civic Stadium, and some echo of someone talking loud, microphone-echo, coming up with the crowd noise and then big church music. I leaned against the stone wall, took a swig, and when my head went back it got in bushes hanging over the stone wall and I kept it there for a second, leaves in my face, swallowed beer, leaned up, gave James the bottle. James said to Jody that he was the one who got the bum to buy for us and I said I was the one who did the last deal that got the funds to buy the booze, and then Branch got up again and said, "What is you guys' *fucking* problem?"

"We're snuffed," James said. "We're totally snuffed out"—the church noise went up and James got up, looked at the stadium lights—"because of that, two days, two nights of them, the rollers, the thumpers, down there," and I walked a couple steps down and James said, "Fuckin' Billy Idol," spitting his words around, probably fairly buzzed, and Nikki said, "Fucking Billy *Graham*," and I walked down some more steps, walking around and past Nikki and Jody, holding onto the stairwell and picking off pieces of bush-leaves, and my shoe snagged a bump and I missed a step and fell on my butt and elbow and slid down against the wall, bush pieces falling on me, James running down, handing me the rest of the forty, and I swigged some, ended up killing it, parked the empty one stair up.

Nikki came down, Branch looked over me, said, "Where the fuck're you going?"

I pointed down the stairs, said, "These stairs go down here, and then wind around down there, and then after that they come out at the front, right in front of the park and then . . ." James moved the bottle and sat down by me and I rubbed the back of my head.

"Then it's downtown," Jody said, somewhere on the steps.

"Then I'm downtown," I said.

Branch got a hand in a jeans pocket, got out some money and

Nikki asked why the funds check and Branch bent down, kind of slapped my face and said it was because it was time that two of us got a paid vacation.

We got down Burnside okay—James needing to piss, pissing on the pole under the big blue Volvo sign, caught in car-light but nobody honked—Branch walking by me, on the street side of me, shoving me over when I got too close to traffic, but the street wasn't even that busy, fairly carless until James zipped up, we got moving again, got down to about Eighteenth, and then there were cars everywhere, moving, parked, stalled all over, and buses—white and orange—cramming space up Eighteenth, coming from Civic, and people, mass people—a few in front of us, but most around and behind us, walking down both sidewalks, using the space on Eighteenth that the cars couldn't take—and they were close and talking and loud.

We walked real fast and went over 405, then crossed Burnside to Stark, and Jody kept me up because I was falling back, and Nikki kept James up and Branch kept ahead, and we kept ahead of the church-bunch, and I got up to Branch when we'd slowed down, about Twelfth, still moving down Stark, and asked where the vacation was, but he didn't say anything, and I looked back and the people-lines weren't too far behind us even though they weren't walking fast. A few church-people in front of us got into cars and started up and got into traffic, and a few people ahead made a little line up into a parking garage on Eleventh—a bunch of garage cars, already stalled, were trying to get out.

We kept on Stark, hit the middle of the fag-strip, and some cruisers and barguys hung out in front of the clubs but the street and side streets were taken up by parked cars, and Nikki got up to me, said,

"The Graham crackers are cramping," and then Branch stopped, start of Tenth, turned, laughed, and we looked back and laughed because the people were still coming—two big lines—one, on the other sidewalk, turning around the Eagle, and coming down in front of Silverado, and one line of people on our sidewalk—just hitting the corner before the Brig. Branch walked us to the front of the Brig, and a few barguys'd come out, were scoping the street scene and we sat on the Brig' steps, and I looked around and more barguys and girls were watching—by the door—and a cop—leaned up on the Brig's big ship-steering-wheel stuck by the door—talked and laughed into a walkie-talkie, and turned, and then shook hands with a bargirl who'd come up behind him, and then I looked at the line of people coming in front of us, and the bargirl who'd been talking to the cop came down and held out a handful of wrapped rubbers, asked Branch and Nikki and Jody and James and me if we'd hand them out—she said, "Offer 'em these would ya?" and Branch said, "No thanks," and James laughed, and the bargirl backed off, and handed the cop a rubber, and the cop looked at it and laughed into his walkie-talkie, and then I turned around and the sidewalks were filled and tons of people walked in front of us, none of them looking at us, except for a few kids, little kids.

Nobody said too much but Branch said something to me, said something about the people going by but I didn't hear, and I said to Nikki that I had to piss and I got up, got in the sidewalk line, got around a man, another man, a kid and a woman, then got out of the line, out from the people, and off Tenth, around a parking lot that was trying to clear out at the corner of Ninth, and I walked into an alley between a couple black buildings on Ninth, across from O'Bryant Park, and stood in front of an alley wall, next to a guy, older, who was already whipped-out, pissing. I pissed, and, when I was done, the guy was still there, pulling on himself, and he asked if I wanted some of him, and I looked around—only two or three people going by the alley—but I said no, fixed my jeans up, and said, "I've gotta go."

"Where're you going?" he said, fixing up his pants, and he got closer, but didn't move in, pulled a pipe out of his pocket, fingered it, looked like loading it.

"I'm going on vacation," I said.

"Where's that?" he said.

"I think . . . not far I think," I said.

He pulled out a lighter, lit a hit, sucked, asked under smoke if I had time for a hit, and I took the lighter and the pipe, did a hit, choked on smoke, and the guy laughed and took the pipe back and said he should've said that it was killer shit—"Corvallis killer bud," he said, then said, "Are you one of them?" pointed his pipe to the street, and I said no, real quick, figuring he meant the church-street people, but I turned around and saw Branch and everybody at the head of the alley, and I said, "Oh—yeah—I'm with them," and burped smoke and James said loud down the alley, "C'mon—crowd's gone," and I got to them, got to Nikki, and we started walking and she looked at my face, looked at my eyes and asked how many hits, and I said, "One is all," and she said, "Baby looks *baked.*"

Branch and an older guy stood in front of a metal door in a doorway cut into a building somewhere downtown, still on Stark, and we were right across, in front of the Blitz brewery on Burnside, and the side-walks and the streets were calmer—regular cruising, car-fruits, couple of cops—and there were lights lighting doorways at other buildings, at the bars, and around us, but not where Branch was—Branch and the guy talked in a big block of dark.

Branch yelled, "Hey—" and it bounced over to us and we crossed Burnside, and Branch came into street-light, got out some of the funds, then got my shoulder and James's, got us in the doorway dark, and pointed to the guy in the dark, said, "This is Mike," and, "Mike's cutting two very cool deals," and, "Mike knows the rules, Mike *is* the rules. Obey Mike." Mike opened the metal door behind him and some light came out and I heard Jody say, "Oh, it's a dinger thing, a guy, wiener, dinger thing," and I turned and looked for Nikki but she was already back crossing Burnside with Jody, and James went in and Mike still held the door and Branch said, "This is cool, this is the good shit," and I went in and Branch said, "See you in twelve hours"— quick—in the crack of the metal door, closing. There was another door inside and Mike said, "Hey," and a buzz went off, and Mike opened the door and there were stairs, carpeted, right in front of us, but Mike took us off to the side, behind a counter, where another guy was buzzing someone else in, and Mike took us back more, into a room with a stack of stereo stuff hooked up and going, playing something low, and there were thumps around, not from stereo noise, but thumps right above us, ceiling noise.

Mike went back around front, and I looked out front—could see the guy who'd come in behind us—and he was holding up a black plastic card, and the guy behind the counter took it and looked at it and wrote something down in a notebook, then gave the card back, and the guy who'd come in put the card in his wallet and gave counterguy some money—some ones, a five—and counterguy rang the cash in a cash register, turned his notebook around, and the other guy took counterguy's pen and wrote in the book, and counterguy handed him a towel and a string with a key, and they both said thanks, and the guy who'd come in put the towel under his arm, put the string-key around his neck and walked upstairs.

James said, "He was kinda hot," and then Mike came back, holding two string-keys, and he gave them to us and we put them around our necks and I looked at mine and it had a number—417—and looked at James's—416.

Mike said, "Tip-top floor," then gave us each a towel, then told us some things—to be cool, be fairly quiet, be safe—then pulled out a thing of Tic Tacs, said, "Here," shook some out in our hands, and we crunched them in our mouths and the door buzzer buzzed and the ceiling thumped louder.

We walked upstairs and some guys came by, four or five, out of a second-floor door—a couple older, a few not older, one that looked almost our age—just wearing towels, walking fast around us, up, to the door above us, and I rubbed my eyes, heard more thumping and James followed them, took the steps up by two, and I followed him, into the third-floor door—a guy, wearing clothes, next to the door— dumping new, wrapped rubbers into a plastic box on the wall, half- empty.

There was a long hall, carpeted everywhere, doors on both sides, and guys in towels walking around, stroking under their towels, watching everything, stopping at doors and looking in. I caught James turning a corner, going down a side hall, and the group of guys we'd seen were gone, but one of them, the one about our age, unlocked a door with his string-key and opened the door and went in and kept his door open, and James walked by the open door, and then I walked by, and the room was bright, and the bed pretty big, and a guy-guy viddie was playing on a TV, and the guy in the room was sitting on the bed with his towel off, and James came back by me and flicked my key and it jingled, and then he went in, sat on the bed, watched the viddie, kept the door open.

I leaned back to the wall, checked out the big hall because two guys were kissing in another doorway and their towels'd dropped off and one guy's hard-on bounced on the other guy's almost-hard dick until it was hard, and then they quit kissing and went into their room.

James had his shirt off in a wad by his towel, and the guy on the bed kissed James's neck and then one of James's nipples for a while, once in a while missing the nipple and kissing James's key, and in the viddie behind them I could see someone getting fisted—zoom-shot of a plastic-wrapped hand going up a guy's butt—and a guy walked by me, and stopped and stood by me, and watched the guy on the bed kissing James on the lips. The guy in the viddie getting fisted got loud, made noise, way over the music that was mazing around in the hall real low, and the guy standing next to me walked away and, under his towel, scratched his butt.

James reached around, picked up his shirt and his towel, and got up, and the guy on the bed leaned up, reached up, and got James's face and kissed him real hard, and then James came out to the hall, came back to me, and the guy in the room leaned back, flat on the bed, fingered his balls, watched us leave.

"Why'd you stop?" I said, walking the big hall.

"Because I want to see more," James said, fingering his key.

"We have to take our clothes off," I said, pushed the door to the stairway.

We got to the fourth floor and James yawned, and I rubbed my eyes, and there was a cart in the hall with a garbage can and cleaning stuff on it, and a guy came out of a room, a bathroom, pulled off some plastic gloves and squeezed a sponge into a bucket, and when we walked by there was still a lot of splatter on the toilet seat and floor and the guy said, "This is why the no booze rule," and James, ahead a little bit, found our doors, and opened his and I opened mine and reached in for a light. Some guys came behind us—stopped and watched—so we closed our doors, and James said, "These're small," and I could hear him because the rooms weren't real rooms but walls put together, with a bed and a locker, and a pillow on the bed with a wrapped rubber in the middle of the pillow. Light came in from James's room and a couple others because the room-walls didn't go all the way up, meet the ceiling.

I got off my shirt and shoes and socks, and then got my jeans off, and James'd been quiet for quite a while, too long, so I said, "James." James didn't say anything. I pulled my underwear off and pulled the towel around and twisted it tight and sat on the bed and the bed creaked and I sat for maybe a full two minutes and then I said, "James," but James didn't say anything. I leaned back, head to the wall, and listened to James's room and there was nothing, then a creak, then snoring. I untwisted my towel.

I slid down, head from wall to pillow, ear crunching the wrapped rubber, and I pulled it out of my ear, flicked it, closed my eyes, kept out all the room-light. James snored big and his bed creaked and his key jangled and he coughed, then snored normal. The floor outside thumped and the music mazed around, and I smelled smoke because someone a wall or two away'd lit up, and I smelled bleach because the cleaning guy must've still been at the bathroom, and then his cart creaked, and the wheels went by, and a few walls over, on one side, I heard more creaks, steady, and low fuck-noise, and a few walls over, on my other side, heard creaks and maybe kissing.

*   *   *

A creak woke me up. Room-light'd mixed with the start of some daylight from somewhere, and my towel'd come off but I wasn't cold. I got up, wrapped my towel, opened the door, and looked into the hall and a guy—different cleaning guy than the one I'd first seen— was dumping ashtrays and picking up tubes of lube in a room across from me. I walked out and asked the guy what time it was and he said near five, and I asked the guy if there were showers and he said two floors down, and then he bagged some trash and put it in the garbage can and wheeled the cart around a corner. I stood and looked the hall up and down and it was empty and quiet. Night noise'd stopped but the music was there.

I looked in James's room and he was balled up, back facing me, shirt off but the rest of his clothes still on. I turned his light off and had started to click his door shut and I heard, "Davy," so I looked back in and he was yawning but still balled. "What time is it?" he said.

"Five," I said.

"We missed the slither," he said, and yawned and turned and put his head back in the pillow.

I stood under warm water in the empty showers and got a handful of soap from the wall-soap and soaped up my hair and armpits and pissed, then soaped my dick and dick-hair, then did my legs and feet and soaped my face. Then I stood and soaked for a while, till all of it was off, till the water went cold.

I toweled my hair, twisted the towel to my middle and went into a sauna room, right off the showers. It was on and hot, and a guy, not old, was sitting on a high bench, leaned back, sweating. I climbed up next to him and undid his towel and he rubbed my shoulders and his dick was up and big and red and I sucked on it and he felt my back, rubbed the shower-water in, and when my back was dry, and my hair was almost dry, and my face was hot and close to sweating, I stopped and got down and left.

Daylight came in way more in the stairway, coming in big from a skylight on fourth, and the fourth-floor hall was brighter than the second or the third. I got to James's door and it was locked and I knocked and said his name but it didn't open. I walked down the main hall and no one was around, awake. I got into a side hall and it was dead too, but one door was open and I walked by and a guy was on his bed, twisting his balls around, and he asked if I wanted to get sucked and I looked back up the hall and it was empty. I looked around and the other side was clear, and there was a square piece of board where a window was, but there was no light coming in at all through the wood, and there was a sticker on the wood that said DO NOT OPEN, written huge, and I turned back and looked at the guy, and walked into the room and dropped my towel and stood by the bed.

He sucked, and a few seconds went by, and I turned around and James was there, hair wet, watching in the hall. I moved back from the bed and my dick came out of the guy's mouth and I grabbed my towel, got out of the room, closed the door.

James said, "Why'd you stop?"

I said, " 'Cause we came here for good slither and that wasn't it."

James said someone in the showers said that there was a porno room that needed checking out and it was on the fourth, James said, around the corner from us. We wandered around past a couple more doors that weren't open. At the end of the side hall was a room with no door and low porn-noise coming out and James and I walked in, sat on the bottom part of a floor that was leveled up, like big steps, to a strip of wall-mirror—two older guys on a middle shelf, one smoking, one, towel open, twisting his balls, and one way older guy on the top shelf, flat, sleeping, back to us, fogging up his part of the mirror.

There was fucking in the mirror-strip, porno pictures bouncing back from three TVs set across a cage right in front of us, bars in front of a room, real small, way dark, with a bed cut into a wall, with a pillow, ripped wrappers for rubbers on the floor. The bars were big and spread out. I got up and got through them and James followed. We stood and I rubbed James's shoulders and looked out the bars in the mirror-flicker, porn-nasty TV-light, and the smoking middle-shelf guy pushed out his cigarette, and the other middle-shelf guy moved his hand up, started twisting his dick instead of his balls. I looked at James and kissed him. James kissed my chin and neck and shoulder. Someone else came in the porno room, naked, rubbing wet head with his towel. He looked up at the TVs and then down to the cage, to me and James, and then he sat on a low shelf right in front of us and rubbed his dick, and the smoking middle-shelf guy lit another smoke, and the guy twisting his dick was hard, and beating slow, and he nudged the top-shelf guy's foot and the top-shelf sleeping guy sat up, saw us in the mirror-strip, then turned around, sat up all the way.

I turned James around and rubbed his shoulders and back and rubbed his butt and kissed the back of his neck, up, into wet hair, and he got over to the bed and kicked back a couple ripped rubber wrappers on the floor and I picked and flicked a used one by the pillow. Then he got on the bed, on his stomach, and I spit in my hand a couple times, got him wet, and he reached around, got me going, then spit in his hand, got my dick wet and real hard and I got up, I got in him.

I pushed and James pulled so I pushed slower and James pushed back and I looked back through the bars and a few more guys'd come in and most of them were sitting on the low shelf except for the top-shelf guy who'd slid to the middle shelf and everybody was beating.

I moved in and out in James and pulled him up some, and felt around his chest and arms. I got his hand on his dick and got him into beating himself, and then when I got fucking faster I pulled his hand off his dick, put on mine, and started beating him, and got my other hand up around his chin and put some fingers in his mouth, and he pushed back hard on my dick and bit my middle finger—bit it, bit it, kissed it—came on my other hand, and I rubbed the wet around his dick and balls and belly button and then let go in his butt. For about a minute, or maybe two or three, I stayed on him, stayed in him. I rubbed his face and his chest and kissed his hair and his neck and he turned over and I kissed his mouth.

James slid over, got on his side, and I slid down in back of him, held him, looked around through the bars and a couple guys were smoking, a couple guys were gone, and a couple were still beating.

I rubbed James a while and when his breathing got real steady I got my head on the pillow, kept eyes open, looked over his hair, watched between the bars, and there was smoke and porn-flicker and a couple more guys got off, got liquid, and wiped off and got up and thumped out, and some more guys came in, sat on the shelves, and I spooned tight to James. Nobody crawled in the cage.

There were no trails going around anywhere because there were hardly any trees, only a few, small patches in spots around the edges of the park, some behind the greenhouse, and up by the parking lot and a few beside East Prospect, the road entering the park, but all of them, it looked like, first walking in, for decoration. Same for bushes, except for one big clump around the parking circle in front of the greenhouse, but we were walking in a little before sunset and the bush-clump, so close to park-traffic, was probably just a total-dark slither-spot.

There was grass everywhere, a huge hill of it under the parking lot, and there was one road, going around the grass-hill, coming down from the parking lot, and we were on it, jut coming under the hill, and even down at the bottom of the park we could still see the Space Needle and the whole city, small building-tops too, only a few trees to block anything.

I said to Nikki, "Not many trees, maybe not much slither," but Nikki said, "This is a real-city park, so it's here, it's prob'ly all over at night, *prob'ly just in a couple spots at day, but more in the open, I'll bet you, because this is a real city," and coming down a little further we could see two cars and a pickup parked on the side of the road, truck behind the cars, but the short-bushes next to the road were empty and coming up to the first car, I squinted and shaded my eyes to see into the back window and there was nobody and I said, "It's not in the cars," and Nikki pulled on my T-shirt sleeve, said, "Davy, it's here, though." I looked up and past the second car, laying in the bed of the pickup was a guy, no pants on, legs open, knees up, asshole showing. A car came behind us, fairly fast, we moved off the road some and truck-guy's knees wiggled and one of his hands waved but the car kept going and we walked around the truck and there was another man, standing, back to us, in a low bush, clothes on, hands on hips and I said to Nikki, "Just whizzing," but a beeper-noise went off just as we came around him and a kid, my age, stood up in front of the guy—guy's fly open, dick out—pulled a beeper out of his back jeans pocket, clicked it off, stuck it back into his back pocket then went back down into the bush, turned his head up, licked under the guy's dickhead.*

There were a couple newspaper sections spread out in some road-grass and Nikki looked at them, picked one page up, front page, and right under where it said Seattle Post-Intelligencer, *it said that Jerry Garcia was dead and Nikki read some of the story, fairly big, then saw me watching her reading and dropped the page back in the grass. I didn't see the date of the paper so I asked Nikki and she just said, "It's old, I think, a few days probably," and started walking and I said, "You think Jody—?" and Nikki said, "Oh, yeah—wherever she is—she knows."*

Another car came behind us fast but slowed just ahead of us, then stopped. Another kid, my age, got out of the passenger side, closed the door, stuck a money-wad into his back pocket, then the car drove up the rest of the road and the kid crossed the road in front of us, sat on some hill-bottom, looked at me and Nikki, and pulled up the bottom of his T-shirt, rubbed his belly button, then got the shirt up higher, pinched his nipples.

"See," Nikki said, "slither's here."

I nodded and while we walked by the kid, I pulled my T-shirt off.

Some Ground
Movement

Some Ground
Movement

Me and James came out of the bathhouse into bright afternoon light and squinted, and two guys walking in front of us whistled, and one said, "Shame," and the other one said, "You boys know you missed Sunday school," and James said, "Oh—Church of the Stark Street trolls?" and the guys both turned their heads, walked fast across Twelfth and Nikki came up Stark, running around the guys, rubbing her eyes and she said loud, "They fuckin' got Jody," tripped in the crosswalk, fell on the street. I ran up to her, got on my knees and got her arms, and a car stopped in front of our heads and honked and James—at the curb—yelled, "What—what??" I got Nikki up, got her walking fast, holding her elbows tight, and there were blood spots on her arms and I touched her hands, turned them over, and some of her fingertips were scraped and bleeding so I got a few in my mouth then we got over the curb onto the sidewalk and she pulled her hands back, sucked her own fingers. She backed up from me and James, stood in front of the BH door, got her fingers out of her mouth, rubbed them on her jeans, closed her eyes a second, then opened them and said, "We were workin'—just Sunday morning shit—fuck, it wasn't even busy—and I was pissing—just down between a couple cars in 7-Eleven's lot—and this car came up to Jody and wanted—must've been a blowjob 'cause she said eight dollars— and the car went off and things were cool and I was still pissing, then there were fuckin' lights and I got my pants up and people were comin' out of 7-Eleven and up to the street, and a little ways up Eighty-second—the car—was stopped—" James got close to her, got an arm out but she got her hands up, got back more and a guy came out of the BH door and Nikki moved out of his way, stood flat against the building, said, "There were cop cars, Davy, blockin' cars on Holgate and all up Eighty-second, and girls gettin' cuffed and Jody—in cuffs and cryin'—standin', shakin' her head, and cryin'—cops standin' around her talkin' at her and the guy—the stupid asshole that hooked her up was—fuckin' fake—a fake john—a real cop—standin', talkin' with the other ones—then the 7-Eleven guy came out, came right up to me, said, 'You two're together, aren't you?' and I —I—" Nikki slid some down the building-side and me and James got to her, each got an arm, kept it up and she said, "Davy—I just jammed," and she closed her eyes and bent her head and tears and snot came off her face, hit the sidewalk. I got my arm all the way around her, got my face under her hair and kissed the back of her neck and around to her throat and James let go of her, got in front of her on his knees and said, "You had to jam." Nikki nodded, got her hands up to her eyes, slid all the way down to the sidewalk.

I said, "Where's Branch?" and crouched down next to James, and Nikki coughed, got some air, then said, "He went to look for her because, when, when I got to the DH and told him everything he said maybe they were just questioning her so he took off to look for her, but, but, but—" She shook her head and two people, guy and a girl, walking around the three of us, tripped a little over Nikki's boots and the girl didn't fall but the guy started to, got a hand on James's neck and the guy said, "Sorry," and Nikki looked up at me and said, "I looked back one time when I was running and she was in the back of a cop car, and, Davy, she ain't comin' back."

James wiped her nose, said, "Branch made you guys go, didn't he?" and I looked at him, and Nikki said, "No, we were just—doin' a Sunday—" but James said fast, "You guys don't do Sundays that much, though, so he must've—" and Nikki said, "No, James, we do Sundays—" and I stood up, said to James, "Man, fuckin' shut up," and James looked up at me then looked around and I touched Nikki's shoulder, said, "C'mon, okay?" and James stood up, too, got a hand out. Nikki rubbed her eyes more, then stood up and James said to her, "Nik, the DH?" and Nikki said, "Anywhere, inside."

We sat in the DH and I had Nikki between my legs, my arms around her middle, and James sat under the big window, by Jody's stuff, until it got dark, then me and Nikki laid down but James stayed sitting up, next to the window, and we slept some until someone coming in woke us up and Nikki got up on an elbow real fast and looked but James said loud, "It's just him."

Branch, getting up from coming in, looked at James, said, "What the fuck is that?"

James had his head down, shook it.

Nikki said, "Branch, did you see—did you find out—?"

"It was cleared," he said, untying a boot, "the whole street," he pulled the boot off, started untying the other one and when he got it off, he stood both boots up and looked at Nikki and said, "I talked to the dude at the 7-Eleven, Nik, and the guy said they hauled them off. And the dude hasn't seen any of them, none of the girls."

Nikki got flat on the floor again and she said, "What's gonna happen to her?"

Branch backed up to his sleep-space under the window, got flat, and said, "They'll send her home if she really didn't get kicked out, like she said. If she got booted and the family don't want her, then some home, somethin', foster or group or whatever. Either way, it's Idaho for her." He rubbed his socks, said, "Fuck, I *liked* her—"

"Her fucking earning power?" James said, head up, and Branch, still flat, said fast, loud, "What's your *fuckin'* problem, faggot?" and James said, "You just had to have somebody working at all times, Branch—we were on vacation so you had to send the girls out to make up the loss—" and Branch yelled up to the ceiling, "I didn't send them there!"

Nikki said low, "It was just us doing Sunday."

James said loud, "Branch, it's you—it's *you!*"

I said loud, *"James!"* and he looked at me and I said, "Shut your shit."

After a couple seconds of quiet, Branch said, "Thanks," real low, turned over, and Nikki pushed back into me and I got my head on her shoulder, watched James for a while, till I started falling asleep, but I never saw him go flat.

In early morning, Nikki was on top of me, talking into my face, and I caught "—don't wanna get picked up, Davy," opened my eyes and looked down and she had all her clothes on, boots, too, and I said, "What?"

"I don't wanna go back there, I don't wanna get picked up," she said and I grabbed her arms real fast, said, "What're you gonna do?"

Some of her fingers touched my chin. "Oh, no, I'm not jammin'," she said.

I said again, "What're you gonna do?"

She looked around the DH, then back down at me, said, "Anything else," then got up, went slow to the window, started crawling out and James, head slumped down to his chest, snoring low, jerked his shoulders a second when the last part of one of Nikki's boots tapped the windowsill.

Later in the morning, me, James and Branch were all up and getting clothes on and I was tying a boot real slow, then stopped. Branch, everything on, stood up, looked at me.

James, sitting, buttoning his jeans, looked at me, said, "What's up?"

Branch said, "Davy, you just wanna hang today?" and I nodded, then he said, "Wait for her, make sure, y'know, make sure she makes it back?" and I said, "Yeah, I do," and he said that was cool, looked at James, said, "It's you and me," then said to me, "Some A from Max is what we'll be gettin' rid of, Davy. We'll hang close, not go to the zoo or park, just hit Lincoln High and O'Bryant so we can stay downtown," then he looked back at James, standing up, said, "That okay with you?"

James looked at me, then nodded at Branch.

Branch said, "Cool, good," and James started out the window and Branch said to me, "Wherever she jammed, Davy—Nik, Nikki—*she'll* be back."

I said, "I know," finished doing my boot.

I sat on the Yamhill Street side of Pioneer Square, on the top steps close to the MAX-benches, watched a late-afternoon MAX-train let off a bunch of people, and the people on the benches got up, got in the train, then it closed up and went down Yamhill and I looked at heads and faces in the crowd that got off and after a minute or so the crowd-people were off walking in all different directions, none of them staying in the Square.

I went down further in the Square, sat in front of some kids holding and tapping empty Starbucks cups, sitting under the man-holding-the-umbrella statue, and I got a Snickers, half-eaten, out of my back pocket, took a bite, then held the rest up to chuck in the Square and one of the kids behind me said, "Back here, if you don't want it," and I held it back and somebody took it, and I spit a nut-chunk in the pit and Nikki was coming into the Square from Sixth. I got down fast into the pit, got around a skateboarder, got to her and she said, "You're not workin'."

"No," I said, "I was waitin'."

She smiled, "I'm way okay, Davy."

I got closer and looked at her eyes.

"No, I'm not buzzin'," she said. "I'm not on nothin'. I'm *real*, Davy. And—I'm legit. Almost. I'm *employed*."

I said, "Where at? Where'd you get it?" and "How'd you get it?"

She said, "I went walkin' everywhere, around here all day till I just found somethin'," she turned, pointed a ways past Sixth Avenue. "Over there, doin' cleanup at this old beat-up restaurant. I just knocked on the back door, said I was looking for work and the lady said she needed cleanup, tonight, for a few nights, pay under-the-table, and it's late and the place's beat-up, but it's close to here, and you, and—"

I kissed her neck, rubbed her hair.

"It's on Third," she said.

I pulled back and looked at her. "There's a viddie-place there," I said and she nodded, said, "Right next door," and I said, "Could be, sometime, I'll be doin' slither there," and she said, "Yeah, and, hey, maybe y'know sometime—we could—*do lunch* together." She touched my chin and I smiled a little and behind her the skateboarder said loud, "Shit!" and got his board up, looked at it close, said, "A fuckin' split," flicked the bottom wheels.

That night, right after dark, all of us were walking down Burnside, toward the bridge, and going by the Skidmore Fountain, Nikki, carrying Jody's bag, said, "Branch, why can't you guys try for like what I got?"

James, back some, behind her, said fast, "Mo' money, mo' money, mo' money, right, Branch?"

Branch, walking up with me, looked at me and shook his head a little, then said back to James, "Yeah, that's part of it. We're takin' home everything we make, nobody takin' a cut, no boss, no taxes. Plus," he turned around, slowed walking, looked at Nikki, said, "You're lucky, Nik. You're a girl. Cops're coming down, right now, on girls, all that Eighty-second shit, so for under-the-table gigs girls can work them better. But for guys, the cops don't bother us, our slither, so we're actually pretty safe," and James said, "Unless we knife a cop—" and him and Branch and me laughed but Nikki didn't, said, "Yeah, you might as well stay with slither."

I looked back and Nikki was watching the water shoot up and the lights in the fountain.

We started up the bridge and Branch slowed up some again, said loud back, "You sure you wanna do this?" and Nikki said loud, up, "You asked that goin' out of the DH, then goin' by Chinatown, and I'm still sure and I wanna get this done before work so don't ask me anymore," and we were up further on the bridge and I said, "How about here?"

Nikki stopped, got close to the rail, looked over and said, "Here's good," got Jody's bag off her shoulder, got it up on the rail and the rest of us stopped walking ahead and got behind her. She kept both her hands on the bag and stared down at the Willamette a couple seconds, till James said, "Is there anything you're saving?"

"Tampons," she said, not looking up from the water.

Branch looked around Nikki at James, said, "She's not fuckin' dead," and Nikki looked up, at Branch, and he said, "The Dead'll be through here, again, no doubt at all. And she'll be there, I'll bet you."

Nikki said, "Yeah, right, totally," nodded, patted the bag and there was a low tinkle.

James said, "Not even one of the candles?"

Nikki said, "No," looked at James, said, "I hate the smell of them fuckers," started to push the bag over the rail and Branch reached over fast, said, "Hold up," and she quit pushing the bag. Branch got his hands into the bag, pulled out the knife.

James said, "You don't need that."

Branch held it up, said, "Not for me," rubbed the blade with his fingers then held it out, by the blade, to Nikki.

Nikki looked at the knife, looked at me, then said to Branch, "I don't need that."

Branch said, "Yeah you do. I told you, we're guys, we're safe. You're a girl, take it."

Nikki blew air up to the front of her hair, looked at James, shook her head.

I said, "Maybe you ought to," and she looked back at me, then I said, "Okay?"

James said, "Isn't that—what she had it for—protection?" and

Branch said, "Yeah," and Nikki took it by the handle, held it up in front of my face and I took it, put it in her back pocket.

"There," James said, "feel safer?"

Nikki said, "Whatever," pushed the bag over the rail, said, "I gotta go to work," and the bag made a fairly big splash and James, looking over the rail, said, "Hmm. The Dead tapes aren't sinking."

Nikki walked around James and started back down the bridge and Branch and James got moving behind her but I ran, got close to her back and pulled some of her T-shirt out of the back of her jeans, put it over the tip of the knife-blade, sticking up some out of her pocket.

Z z

A couple days later was the first of August and that night me, Branch and James were across the Burnside bridge, on Southeast Pine Street, right by La Luna, standing around Max, sitting in his car.

It was way late and whatever band had played was gone and posters were all over the alley and two bums hung around but no groupies or cops. Me and James passed an Olde English forty-ouncer back and forth and Branch twisted his hat around in his fingers and leaned into the car, talked close to Max. Then Max took Branch's hat, leaned down in the car, then came up and gave Branch back his hat. Branch held the hat tight, kept it wadded, walked by me and James, tagged my arm, said to both of us, "C'mon," and Max closed the car door.

Out of the alley and a little ways from La Luna, Branch stopped and said, "He's gonna wait another hour here, he's got crank for the roadies but he said it'd be a fat hour, so we should have tons of time."

Me and James stopped walking and he said, "For what exactly?"

I took a big drink from the bottle, handed it to James, but Branch got the bottle fast, said, "That," gave me the hat-wad, got a big drink.

I unwrung it, looked at the white and black and yellow pills inside, in an open Ziploc, shook them around in the hat.

Branch said, "Don't lose any of 'em."

"I'm not touchin' 'em," I said, stopped shaking them.

"You know they're not for gettin' off," Branch said, and I said I knew, and Branch said to try one—just down one—and I said, "I'm not touchin' 'em."

Branch gave the bottle to James and James looked over at me, into the hat, said, "They look like some kind of happy shit," then stepped back, took a drink—too big a drink—spilling some on me, tripping back—tripping on a bootstring—me saving the bottle.

Branch took the hat back, zipped the bag up, put the hat on. He said, "Jeez—Christ—everything's not for getting off," and started walking again. I stood by James—stopped to tie his boot—a car light coming up, lighting up James's bootstrings, Branch headed off a side street, toward Burnside and the bridge and downtown—and James asked loud what was up with our place.

Branch stopped, turned, said loud, "We do got it."

James got up. I got a drink.

"Max said start of next week," he walked fast back to us, patted the top of his hat, said, "That's kind of what this stuff's for. We're gettin' a new place so it's like a whole new start on everything."

James got close to Branch, patted his hat, said, "So what *is* this shit?"

Branch said, " 'Shit, shit'? This isn't shit." He looked at both of us. "You don't even fuckin' understand—you don't even know what these are, do you? This isn't *shit,* assholes. These little fuckers—they can be life. Assholes—*life!*"

I put the bottle down on the street. Branch got the hat off, unzipped the bag, took out a black one—got the bottle—took the pill and a drink.

He held the bottle low and said, "Safeties—that's what it is, okay? Listen—pounding down a couple of these a day for—what?—couple weeks?—is gonna make us safe, all of us. What Max was sayin' was that we'll beef up the immunes. Sometimes the deals—*you know*—don't wanna fuck with the rubber shit, but now, see, with these, it won't matter. We'll be safe even if they don't wanna."

James pointed at Branch's pill-bag and said, "Antibiotics," and Branch got walking again, holding the hat tight and shook his head, said, "It's Z, better, way better, *A-Z-T,*" and James said, "I didn't know you could score stuff, that's—*you know*—good for you," and Branch said, "Max gets anything," patted his back, then front jeans pockets, said, "Street-shit, to sell, that goes here," then held up his hat-wad, said, "But life, that'll go here," then we came around a house and right into Burnside and Branch said we needed to use the hour to get some fast funds to get more Z from Max.

Branch drank some more and took another pill and he checked the street, and caught an opening between cars—jammed—and we crossed close behind him, closer to the bridge and downtown.

I looked at James, said to him, "Z?" and he shrugged and I said, "Nikki's gonna be gettin' back to the DH in a while," and Branch looked at me and I said, "We should be there."

"We need to be gettin' funds for this," Branch said, patting his hat again.

"This is bullshit," I said, and Branch came up behind me, swung an arm and the bottle around me, kept me moving.

"Not bullshit," Branch said. "It's life. It's what we need about now, with Jody jammed. What I just took—another day—no!—a whole fucking extra week added to me."

"It's shit," I said.

"It's not shit."

I pushed him off. "Fuck—do we look sick?" I said. "Do I look sick? You think I got it?"

"Think about it—"

"You think *I got it?*"

His face was in mine. *"Think about it!* Who the fuck haven't you fucked with?" He waved his hand over cars going by and city-lights past the bridge. "The whole city, just about! Plus Nikki and Jimbo, here, and *me,* dude—remember the viddie? That was *me* fuckin' *you*—and I'm from fuckin' Oakland—*California*—so you haveta have somethin', Davy, you gotta have it!"

I backed up, looked over him at the cars going over the bridge, into town.

James got the bottle from Branch, put his hand on Branch's hat-wad and Branch opened it up, and James took a couple pills and started to drink but I put my hand on the bottle.

Branch gave me a black one and a yellow one, then dropped two more yellow ones into my open hand and I downed everything.

"We'll hit Hart's 'cause it's got the holes," Branch said, bag zipped, hat on his head. "And 'cause it's by Nik, too, okay? Keep an eye on everybody and start pullin' clean deals—clean start"—he spit, said, "Get our bucks, jam back here to Max, and be set, be totally set—for life—okay?"

I handed James the bottle, what was left—not much—said, "Kill it," and he said, "Oh, ick, fucking Davy backwash," but finished it with his drugs. He chucked the bottle between some cars, clinking it back almost to Pine Street, and then we were moving again, already past midbridge, cruising the downside.

We got to Southwest Third and I looked at the restaurant across from Hart's but there were only a couple lights on inside and the BLUE SEA restaurant sign was off outside and no one was sitting at any tables but there were a couple shadows, in the back, one pushing a broom, and James said, "Girl's working hard," and Branch, ahead a little, said, "Fuckin' A—not *him*," stopped, pointed at a kid-kid—twelve, thirteen—standing under the red Hart's sign. We stopped behind Branch and James said, "Who?" and Branch turned, said, "Fuckin' baby-slither," and I looked close at the kid-kid, then said to James that the kid-kid had gotten into Branch's way, a few times.

James, face over Branch's shoulder, said, "He's just a dorky little kid," and I said, "Yeah, but he's just like us," and Branch said, "He freaks out the deals," and James said, "Well, he's slithering here, so *some*body must want him," and Branch said, "Well, I fuckin' don't want him here," started moving ahead and I went forward fast, got Branch's arm, but the kid-kid looked over at us, looked at Branch a long second, then took off around the corner of Third.

James said, "We sure don't have time for this shit," and Branch said, "I know, you're right," and I pushed around both of them, got the Hart's door open.

We came out of the dark into Hart's lights and they were bright, and Branch said, "These're new," looking at the ceiling lights, and big lights over the magazine rack, and I said, "Guess we haven't been here in a while," and James said, "Floodlights and slither definitely clash," and further in, Branch said, "That's new," pointed at a little TV on the counter in front of the counterguy, Blazer game going, and going by the counter to the booths, Branch said, "Score?" and the guy, finger-wiping a corner of the TV screen, said, "Tied at seventy-eight," and I said, "Who?" and the guy said, "Golden State," and we got into the start of the first hall, guys mazing around, and James said, "Hold our calls."

New lights were up down the halls too, and most of the guys—going up and down, going from booth to booth, lots of new light—kept their heads low.

A guy in a suit came out of a midhall booth, jingling his keys, finger-flicking a car keyring and James said, "Dibs on Trump," followed him around the corner, and then somebody else—coming from the front—came by close, tapped Branch's and my butt with a rolled-up *Hustler* and Branch said, "Davy—scratch 'n' sniff centerfold—the new *Hustler*—you gotta see it," tagged my arm and we followed the guy that'd tagged our butts down the hall and the guy took the first booth on the left, looking at us right before closing the door. Branch said, "We got him," went ahead fast, and a ways behind Branch and the booths and the people, an old guy was opening a door under a red Emergency Exit sign, and I kept walking towards Branch and he had the *Hustler*-guy's booth-door open and said inside, "Dude—up for two?" and behind him the kid-kid came in, under the old guy's arm and the old guy patted the kid-kid's shoulder, pushed him in more and I got to Branch and got a hand on his shoulder, said, "You take him, he's not hot," and, "I want my own slither," and pushed Branch inside. He said, "Fine—fuck—whatever," closed the booth door and the kid-kid came up through the hall, old guy following him close, looking down at his butt. "Score, dammit, Robinson!" came down from the front then the counterguy yelled, "Get with it, Cliff!" and the kid-kid and the old guy went around the hall-corner and I walked fast up to them, pushed the old guy over some, said down to the kid-kid, "Dude—you gotta get out," and he stopped, looked at me. "My friend—he don't like you here," and the little kid smiled, said, "He's not gonna do nothin' to me inside," and the old guy came back up and I said to him, "You're gonna get snuffed bringin' a little kid-kid in," and the old guy said, "Not if we find a booth in the back there," and I said, "You're gonna fuck it up for everybody," got close to the guy fast and rubbed his crotch hard, then the OCCUPIED light went out on a booth behind him and another old guy came out and I pushed the old guy I was rubbing inside, looked at the kid-kid, said, "Jam—okay?" real fast, then got in the booth with the old guy, closed the door, said, "Drop some quarters," got on my knees while he got in his pockets for change and he got some in the wall-box and I got his dick out, sucked on it, and he got a Kleenex-wad out of his shirt-pocket, stuck it in the peephole in the wall under the viddie-channel box.

Little later, the old guy came and I spit in a coffee-can full of butts in a corner, said, "Me and my friends're playin' safer," then the viddie went out and I got out of the booth, starting walking down the hall. I turned the hall-corner, saw James at the end of the next one and went fast down to him and, "*Goddammit,* Strickland—shoulda got your shit together," came down from the front.

James patted his front pocket, said, "*Fifteen*—the suit tipped—how about you, boy?" and I shook my head, said, "Nothing," and James said, "He stiffed you?" and I nodded, said, "He jammed out of the booth way fast," and then James said, "You played it clean, right?" and I said I did, said I spit, then James asked if Branch got a deal and I said, "Yeah," and he said, "Then his take plus mine is just maybe enough for Max's Z-stuff," and I said, "I know where he is," and we went back around to the hall I'd been in, looked at the last booth on the left but the OCCUPIED light was off and the door was open some and I pulled it open and no one was inside and James said, "Oh, he must've known you were worthless tonight," stepped out some and elbowed my arm, said, "Since he's already got another deal going," stepped back inside, looked around, said, "I was gonna actually try to whip up one more guy—had this one other guy I was following but—turns out he's following that kid—that little kid"—and I said, "He's still here—that kid's still here?" James said, "Yeah—getting every freak here to follow him"—and I said, "Where, what hall?"

James waved a hand back, said, "One over—last I saw—so what?"

I started away from the empty booth and James came out, said, "So what's up with that little slither?"—followed me to the start of the next hall and I said, "Branch doesn't like him"—saw the first booth closed, light on over the door, got around a guy standing across from the door, got my ear up to it, heard video-noise and the guy I'd gotten around said, "You dig leather?" and James, behind him, said to me, "So Branch doesn't like him—so what?—Branch doesn't like *me*," I looked at the guy, said, "That's what in there?" and he nodded, said, "Leather vest, no shirt, nice 'stache," and I looked up at the next booth—light lit up—went to it, got my ear to the door and James said, "Davy—so *what?*"—and I said, "This is different, he gets weird, he could—get wrong—" and James got in front of me, held his hands up, said—"What's 'wrong'?" and I looked at the booth-door right beside the one I was listening to—open some, no light on over it—and I said, "Check the hole in there, tell me what you see in here." James went in the booth and a guy came around the hall corner, smiled at me and I closed my eyes, got my ear closer, heard tokens or quarters going down and a couple voices, then James said, "They're just kissing"—and I said loud "Who?" and James said, "A man and a woman—and they heard us—they stopped kissing"—and James said loud, "Guy and a chick—*here* at Hart's—Ha!" and I backed off the booth-door, looked up, and the next three booths had their OCCUPIED lights on, and I went to the first—got an ear on the door, listened close, just heard noise from the video—got my ear on the next door—middle of the three—heard hard breathing, coughing, then, "Okay—let me go and I'll go—" then James came up to me, got his ear close and we both heard Branch say, "Yeah, you fuckin' think okay—" and I hit the door with my fist, said, *"Branch!"* James tried the door-handle— locked—and the other voice behind the door said, "Hey—get this open—" and I said "Branch!" again, shook the handle and James looked at me, knocked on the next door down, said real low, "Buddy— you gotta drop quarters," and a guy, inside, said, "They're in," and James knocked harder and said lower, "You gotta drop some quar- ters"—and the guy inside said louder, "I got three bucks in"—then opened his door—looked up—said, "See, the goddamn light's on"— and James pushed the door all the way open, went in fast, and I got in after him, pushing the guy—holding up his pants and belt with one hand, covering up his dick with the other—into the hall—and James—already on his knees on the floor in front of the wall-hole under the viddie-channel box—said, "Davy." I got to the floor, pushed James off the wall-hole and looked through and Branch had the kid- kid by the throat in a corner of the booth—both hands tight around his neck, fingers digging marks, kid's hands up, fingers pulling on Branch's—and the guy in the hall said, "Hey—you two don't even work here"—and James said, "Get the guy that does"—and Branch looked around the kid-kid's neck—saw my eye in the hole—and said, "Davy? Hey—this is *our* slither, Davy"—and two spots of blood came up, under both Branch's middle fingers, and the kid coughed hard again, looked at me, and the vid-light in Branch's booth went out and I said, "Branch—fuck—give him up!"—into the hole then—"What's going on?" came loud down the hall. James pulled me off the hole, we got into the hall and the guy that we'd taken the booth from—pants up, belt buckled—was walking fast up to us, pointing at Branch's booth, counterguy, next to him, holding up a key, and the pants-guy said, "There—that's the booth—source of all this shit—" and the counterguy got the key in Branch's doorknob and the pants-guy—pointing at me and James—said, "Three bucks—you two owe me—" and Branch's door came open wide and the kid-kid came out fast—coughing, holding his neck, pushing me over—and I went down, James's boots keeping me from hitting the floor. The kid-kid headed to the exit door—his T-shirt collar—ripped and flapping—flipped around his face when he opened the door, then got caught in the door when he went out and he must've let it rip off because the door closed, the collar-chunk hung, and he didn't come back in. I looked at Branch, standing in the back of his booth, looking at me through the flicking light coming through the hole in the wall from the viddie still playing next door—and his hat was on the floor, next to the pill-bag, ripped, and pills were all over. Counterguy said, "Out," looking at Branch too, then said it again, to James and me, and then to the pants-guy he said, "You too," and the pants-guy started to talk but the counterguy cut him fast—said, "Just all of you—now—*out*"—and—"None of you are coming back"—and the pants-guy went down to and out the back exit and James got my elbow, started moving us the other way, to the front exit. The counterguy went in Branch's booth and pulled him out, pushed him in the hall after us, said he didn't know what was going on but it wouldn't be going on anymore in his place, and Branch followed us slow with his head down, wadding his hat in his hands, and the counterguy, in the booth, said loud, "And drugs. Drugs—on my floor—right out here in the open," came out with a handful of the pills and dropped them into a garbage can by the exit.

* * *

Me and James were out and standing in front of the Hart's door a couple seconds before Branch, and James, looking down Third, said to me, "You've seen him get like that?" and I said, "Not that bad," then, "We just—have to watch him—keep an eye on him—and it'll be cool—" and James shook his head, said, "Davy, it's not cool if we have to watch him."

Then the Hart's door jingled, Branch came out, still holding his hat, and James said to him, "Where to now?"

Branch said, "Not back in there, I tried talking to the guy, but we're out, totally out of that game."

"Which way now?" James said.

Branch came up between us, started heading toward Burnside. Me and James followed and I looked back at Nikki's restaurant, all the lights were off, and Branch, staying ahead, said back to me, "She still there?" and I said, "No," that it looked closed and she was probably at the DH, and James said low to me, looking at the sidewalk, "Where're we going?" and Branch said, still not looking back, "James, you didn't see anything worth talkin' about," and James slowed up, said, "I *wasn't* talking about—" but, Branch said, "I was gettin' rid of somethin' that's been in the way since before you—" but James, stopped on Burnside, said loud, "I wasn't talking about what you did."

Branch quit talking, shook his head, turned the corner, kept walking, heading toward the bridge.

James yelled, "Where're you fucking *going*!" and then, not as loud, said, "Branch, it's been over an hour and we missed Max and we don't have the money."

Branch stopped, just at the start of the bridge, said, "Yeah, you're right," looked around at the water, then the traffic, then opened his hat, looked in it. He said, "Let's, uh, um, go," and I said, "Just—DH it—Branch?" and he nodded, started walking back toward us, still looking in his hat, and he laughed a couple times, and, up to us, said, "Leftovers, here," picked out two pills still in his hat, flicked them on Burnside, then smoothed the hat out on his leg, and put it on, brim in front.

I watched Branch move around in his sleep-space, long time later, Nikki balled high up my side, snoring in my armpit, James in his corner, out of the street-light, and then Branch coughed snot loud, moved it in his mouth, swallowed it down, said, "Freak's in our shit, man," and then, "Uhn-hunh," and quit moving, stretched out more on the floor, his feet taking up old Jody sleep-space. I closed my eyes, rubbed Nikki's head, then heard moving in James's corner and looked over, couldn't see what he was doing, then he came out of the dark, standing up, boots on, and he stepped over Branch, started out the window. I moved Nikki off me onto a shirt-wad, got my boots, laced fast, got out the window.

I got around the front of the DH and James was already crossing Couch, hitting Burnside, heading past the Burnside Burger King, and he stayed on Burnside, going west, and I stayed back fairly far because he'd slowed down, and he didn't get fast again till Fourteenth, and then he ran across the overpass into northwest downtown, so I ran, but not real fast, still kept space between us.

He got up almost to the park, then turned on Twenty-third. When I turned Twenty-third he was walking slow, looking in the closed store windows, reaching up and flicking the lights hanging in the sidewalk trees, then he turned down Flanders.

He was standing on the sidewalk across from our building, looking up at it, and he didn't look at me when I came down the street, and, stopping up next to him, I said, "You saw me a long time ago, hunh?" and he said, "Oh, yeah," then smiled and said, "This neighborhood's so cool. Like, nine coffee-spots."

There was laughing and I looked up Flanders and five or six people were walking down Twenty-third, holding, shaking ice in their coffee cups, and James said, "Great fucking building, too," then he said, "Ready to go back?"

I said "Sure," we both turned, walked, then at the corner of the street, he looked back, said, "Great fucking building," again, and I leaned back, saw he was looking too high, at the top floor, over all the scaffolding, and I said, "Yeah, James, but we're there," pointed across him, down to the basement, and he nodded, cut in front of me, took the lead home.

Perfect Kiss

Next morning Branch was up real early and he kicked my feet hard with his boots, said, "I'm gettin' an early start on slither, maybe score a jogger," and he backed up and crawled out and after his last boot went out the window, Nikki rolled over, got her head on my chest, said, "Your chest just went down," and I said, "What?" and she rubbed the top of my chest, up to the start of my neck, said, "You were tight all night, like you were holding your breath," then touched a shoulder, then pounded on my arm real light and said, "See, you're hard all over, been tight all night," and I shook some, and she looked down, said, "And your boots're on." I said, "I went for a walk."

She got her head and hands off me, rolled over, stayed on her back. I looked over at James, still sleeping, blanket almost off of him, a lot of his back showing, and the whole back of his head, face in his jeans-wad.

"What got you up?" Nikki said.

"James," I said, turned over, got one arm under her, one arm around her and after a couple seconds she spooned back into me and I got my face into her neck, mouth up to her ear and then I said, "It's just shit. Branch had some pills and lost them and Branch was pissed and James got mad and I told James we just gotta watch—" I backed off her ear and then kissed the bottom of it, real quick, said, "—out for each other."

She nodded, put her feet bottoms up to my ankles and rubbed.

"We—fucked up—blew the deal," I said, "Was a one-time shot, too. Might not get a shot at the shit again." I moved my mouth over the back of her ear, then closed my eyes, moved my whole face around, in the back of her head, pulled her tighter, tits into my arm.

"What else?" she said low.

I shook my head slow at the top of her back. She got her toenails into some of my ankle-hair.

"These pills—we could've used them—ourselves," I said. "They were for, uhm, in case we—get something—or maybe got something—and what if—we got something."

Her shoulders shrugged. Her big-toe-bottom rubbed my anklebone and she yawned.

"All the stuff," I said, "With everybody, and you—"

"I gotta sleep," Nikki said, an elbow going into a couple of my ribs. "Let's sleep, 'cause you were right, it's just shit."

I looked over at James and his head was turned up some, one eye was open and he was looking at us, a whole side of his face showing in a big chunk of window-light, and we looked at each other a couple seconds, then his eye went closed and I turned and nodded in Nikki's neck.

*   *   *

There was stubble in my back and a hand around my dick, not much later, little more light in the place, and after my eyes got open I started to turn my head but James's mouth came up and pushed down hard on my ear and he said, "It's louder in here without Jody," and I said, "What?"

"Everything echoes because there's more"—he pulled his mouth off my ear—"too much space."

Nikki moved and turned on her back, one tit over, one tit under my arm. I looked at her and an eye came open and she said, "What about space?" and coughed, rubbed the closed eye.

"Branch said next week we'll be in," I said, and she smiled, both eyes open, and I turned and looked at the ceiling.

"Davy, that's good shit," she said, then she got her head up, looked over me to James and he said, "Yeah, Davy, say goodbye to the Burnside Benson," but I didn't say anything or look at them, kept looking up.

Nikki moved off me. James got his mouth back on my ear and said, "We maybe *don't* have it," and I looked at him, then Nikki said, "Yeah, Davy, it could totally be that, too," then I looked at my chest.

Nikki put her head up, chin on a nipple, looked over at James a couple seconds then smiled, looked at me and said, "Davy, close your eyes."

I closed my eyes, said, "Okay, what's this for?" and James said, "Morning mind-fuck because we're bored and you're talking shit," and Nikki pulled the blanket up more, all the way to my chin, then got under the blanket, climbed over me, got down to my legs then Nikki scooted lower and four hands started pulling my legs apart but I pushed back and Nikki said, "Davy," and I quit pushing and moved my legs apart. Nikki and James moved around under the blanket, between my leg-space, and James said, "Don't peek, dick," and I said I wasn't, kept my eyes tight and a mouth came on my dick and fingers felt around hairs on the bottom of my balls, and I laughed a little but got hard fast.

The mouth came off my dick and two tongues licked on and under my dickhead and a whole hand got around my dick and another bunch of fingers flicked under my balls. I put a hand under the blanket, started to feel around some hair, then a hand took my hand off, and I pulled it out of the blanket, kept it by my side, both hands by my side, and a mouth went down all the way on my dick and came up, then another went down fast, all the way, and I leaned my head back, stayed flat, till I started to come. When I started coming I leaned up some and opened my eyes but their heads were still under the blanket, one mouth going on my dick, and they were both moving around, then my eyes went closed and it all came out. Hands felt up my stomach and the blanket went up and I looked out at my stomach and down at my dick and there wasn't any jizz and I looked at Nikki and James—looking up—looked close at them, looked at their mouths and around their mouths—but nobody had jizz spots.

I said, "Okay—who—?" and they both smiled, then James scooted out of the blanket some, turned and scrunched, butt to my knee and Nikki got her head out of the blanket and kissed my chin, fairly fast, then put her face-side on my chest and closed her eyes.

I put a finger on my chin and rubbed the finger around, put the finger in my mouth and there was no salt-taste. I looked over at James and he had a lot of the blanket and his hair was in my ribs and he'd started sleeping. I looked at Nikki and her eyes were still closed and her smile was gone and she was taking long breaths, too. I got my head down, stayed flat, rubbed James's hair and Nikki's back, started sleeping and then James burped and everybody laughed low, but it echoed fairly big.

*   *   *

Afternoon, in the park, I was on my knees, mouth full, holding jizz, and the guy I'd done finished buttoning up, gave me two fives, one on each shoulder, and said, "The extra's for taking it," and I looked at one of my boots and tightened up a couple strings, nodded and he turned, started down the trail and when he was down fairly far I spit, stood, spit two, three more times. Branch came up, out of some bushes just off the trail.

I said, "How long you been there for?" and he got closer.

"Dude, I wasn't stalkin' you, I been tryin' to get to you to tell you some news. But you and James—been snuffin' me all damn day—walkin' the total other way when I'd come up or James, movin' up to the swings when I'd—"

"What news?" I said.

"I saw Max, tracked him down, real early today and he says we can move in tomorrow night." He looked down at the trail, moved dirt with his boot-toe, said, "I told him that we needed this bad. Real bad right now." He looked at me, said, "Told him I was—fuckin' things up—and needed some real floor-space to—settle down on."

I looked down over at the big fountain and a couple cars'd left but James was walking down from the swings and a couple new cars came, slowed, parked in front of the fountain.

"I also got a deal rigged up," Branch said, "Later, late afernooner, all of us, and Davy, it's with Mike—bathhouse Mike. He was slitherin' around here in the AM, and, uh, well, if we give him a good time today, he'll let us into the BH, couple weekends out of the month, free, no card, no fees, dude."

James sat on the fountain-edge, got his knees up to his chin. I looked over, back down at the pile of trail-dirt Branch's boot'd made.

"So, Davy," he said, "We got space—and—vacation space."

I kicked some of his pile, then nodded and said, "Cool," then looked at him. "Yeah," I said.

"*Go home, Kent!*" came up from the fountain and I turned and James was standing and laughing by a car, and a hand came out of the driver's window and a finger pointed at James and out of the car came, "*Go home, James!*" and James laughed harder, bent over, came up with his hands on the driver's door and the driver-guy's finger came out more, touched, did circles on James's chin.

"That car—" Branch said.

"Hasn't been around in a while," I said, then James came around the front of the car, got the other door open and I started taking a couple steps down the trail and James got in the car, rolled the window down some and looked at me over the window-edge and I ran.

Branch yelled down, "Davy—you're *trippin'*!"—and the car went around the fountain, the hill, toward the exit, and James's head was straight ahead and I got to the fountain and the car got a little faster, going down the hill, then a car—parked on the side of the road right in front of the exit—pulled out in front of James and Kent and I cut up the hill, low and fast, pushing some in the ground with my hands, then got to the top, cut through the swings and ran down, through bushes, down the other side of the hill in front of the exit and the car blocking Kent's car went by me and out of the park and I came down, on my knees, on the road, in front of them. Kent's car braked at my boot-toes.

"What the hell's the matter with you?" Kent yelled, head out the window.

I stood up and James was looking down.

I rubbed mud off my hands onto my jeans. Kent honked once, then looked at James and James got a hand on his seatbelt, rubbed it up and down, then looked out at me. I went fast to his window and James got it down all the way and I looked inside, saw James pulling some of his shirt over the barrel of the toy-gun on the cover of his Foo Fighters CD, sitting on his leg, and he looked at me, let go of his shirt, said, "You can ditch the rest of my shit—or keep the tunes if you want—" and I grabbed his seatbelt-strap, said, "You had that stuck there, with you, all day, waitin'?" He nodded, looked down again and Kent said, "There are cars coming behind me, guys," and I pulled some more on the seatbelt-strap, said, "It's Branch"—and James said fast, "It's Branch plus I want a shower but it's not you"—and I said, "Yeah—but if we *watch* him"—and James said, "I want to look— somewhere else—start over, *my* park—" and a car behind Kent's honked and Kent said, "There's a car really wanting out here"—and I said, "He's gettin' us space and —we *owe* him—" and other car-honks came and James—shaking his head, tapping the top of his CD case— said, "Davy, the guy is a gun and I'm a pussy—I don't want to deal with him and—maybe—I can do better than a basement—" then Kent got a hand on James's shoulder, said, "James," I let go of his seatbelt—and James looked ahead and I leaned in the car, got my mouth around his, kissed hard, then the car went forward and I went back, fell in the bushes, rubbed my mouth, looked at James, looking back at me, rubbing his mouth, and the other car came by me, then another, after it, and Kent's car was at the end of Lewis and Clark Circle and James quit rubbing his mouth, turned his head straight ahead, then they were out of the park, four cars close, fast, behind them, then I got up out of the bushes, rubbed the back of my head and my butt, then my eyes.

Branch came down the hill, got on the street, in front of me, and I got my hand off my eyes. Branch looked at my hand, flicked off a few little bush-leaves stuck between my fingers, then looked at me, said, "Davy, hey, man, *fags* cry."

An hour or so later, I was on the fountain-edge, knees up to my chin, looking up at the guys on the trails, Branch, by me, talking.

"You can't be hangin' him jammin' on me at all 'cause you know it's not me, it's him, okay?"

He pointed around me but I didn't look around, or at him, kept my head straight.

"I didn't do that. Davy, that's his shit, leaving. I'm fuckin' still here."

He pointed at himself, then two cars started pulling around us slow and Branch looked at the driver and I looked down between my knees.

"That kid-kid," I said. "I saw that. James saw that."

"I scared the kid is all."

I looked at the trails again.

"All of us," he said. "What's left, I mean, we just need to stay cool and stick together. It's back to you, me, and Nik."

He smiled, then looked behind him, at another car coming up to the fountain and said, "That's Mike," looked back at me. "Can you just get over it, get it up, for now, for this, and deal?"

The car stopped and Mike waved, then leaned over, unlocked the other door and Branch got off the fountain-edge.

"Dude," Branch said, rubbing one of my boot-toes, "with or without him, *we're* still hooked," and I got my legs straight, then got up.

Piss & Quiet

That night, I was standing in my underwear in a big bedroom in a house on Canyon, next to the park, close under Portland Heights, talking on the phone and holding some beer in a glass, Branch and Mike way behind me, on the bed, Mike, shirt off, belt undone, pants down some, Branch in his underwear, TV in front of them, on, viddie going. I said into the phone, "Nikki?"

There was noise in the back, where she was at, so I said her name again and she said, "What's wrong?"

"I'm drunk."

"Where're you at?"

"A deal's place. Mike's house. This afternoon deal went into night."

"Okay, cool, that's what I figured."

"I'm drunk."

"Davy—I'm busy. I'm closin' up. I can't talk."

I put the beer on a table and turned around and looked at the TV and then at Branch and the older guy, and they were feeling around down each other's underwear and kissing and laughing. "The viddie's going," I said.

"What viddie?"

"The one that's got us in it. Branch. And me. And James. It's playing—"

"He's got it?"

"Uhn-hmm. Mike's got it and you know what? He plays it sometimes, he says, once in a while, in the BH, in the viddie room at the bathhouse, and right now, it's playing, right here. And they're laughing."

"Branch and Mike?"

"Uhn-hmm."

"It's not funny."

"No. It's not funny."

"Davy—I can't talk and I can't do nothin'."

"I'm drunk."

"I know, and I can't do nothin'."

"I'm drunk and—James jammed."

"Oh. Oh, shit. When?"

"Today—in the park—but he's here—" I laughed, burped, said, "Caught—on tape."

"You're drunk."

"I know that."

"Right, okay. I can't do nothin'. Can you just go lay down? That's what you need to do. Just say you're tired and go lay down a while."

I said, "I can do that," and Nikki said, "Mmm-hmm," and I put the phone down and looked over at Mike going down on Branch, and Branch pushing Mike's pants way down, and I looked further over, into the other big room with a couch, and then Branch was looking up at me, moving his head for me to come over but I went into the bathroom, a couple steps from the phone, on my side of the room.

I turned on the light and a fan came on. There was a tub with a plastic curtain covering it up halfway and I turned off the light and the fan went out and I pushed the door but it didn't totally shut and I felt around the sink and my knee nailed the toilet and I felt around more because there wasn't much bedroom-light coming in from the door-crack and I felt plastic, touched the tub, pulled the plastic, put my leg over, then the other, and sat in the tub. I put my head back but the tub-spout was back there so I turned around, got backwards in the tub, and put my head back to the cold rim and then the bed-room light went out, just video-flicker left around the walls and ceiling. I pulled the plastic over to my head, closed the curtain all the way, put my feet up, shut my eyes.

Light, wind woke me up, and I squinted at the bathroom bulb, heard the growly fan spinning, heard a long trail of piss hitting toilet water and I bent up and rubbed my eyes and the back of my head and I was cold. The pissing quit and I heard a zip and the plastic got pulled and Mike said something but a huge wad of beer breath came with what he said and I closed my eyes for a second and then he bent down to the tub and put his head on the rim next to my head and I held my breath and heard him say "I need to fuck you."

I started to stand up and fell into the plastic and Mike got me up, got his arms around me, and I stepped out of the tub and he pushed down my underwear and I started to walk and reached for the door and he said, "In here's fine." He turned me around and held onto my butt and looked over my shoulder and put some fingers around my dick and I was hard some, and he said that I looked bigger in the video. I looked behind in the door-crack and Branch was in a scrunched lump under the bedcovers and I said to Mike, "You . . .

didn't you just give it to Branch?" and looked over, and Mike put a couple fingers in his mouth and got them spitty, said, "I just *got* it from him," and put a finger next to, then into my butt, said, "Now I want to fuck you," turned the first finger around some, and put in the other, and held my stomach with his other hand, kept me up and still.

His front hand stopped holding me and he unzipped and worked his dick, and one of the fingers went in way far, and I moved forward some, and he took his dick hand and moved me, got me standing in front of the toilet. I put a hand on the tank to keep up and looked at the water and it was mostly piss and Mike put my other hand on his dick and put his mouth on the side of my mouth, then kissed the side of my face, then put his tongue inside my ear and said, kind of laughing, "Son, you reek of about a half-rack of Henry's'd be my guess—that what you'd say?"

He pulled the fingers out and held onto my butt some more, and then put one of the fingers under my nose and I said, "I reek," and he laughed and kept the finger there a while, and I sniffed butt for a while, then he pushed on my shoulders and I went down, the floor cold on my knees, and I saw that his pants weren't down very far, just open at the fly, and he undid his belt some more and the pants and underwear went down some more, about to my ear, and his belt buckle, loosened up, next to my ear, made noise, k-jangled, while he pulled up and down on his dick. He pulled my butt apart and got me wet but didn't put fingers in. He moved behind me, and moved me so my back was low and my butt was up. He put my hands up to the tank and put my chin on the seat and I said, "Do you have rubbers?" and he said yeah, but that they were in his car, and then he put a hand around my middle and pushed my head down and I reached up and flushed the tank and he laughed a little, said, "Whoops," said he never flushed much because he lived alone, and then pushed his dick into my butthole and I looked down, watched the piss-water go around and out, come up clear.

He pushed in more, pushed me up more, my chin coming off the rim, toward bowl-water, so I scooted my face around the rim, kept it from hitting water, my nose fairly close to the tank, and Mike's belt buckle tapped the toilet, k-jangled in my ear about three times as loud and faster, following the fuck-rhythm, and around that there was the hum of the light-fan and the hissing toilet water settling and under that maybe a few of my grunts because my stomach was squeezed up to the belly of the bowl.

I said real low, "That jangle," and he said, "Belt buckle buggin' you?" but didn't stop fucking, and I said low, "Sounds like somethin'," and he said, "Mmm-hmm," pushed up further and held it in so the k-jangle stopped a second and some of my breath went out and I said, "Quarters droppin'."

Then I held onto the tank tight and closed my eyes but they didn't stay closed because it was cold and bright and loud, and Mike put the reeky finger back up under my nose, then into my mouth, and I whiffed my shit, and then tasted my shit, and I said, "Stop it," and his dick pushed up more and my breath went out again and I spit out the finger and turned my head and the finger dug around for my mouth, got going in, and I got my breath and said, "Stop it."

Mike said, "What?" and pumped some more and said no, because he was close, and I reached back and pulled him out and reached over and wiped fuck slime on the plastic curtain and climbed up, my hand slipping—elbow hitting toilet water—head hitting the tank, but I got up by the other hand, and my legs—close to asleep—got straight, and I got the elbow out of water and kept my hand up, pushing Mike back because he was reaching up.

I got hold of my underwear and Mike, still down, looking up, beating off by the tub, said, "Don't move—stay a sec," and I stopped and he dribbled and shot, made spots on the plastic, then dribbled a couple spots more on the floor and I pulled up my shorts and got to the bedroom.

Branch was sitting on the bed, shirt on, jeans on, pulling socks on. The TV was dead snow—on, but nothing playing—snow noise hissing low. I got my pants, shirt, socks, boots off the floor, threw the socks, pulled on my jeans.

Branch said, "We need to stay for payoff."

"You."

"No—fuck it," he said, "Let's go."

Mike, at the bathroom doorstop, said the deal was for all night, toweled his balls and dick, threw his wad of pants and belt and socks to the bed and the buckle clanked the pillow behind Branch. Branch got up.

"You stay," I said, got my shirt on, got into my boots, laced fast. Branch got beside me. I tied both boots and said, "I'm going, you're stayin', that's all that's gonna happen."

"You're fuckin' wasted."

"And you're staying," I said.

I got to the other room, and the door, and Branch followed partway, and Mike said, "Somebody needs to stay," and Branch said loud at the couch, "You're fucking wasted," and I undid the door and opened it and didn't look at Branch and said, "You stay here—and then—you stay away"—and looked at him—"from me"—and then left.

I ran down through Portland Heights then slowed, out of breath, stumbling some, through the park and then walked when I got out of the park onto Burnside, the rest of the way to the Dead Hotel.

When I got through the window I stayed on my knees, crawled to the corner and James's stuff. I grabbed handfuls of stuff—CDs, tapes, socks, shirts—put them hard into his backpack. I rubbed my eyes and looked around at Branch's wad of sleeping blankets, and me and Nikki's sleeping-wad, then zipped up James's pack, got it over a shoulder, then walked back to the window and crawled back out.

I walked slow, back up Burnside, then through the park and my face was sweating, going up the high trail, so I got the backpack off, held it, pulled off my shirt, got it wadded and wiped my face, then I saw a fairly big tree, off to the top of the trail, getting lit up, then going dark and I got to it, dropped the pack and sat. Lights came up under me and I looked down the hillside and Burnside was under me, bunch of cars going by, all at once, then none and dark.

I reached around, pulled the pack in, up under my back, then stretched out my legs, got the shirt-wad in the middle of my chest, scooted down, more in the dirt, got my head on James's pack.

The guy pulled my shirt up, I got my arms up and before it got over my head he kissed my mouth fast then the shirt went over my chin, face, hair, then off onto a long glass table, covering up his keys. He kissed my neck, felt my back, then my crotch, then popped a middle button in my jeans, got a finger in, fingered my dick out, then used his whole hand, got me hard, then said it was a great, gorgeous day and it looked like I needed some sun, backed up and pulled the curtains open and a ton of light came in the big room and I squinted then looked at the Space Needle, middle of the window, up over the tops of the trees down the hill.

He tapped the window, a big patch of bright blue, and said, "This could be it for nice days for a while. Although last summer," he moved around a couch, back up me, "the heat hung around quite a while," he undid the rest of my jeans buttons, "well into September, I remember," then he kissed my neck again, said I needed a bath, and I said, "I can't, like, do the whole night," told him I had a buddy waiting for me in the park, that we didn't like being apart for too long a stretch, and he said, "A buddy? You should have mentioned that you had a friend—" and I said, "Buddy's a she," and he nodded, laughed a little in my neck, said a low, "Oh," in my ear. Then he backed up, kept a hand out, under my dick, fingers in my ball-hair, said, "I understand. You have to watch out for each other. That's a smart plan, David." He let go of all my business, backed up more, smiled, looked at outside, said, "Fab view, isn't it?" and I said, "Yeah," looked around the place in the light, stopped at his stereo, big, and his TV, huge, and he said, "I was very lucky to land this house— I'm still closing on it actually—" and I said, "We didn't ever do rates or anything," and he said, "Oh, right. Well, I just assumed the usual—" and I said, "What's that up here?"

He smiled, sat on the couch-arm. "Something in the neighborhood of one, one hundred-fifty," he said, "That's the usual. But that's also all night."

"I can't do—"

"I understand. How about fifty, for the afternoon—"

"How 'bout nothin'—for the afternoon—this time—just today."

"That's—that's unusual." He scratched his head. "Am I that—"

I bent and grabbed my backpack-strap and held the pack up a little, said, "I got some tunes and a viddie—a video—if we could maybe—have them goin'—" I got over to the stereo, flicked the power on, opened the CD shelf, looked at the guy and he was nodding so I undid the pack, started loading up CDs and he got around me, got a hand in the pack, got the viddie-tape, said, "This—?" and I nodded. I got the shelf full— five CDs—Temple of the Dog, Alice in Chains, Soundgarden's Louder Than Love—all of James's discs except Pet Shop Boys—and the guy loaded the tape in the VCR, turned it on, then the TV, hit play, sat on the carpet and looked at the screen, looked at me sucking James, Branch in the back beating off on a couch, and said, "Where are these buddies?"

then turned and smiled. I said I didn't know, told him to snuff the sound on the viddie, then I hit play on the stereo and the shelf went in and old Soundgarden came on.

Later, I was on my stomach on the carpet, butt up getting fucked, face up in front of the screen, looking at me fucking James, and the guy started whispering in an ear—"Used to have a nice kid like you, you know, regular guy, steady basis, but he took off, like you kids do, but I set him up with a pager, which I can do for you, Davy, and I can just buzz you for this, so you won't have to cruise, can keep you out of the park, away from cops' eyes and—"

"Okay, cool," I said, pushed my elbows hard into the carpet and got my butt back more on his dick, said, "But shut up, okay?" and the guy said, "Sure," bit the bottom of the ear he'd been talking into. I closed my eyes, got my head down, and under all the grunge-noise and low grunts coming out of me and the guy, I thought maybe there was something else, maybe I heard James hum-singing some dance-tune from the City, the last part of that song—"Disco me to ecstasy, Babyford, Babyford, chikki chikki ahh ahh, chikki chikki ahh ahh."

Water woke me up—a big bunch between my

nose and eyes—early in the AM—light rain and lots of fog coming down around me, and right over me, when I wiped my eyes and looked up, was a long branch-tip, dripping big water-drops, another drop rolling down, ready to hit, and I scooted up and it hit my shirt-wad, still sticky. I got up, twisted the water out of it, put it on and looked around, no cars around the fountain or coming in or parked anywhere, nobody on the trails or walking anywhere in the park-fog, and down below me, no cars on Burnside.

I bent down and brushed off James's pack, shook out the flat-spot where my head'd been then picked up, brushed leaves, needles and dirt off the back and bottom, then got each strap around a shoulder and started down the trail, getting thumbs under the front of the straps, then the rest of my fingers around and tight.

I looked around everywhere going out of the park, but it was clear and empty and by the time I got to the exit the rain had stopped, just misty, and the fog was pretty much gone, more AM light coming into the park, then a car came up, took the park-entrance and the guy driving looked at me and I looked away, down the street, shook the pack and heard the tapes and CDs—all of James's shit—rattle, didn't look at the next car coming up.

I turned on Vista, then got to Burnside and crossed and walked Twenty-third till I got to Flanders, then turned and got to the building-steps just up from our building, sat on the second-to-bottom step, behind the blue Sani-Pac can. The scaffolding was gone around the building and there was nobody painting around it and there were white flowers, now, sticking up in front of the basement window, and I leaned out, looked around the Sani-Pac can and there were more flowers around the corner of the building, in front of the other basement window.

A car, then another, came up Flanders, drivers holding coffee-cups, and I got down some behind the plastic garbage can until they both went by, then I looked back at the building and took another step down, then the door on the building behind me came open. I turned around and two women, talking low and fast, came out, one holding a plastic Plaid Pantry to-go coffee cup and keys, and they both slowed walking and stopped talking and smiled at me, and the woman with the cup and the keys got close to me, still smiling some, stopped and said, "Hon, are you waiting for someone inside?"

The woman behind her stopped at the passenger side of a car by the curb.

I shook my head, said, "No," and she scrunched her face a little, and I said, "I'm just—here," and the woman unscrunched her face and nodded, said, "Excuse me," reached around me and got the Sani-

Pac lid up, dropped her Plaid Pantry cup in, got the lid down and smiled at me again, and went to the driver's side of the car and held the door handle and both of the women looked at me, then I moved around the can, past them, back up Flanders, and when I'd gone by a couple more buildings, I heard the car doors unlock.

Later, almost afternoon, I was sitting on a bench in Tom McCall Park watching a bunch of small boats go down the Willamette, my arm around James's pack and two guys, my age, holding skateboards, walked in front of me over to Skidmore Fountain. They got their boards down in front of the jets, right where the water quit hitting the concrete, 'boarded around the water, did pops between the jets.

I reached around and unzipped James's pack, pulled out his Walkman, then reached in, felt around, pulled out a tape, didn't look at it, put it in, flicked it on and it was Nirvana, "About a Girl," *Bleach*.

I watched the 'boarders till they left, then watched more boats in the water, then just the water, going through *Bleach*, Everclear, all the tapes in the pack, a couple twice, till the start of night when the batteries finally went dead.

Little while into night I was in the middle of the Burnside Bridge, looking over the rail at city-light spots in the water, James's pack on the rail, my arm around it. The headphones were off and the Walkman and everything was inside and the pack was zipped.

A car slowed and I turned and two guys yelled, "Dive, dick," and I yelled quick, "Fuck, no" and the guys laughed and the car went fast down the rest of the bridge. I got my fingers tighter onto the pack, felt over all the places where the CD and tape covers stuck up, felt over them a few times slow, then I said, looking back at the Willamette, "Nothin's goin' over," then got up a wad of spit, leaned up some and spit up over the river, watched the wad come down, hit a light-spot, then I patted the pack, picked it up by a strap and got it over a shoulder then walked down the bridge, back into downtown.

I pushed the pack in first through the window-hole, then I crawled into the DH and Nikki was sitting in James's corner, legs stretched out, boots off, in front of her, head back to the wall, eyes closed, and I landed in hard and got up straight but she didn't open her eyes or move.

"You're—not at work," I said, not getting closer, staying still.

She sniffed up some snot, wiped her nose, kept her head back to the wall.

"Where's Branch at?" I said, and she didn't move or say anything so I said, "We're supposed to be movin', tonight, are we movin'?"

She bit the middle of her bottom lip, looked down, leaned forward and picked up a boot, leaned up and looked at me and threw it hard but it landed a ways in front of me, straight up, on the heel, then fell over and Nikki said, "You little prick—you fuckin' little prick," eyes watery, big and red, and I said, "I was always—comin' back—I'm sorry—" but she said loud, *"How the fuck was I s'posed to know?"*— then she looked down—"I don't know any of what the fuck's goin' on," and I went forward fast, got on the floor, in front of her, on my knees in front of her feet.

"I didn't take none of my shit," I said, looking around at me and Nikki's stuff by our sleep-wad, then said, "See?" but she said, "James didn't take his shit, did he? and Jody—" She got a big breath, bunch of tears from both eyes coming down her face, said, "Well, we had to deal with her fuckin' leftovers, right?"

I looked down, then nodded, then rubbed her toes.

"I didn't go to work 'cause I didn't know for sure about you," she said, talking slower, taking long breaths. " 'Cause you were gone, a while, too long, so I probably lost the job thing, but that's okay," she stopped a long second and I looked up, just over her toes and she said, "But don't you fuckin' ever do that again," and I said I wouldn't, then said that I'd gotten her first, we'd hooked up before getting anybody else—Branch, Jody, James—so I'd stay hooked with her until she wanted to jam and she leaned way forward, rubbed her hands over my fingers still rubbing her toes.

I leaned up between her feet, kissed her chin and she got her head lower till her lips were on mine, then after the lip-kiss she said, "We're gonna be cool, still," then kissed between my eyebrows, said, "Space," and I nodded, said, "Right, uh-hmm," then said, "I won't fuck it up," then Branch's voice echoed around big in the place—"Told her you couldn't jam"—and when I turned Branch's head was in the window-hole, mouth smiling.

"Dead batteries," I said loud to Branch, "I had to come back for new batteries for the Walkman."

Branch, still smiling, head still in the window, said, "Whatever reason," then a couple voices behind him said, "This is it, Branch?" and, "Get in, up there," and Branch turned his head, said down, "Fuckin' hold up," then said back to me and Nikki, "I got some surprises, for us."

He started crawling in all the way and I looked at Nikki but she shrugged, said, "He went to look for you, told me to hang here for you," then, after Branch'd got in, another head came up to the window-hole, and another kid, my age, crawled in, and while he was standing up, another guy, my age, crawled in, and another guy was waiting close behind the second guy's boots and a girl, same age, stuck her head up over the guy waiting.

When they all got in and got standing almost all the empty space in the place was taken and I looked at Nikki, then Branch and said, "Who the fuck're these guys?" and one guy said fast, "Davy, don't dis me, roomie," and Branch looked at the guy, then pointed at him, said, "That's Patrick," and pointed at the others, one by one, said, "Craig, Nate, and she's Danika, and Davy, you prob'ly saw them all, sometime, in the Square."

I looked at them in the night-light coming into our corner, said, "Yeah, maybe," and Nikki pointed at Patrick, said, "Maybe you," then Branch said, "Davy, they were just hangin'," and Nikki said, "We need more people," nodded, said, "That's what we need."

I looked at Craig and said, "Maybe you were at—the park—once," and Craig sat, shook his head, said, "No, man, doubt it, I work Stark, only Stark Street," then the others started sitting, but Branch still stood, said, "No, dudes, we've gotta get to the other place, the better place, the *real* space," and he looked at me and Nikki and said, "It's time—total kick-it-out-of-here time—and we've got some celebrating to do and"—he smiled big—"a whole bunch of shit to celebrate with—" Danika laughed loud and Nate tagged Craig's arm, said to him, "You'll *like* it, it's *good,* I've *done* it," and Patrick looked up to Branch, said, "Who is *Max,* anyway?" and Branch said, "Max is everything, dumbass," and Nikki said, "Branch—we got X?"

Branch nodded.

Nikki said low, "Yeah, that's what we need, too."

I said loud to Branch, over everybody else's talking, "Can we do it here?"

Branch said, "Davy, here? But we could be wakin' up on a real floor in the AM."

Nikki said to me, "One last thing here—that's kind of it," and I said that was it and Branch nodded, sat down, said, "No problem,

Davy, no problem at all you guys." He got a couple dollars out of his back pocket, turned and told Craig to go get some Big Gulps, bring them back because we were doing the drugs here and Craig got up, said, "Why the fuck me?" and Patrick said, " 'Cause you move the fastest," and Danika said, "And you're the *easi*-est and the *cheap*-est," and Nate laughed and Craig started through the window but came back through because someone else was coming in.

Shoulders came up outside the window and hands reached inside and the head was down and Craig said to the head, "Took you long enough," and the head came in the window and the face came up and it was the kid-kid and he said, "Had to piss—and there's no dark places in that alley there—light all over," and he got in, got standing, and I looked at Branch, getting over to the kid. Branch brushed dirt off the back of the kid-kid's T-shirt, new, no ripped collar, and I looked at his neck and there were a couple dark fingerprints on the side and one small blood-scab. Branch saw me looking, rubbed a finger over the scab, and said over the kid-kid's shoulder to me, "Davy— Curtis, Curtis—Davy. This is a total clean start, Davy—" Branch looked at me—"With everybody, all bad shit goes good," and the kid-kid looked at me, said, "Hey, Davy," looked up to Branch and said, "Hey, thanks." Branch backed up, got out a folded wad of newspaper from his back pocket, said loud, "We gotta cut this shit," then asked loud if anybody had a card or a knife, and Nikki, up, standing a little ways out of the corner, next to Danika, said loud, "Hey—*duh!*" went over to our sleep-shit and clothes and pulled Jody's knife from under our backpack and Danika laughed loud, said, "What's *that* supposed to be?" and Nikki said, "Protection, duh," then laughed, and Curtis said, "Man, we need some cool light in here," and Nikki's laughing got a little louder, and I looked at her, said, "Nikki—what?" Then Nikki went back to our sleep-shit, got a hand under some of her shirts, dug a second, pulled out a small candle, and I said, "Jody," and Branch said, "You fuckin' saved one," and Curtis said, "That little thing?" and Branch said, "Shut up, okay, it'll be fuckin' cool," and Danika, reaching in her back jeans pocket, went over to Nikki, pulled out a lighter and said, "Nik, I got that," bent and flicked up fire.

A while after Craig'd come back I was sitting up to the wall in James's corner, kicking one of the empty Big Gulp cups with my boot-toe and Nikki, sitting with Danika under the window, looked over Danika at me and I nodded my head a little, said, "Yeah—on." The candle was in the middle of the floor and Patrick, Craig and Branch and Curtis were around it, talking fast and loud and Curtis said, "Whoa—wait!" and everybody shut up and he said, "*There!*—Fuckin' *finally!*" and got a hand up, high-fived Patrick, Craig, then Branch and said loud to him, "*On,* man—*on,* dude!" and I leaned my head back, looked at the ceiling a second, then closed my eyes.

Couple seconds later, Branch said loud, over more talking, "Davy—*Davy*—hey—you gotta be gettin' *on,* dude!" and I opened my eyes, looked at him, nodded, and Craig, beside him, holding the knife, gave me a thumbs-up, then ran the thumb over the blade, then put the knife on the floor, sucked the leftover X off his thumb, then I looked next to me fast because the kid-kid—Curtis—had moved over by me, had his hands in James's pack.

I got my hands out fast, around his, held hard and said, "Fuckin' stop," and he looked up, said, "Some cool stuff here," and I said, "It's none of your shit, it's nothin' to do with you," and behind me Branch said loud, "Hey Davy—check his pupes—see how on he is—" and I looked back and Branch was pointing at Curtis, and Nikki, nodding, said, "Look at his eyes," and I turned around. Curtis leaned up and got his eyes open more and his pupils were big and I said loud, "Huge, Branch," and Curtis smiled, said, "I'm flyin' "—then around me— "Told you, B," then I let go of his hands but Curtis reached out, got a hold of one of mine, said, "Davy, look down," and I did and it was shaking. Curtis let go and I got both hands up and for a minute or so, me and everybody watched them shaking, then Curtis looked at his and I looked around and everybody was looking at their hands.

Nikki, turning her hand around, then making a fist, said, "Branch, how much did we get?"

Branch got his hands under his butt then got one out and rubbed his eyebrows and said, "I don't know exactly. I told Max I was getting some people together, told him I didn't know how many, told him—"

"Tell him thanks," Nikki said, and Danika laughed, said loud, "Girl, no doubt," and Nikki and Danika did a low five, then Nikki turned and crawled over to me, sat on her boot-heels and looked at me for a second, then got her arms around me hard, and I got my hands up her back and her arms got tighter and she said, "We're gonna be so cool," then loud, "We're gonna be so *fucking* okay!" and I closed my eyes in her hair for a minute or so, took a lot of long breaths and when I got my eyes open, my hands, still up her back, touching the bottom of her hair, had stopped shaking. I stretched my fingers out then got them tight, got more of her back in my hands.

Someone said, "I'm gettin' sick," and I looked through Nikki's hair and Craig was up, heading fast for the far corner, saying, "Yeah, yeah, for sure sick, here," puked, got on his knees, puked more, then Patrick got up, ran by me and Nikki, got on his knees and puked behind me in James's corner. Then there were arms around my middle but not all the way around me and small hands holding my stomach tight and I looked down just as Curtis was putting his head in my side and I said low, "Kid-kid—you gonna puke?" and he shook his head "No" in my side. I let go of Nikki some and rubbed the top of his head and Nikki looked down, got a hand free and rubbed too, then turned because Danika was crawling over, arms open and Nikki got her arms up, too, got them around her right when Danika said, "Girl," and Nikki said, "Girl," back, patted Danika's hair and Danika bent her head more and behind her Branch was staring at me, eyes watery. I watched him a couple seconds, till some tears came—two—one coming down out of each eye—and they got down to his mouth, then he looked down, got his T-shirt up some and wiped his face and I looked around at Nikki and Danika, then at the pukers and said, "Good thing we're outta here," then back to Branch, but he was crawling, head down, up to me. I said, "You all right?" touched his head and he nodded it, stopped crawling, looked up, smiling, said, "You stay away—from me," laughed, poked at my tit with a finger and I said, "I didn't—I was—James—" and he said, "Yeah, yeah," and Curtis, between us, got an arm off me, around Branch, pulled up both tight, and Branch—head to my head, looking down at Curtis—said, "Davy, okay to keep everybody, and him?" I got a couple big breaths, looked up, watched Nikki's head rock back and forth, eyes closed, on Danika's shoulder, looked at the pukers in the corners, down to coughing and just spit, and I said, "Mmm-hmm," got hands up Curtis's shirt, pulled him more on me, touched his neck-scab. Branch scooted back some and Curtis stretched out, got a hand on my chin and one on my leg, then moved it off my leg onto my crotch and I was hard and he kept that hand there and I kissed the fingers on the other one, feeling around my face, and I closed my eyes, heard Branch say, "Man, perfect vibe," and I said, "Just need tunes," then heard humming, coming close, and I smiled, opened my eyes and Nikki was off Danika, crawling over Curtis, humming Depeche Mode. I kissed her mouth, then a kid-kid finger, then he moved off me, scooted over to

Branch, and Danika came over, leaned in, kissed the back of Nikki's neck, then the side of my face, and her hair came down over my eyes and I blew on it till I could see and Branch was up, at the window-hole, and Curtis was starting to climb out. Danika hugged me and her hair came back on my eyes but through some of it I saw Curtis go all the way out and I got a finger up, pushed all the hair over, and Branch reached around Craig, coming back to sit down, and got the knife from the floor, put it in his back pocket, then started out the window and I said, "Oh," low. I got up and Nikki—getting an arm around my neck—went back some and Danika fell off me—hit the floor—said fast, "Are you sick too?"—and I said, "No"—walking fast to the window, not looking back, and Nikki said, "Where're you goin'?"—and I said, "Air—walk," and Nikki said, "No—stay," and, crawling out, I looked at her, shook my head.

I got down and Branch and Curtis were gone and I looked up and down the alley, walked into big shadow-chunks then got to the corner of the DH and looked around more, didn't see anything, said, "It's good, got to be all good," walked fast to Burnside, looking up and down the cross streets at all the corners, seeing people, but not them. At Burnside, I got a hand up on a corner-restaurant's brick-front, stopped, got air, leaned on a big plastic Sani-Pac can, looked up at the sidewalk, saw Branch and the kid-kid turn behind the Burnside Burger King, heading into the north park blocks.

I ran, fast a few streets, then slowed, hamburger-smell coming up everywhere in front of Burger King, and my stomach rolled and made noise and I stopped moving, got some long breaths, got my mouth and throat tight and swallowed some stomach-shit back down. I looked around behind the outside Burger King tables and saw a shopping cart in the first patch of park-block grass and a bum wadded-up, sleeping in the last grass-square, and heard low talking coming out from behind the big deer-statue in the middle park block. I got moving again, sweat coming down my face so I got my shirt-bottom on it, rubbed it off, let the shirt drop, got up to the deer-statue, then around it, and the kid-kid had his shirt off, and was sitting, back to me, on a deer-hoof and Branch was sitting, too, leaned against the other back leg, facing me but looking at Curtis and smiling and holding the T-shirt, wadded, up to Curtis's chest with one hand. I looked down, got my hand on the back of my neck, rubbed in sweat, said, "Soakin' up sweat," laughed, and Branch said, "Davy," and I looked up and Branch said, "Didn't want to freak the others out," and he held up the knife, pointed back toward the DH with the blade, pulled the shirt-wad off Curtis's front and there was a big X of red on the wadded white T, and Curtis turned around, said, "Davy, you got change for small fries, maybe?"—a blood-drop—coming down from the top corner of an X carved in his tit, next to his nipple, over his heart—ran down, caught another drop that'd started up at the bottom of the X, and the big double-drop fell into his belly button. Branch, still waving the knife, said to me, "His stomach's been a bitch, been making a ton of noise, but I got no cash," and I felt the front of a jeans pocket, then got a finger in, got something out, quit looking at the kid-kid's belly-button blood-puddle, saw that what I had was a viddie-token, said, "Sorry," put the token back in my pocket then pointed the finger at Curtis's chest, to the puddle, and said, "Hey—here—" and Branch leaned in, said, "Uh-oh, Tampax time," wiped the shirt-wad over and around in Curtis's belly button, then over his tit. Then Branch looked at the X, said, "Dammit, and it's not even fuckin' deep enough," and I said, still pointing, "Branch—what—what is that?" and the kid-kid's stomach growled and Branch laughed and Curtis got a hand over his stomach, hit Branch's arm with the other, said, "It's not funny, I'm hungry," and Branch said to him, "Being hungry helps your high, X

works better on an empty stomach," and I said louder, "Branch—
what're you doing?" and Branch and the kid-kid looked at me and
Branch said, "Hey, it's okay here, Davy, alright? I'm calm, kid's cool,
it's all good." He pointed the blade at me, said, "You said you wanted
to keep him," pointed it at Curtis's X, another drop starting down
from the top, said, "So this'll keep him. In case he starts to wander
off he'll just look down and know where he belongs, like branding is
all," and the kid-kid, looking down at the drip going down, said,
"Branded by Branch," and Branch leaned over, got the drop with the
shirt-wad before it got to the kid-kid's belly button, and I said, "You
said clean," and Branch said, "What?" and I said, "You said clean start,
but that's not—clean." Branch wrung the shirt, squeezed a few red
drops on the grass and I said, "That's the same stuff you been doing,"
and he said, "No hands on his neck, no fist in the face, no hurtin'
here, so quit lookin' at me—and look at this—it's not even *fucking*
deep enough," and the kid-kid pushed his chest up, got his head back,
closed his eyes, said to hurry up, he thought he was starting to come
down because the thing was starting to sting, and Branch got the
blade up to the top-tip of the X, started cutting down slow, more
blood coming up, and Curtis's arms tightened, his face scrunched,
and his stomach went off—growled loud—and I reached down fast—
got the knife out of Branch's hand—and he dropped the shirt-wad
from his other one and Curtis's chest came down and he looked over
at me, said, "What gives?" Branch, looking down, shook his head and
I backed up and my head hit the bottom of the deer-mouth and I
rubbed at my hair and Branch—looking at me—laughed—and behind
him, the kid-kid—still bent back some—rubbed the new cut's blood
around with one hand, reached out with the other, said, "Tampax me,
Branch—c'mon—get my shirt—" and I turned, moved around the
side of the deer, walked fast across the park-block grass—and Branch

said loud, "Yeah—jam—that's all you do"—and on the street, just be-hind Burger King, I looked back and Branch threw the shirt-wad at the kid-kid and said to me, "Be useful, Davy—go get funds for fries"—and the kid-kid—pushing the wad hard over his heart with one hand—looked at Branch and said, "Can he get enough to Super-Size?" but I ran to Burnside, and went up, didn't stop or turn.

Coming into the park there was light—from the whole city under-neath—and I looked down and there were a couple blood-spots on my shirt and my hand, too, from the knife, and I pulled at my shirt-collar fast and got the shirt off and wiped my hands on it, then wiped the blade and the knife-handle on it, then I wadded it and chucked it between a bush and tree, put the knife in my back pocket.

I got up the hill after the in-road, past the swings and down the hill to the fountain—got halfway up the middle trail then got my hand on a tree-side and stopped and breathed in—long breaths—and looked around—a guy stood smoking at the top of the trail—and a guy was coming onto the trail, out of the bushes behind him—and the guy smoking started down my way—and I coughed between fast breathing, got in a big wad of air, cut through the bushes right beside me, got on the top trail, went up to the end of the top trail, fell onto the grass at the top of the park.

I looked up, down the grass at the guys walking around the bath-room, guys sitting on the bench on the path in front of the bathroom and some hands came down beside me and I looked at the ground then at the guys' hands hanging down and I rubbed sweat off my face-sides and head, said, "I can't go no more." The guys got me up and one started pulling me back down the trail and the other guy kept holding me still, said, "No, no, no," and I looked at the guy pulling me, then looked back at the bathrooms, started walking forward some, said, "Yeah, okay, there's fine," then we all got moving forward, down the grass, and one of the guys said, "Some summer, some nice warm summer, isn't it?" and the other guy didn't say anything but I nodded into somebody's shoulder.

Later—twenty minutes or maybe a whole half-hour—I heard my name—low and far then louder and echoey—and I looked up from watching the wads of jizz coming down on the middle of my chest and up and down my arm, all over my dick-hair, dick and balls and knee and the sock left on my left foot—and saw the sound was coming in through two vents up high in the other bathroom wall and "David!"—from Nikki—bounced all over the bathroom—walls to stalls to the piss-tub I was in—and I started to sit up some but a hand came around my head, held it down, kept me steady in the tub. The guy pushing my head came around, pushed another guy—standing, shooting—further down, and he pushed another guy, whole tub-line moving, except two guys at the end of the tub—the two guys that'd walked me off the trail—they didn't move, were done shooting, were reached out, rubbing knee and sock jizz around with their hands. Then the crowd around the top of the piss-tub got tighter, their faces got scrunched, came in closer, and they watched the guy holding my head jizz on my face, and for a couple seconds I couldn't see anything but I heard the bathroom door come open, heard Nikki say, "Oh, Davy, what the fuck're you *doin'*—?" and the guy let go of my head and someone got a hand off my arm and I got a hand up, wiped off the eye-jizz just as the guy that'd had my head was moving away, next guy moving up in the tub-line to the front, new guy's dick to my face but I got my head back before he shot, got the jizz mostly on my mouth, some on my chin, no more on my face, and water soaked my hair because when my head went back it went right under the flush-water-spout over the top of the tub and under the water-splash I heard Nikki yell, "Back off," got my head up to look—hit it on the spout when the "God—back off!" bathroom-echo came back—then Nikki's face came down to mine, behind the spout-spray and she yelled, "Why're you *fuckin'* my *trip?*" and behind her her hands pushed back the last guy that'd jizz'd in my face, and her boots kicked at the air in front of the two guys at the end of the tub—dicks soft, hanging over, starting to pee, dribbling some yellow on my sock toe—and Nikki turned, yelled, "Stop it—stop it—stop it!" at them till they turned and put their dicks away.

Nikki said, "Where's Branch and Curtis? What're you up here for? What're you doin' with the knife? Davy—*what's goin' on?*"—then pushed more guys—guys up front—zipping, buttoning, buckling up—off, away—and the water came cold down in my mouth and Nikki—still in my face—said loud, "What's with this shit—hunh?—Davy, are you trippin'?—Trippin' bad?" and she got both her hands out, held onto mine and pulled, started getting me up, out, yelled, *"Don't trip!"*—and I looked at her and she held my chin and then I nodded.

Guys went out the door and I got my hands up on Nikki's shoulders, got a leg out, foot on the floor, shook my head—hair-water, jizz coming off—and Nikki stopped me a second, looked around the bathroom, said, "Clothes—yours—no shirt?" and I shook my head again, got my other leg up over the tub, shook pee off my sock, got on both feet, started walking and Nikki bent, held me up with one hand, started picking up my clothes with the other—and she said, "I know James jammin' is fucked"—she handed me my underwear and I started getting in them—"but we'll be cool, okay?"—the last couple guys went around me, out the bathroom door and my underwear was

up so she handed me my jeans, said, "Watch the fuckin' knife—
stickin' up in the back—" then bent again, looked around on the floor,
said, "Sock—sock—sock"—then she said, "I know you miss James—
I miss Jody—but can you—try with who we got now?" and I stopped
getting my leg into a jeans leg, looked at her and she turned back to
me, said, "You see a sock?" I didn't say anything and she stared at me
for a long second, then said, "Okay—I know—these guys aren't the
same but—they seem cool—and it seems like we should try—" she
bent again, crawled some away, got my other sock, over a pipe, under
the sink, behind a stall-wall, and said, "Just please don't trip anymore"—handed me the sock and I pushed the knife-blade down in
the back jeans pocket, then buttoned up the jeans, started putting on
the sock. Nikki got my boots on the floor in front of the door, held
them up and I pulled up both my socks, took a boot, said, "Nikki—
we gotta jam." I got my foot in the boot all the way and started to
lace up then stood up and Nikki put the other boot down in front of
me, looked up at me.

"I gotta find him," I said. "So bad."

She looked at me a couple more seconds and the bathroom door
came open and an old guy got his head in some, looked at me, started
stepping in, then saw Nikki, bent under me, backed out and the door
shut and then Nikki started finishing lacing up my boot.

"I want him like I got you, now," I said down to her head. "It's like
the same as you—and I know—you and me hooked up first and me
and you—"

"Other foot," she said fast, got the other boot up, open and I put
my foot in and she started lacing and I must've been shaking or swerving because she patted part of her back, said, "Here—get a hand
down," and I put a hand on her and got steady. She tied the last boot
and stood up, said, "More north, you thinkin' that?" and I nodded,

said, "I think—I—don't know where else, Nik," and she said, "Seattle, to start," then got a hold of her shirt-bottom and got it up quite a bit, got it to my face and wiped under my eyes and I said, "I'm not cryin'," and she said, "I know," kept wiping, said, "It's just jizz," and pushed hard all over my face with her shirt.

Water woke us up, next morning—few big drops
of rain hitting my head, rolling down my face and chin onto Nikki's
head—up against my neck—and Nikki's body moved around in my
arms and I moved my head up from the bench, looked out down to
the city—dark rain cloud already passing over us on Pittock-hill, rain
moving over, onto downtown Portland and there were voices up at
Pittock Mansion and Nikki got up in me and we both looked over the
back of the bench. There were ten or a dozen people on the Pittock-
porch, closing umbrellas, and going into the open glass double-doors,
one woman, behind everybody, umbrella still up, saying, "Right in, to
the left please," few times, then when everyone was in, she got her
umbrella down, said, "Directly left of the staircase we'll find the incredible first-floor bathrooms—gentlemen's and ladies'—all marble—"
then got inside, pulled the doors closed.

Nikki turned and sleeved rain off my face, then my chest, then her face and I nodded over to the city, said, "It's all over there now," and she looked up, over us, said, "Not even no sprinkles," asked if I was cold and I leaned up, got arms around her, said, "No," and she said, "Must be nine or ten, or maybe eight"—looked at the Pittock-porch—"that's probably when they start those tours."

I looked back down the hill, the cloud dumping water over buildings, bridges, and a lot of Burnside.

Nikki looked down too, said, "Our shit."

I said, "I know."

"We don't even need—"

"Yeah, we do."

"Well, I can—"

"No, let me."

Wind kicked up and I shook some and Nikki rubbed her shoulder blades into my nipples and I said that I couldn't run all over the place like this, no shirt, and she kind of laughed, said, "Yeah, couple months there'll be real rain, real cold," looked up at me and I said, "We'll need warm space, by then—" and she said fast, "Davy—we'll have it—" and behind her hair blowing the big cloud got to moving out of the city.

We got up to the DH and Nikki said, "You really sure all our shit's still here—" and I said fast, "Branch might've got pissed and chucked it—but—no—no—it's here," then she said, "You think he's—" and I said, "They're all over there, the new space, Nik—or they're out workin'—but no way they're here," then we were under the window-hole and I started to go up but Nikki touched my leg and I came down and she said, "Davy, I don't know why but—" she touched the tip of the blade in my back pocket, said, "That," and I said, "Yeah, okay," pulled it out, gave it to her, and she put it in her front pocket and I got back up, climbed in.

Curtis was inside—only one—on the floor in James's corner, sitting, eyes closed, Walkman phones on his ears, moving his head a little to the beat of something buzzing loud and when I stood up from the floor his eyes got open and his fingers clicked STOP fast and his head got still. He rubbed his hand over his T-shirt, new, not bloody anywhere, then scratched on his left tit and a small spot of red came up. There were a couple of my T-shirts over the puke-pile behind him but puke-smell was everywhere, and everybody's stuff was gone except for me and Nikki's sleep-shit and our clothes and our pack and except for James's pack, unzipped, open by Curtis's feet, James's CDs and tapes on the floor around him. I pointed to the pack and all of James's tunes and Curtis took off the headphones, put the Walkman in the pack, started putting CDs back in their cases, and I went over to him, started putting the full CD cases and the tapes in the pack. He kept his head low while he put the discs in, then I got the last one in the pack and then the last tape, then he handed me the Walkman and I said, "What's in?" and he said, "Nirvana, *Bleach*," and looked up at me. I said, "That's old shit," and he nodded, then I turned, reached across the floor for some of our T-shirts, got some in the pack, zipped it up, then got one left on, then lifted up his T-shirt. Four Simpsons Band-Aids covered up the X and there was a blood-smear around the edge of the bottom-corner Band-Aid and I said, "It itches, huhn?" and the kid-kid looked down, nodded, said, "But it don't hurt," looked at me. "And Branch's been cleaning it up good so it won't need stitches like Danika wants," he said. He pulled the shirt down, rubbed it flat, said, "Branch is getting some—stuff—pills—antibiotics—too—just in case—from—uh—" and I said, "Max," and he said, "Yeah, him," then he laughed, said, "Branch told everybody a bum did it. Said he stole our BK fries too," and he rubbed over it again, said, "It's kinda cool, and cheaper than a tattoo, and it itches, but don't hurt," and I got up, holding the pack, went to the window-hole. I looked at him looking down his shirt-collar, smiling, and I said, "Hey, watch him, watch Branch," and he nodded but didn't look over.

Back outside the DH, Nikki said, "Who—?" and I said fast, "Just the kid-kid," then she said, "I-Five?" and I said, "Yeah, but one more stop, okay?" and she said, "Okay," got a hand up, said, "I'm just followin' here," got behind me out of the alley, patted the pack a couple times.

We got up Stark to the door at the bathhouse and I got the pack off my shoulder and Nikki took it, put it on hers and I said, "Two minutes—most," opened the BH door. A guy inside on my side of the counter was holding up his plastic card to a guy behind the counter and the counterguy started looking at it, then looked over it at me, said, "You—you're not eighteen, are you?"—shook the card at me, said, "Don't even answer that, buddy, you need to go—" and the guy on my side of the counter took his card, looked back at me.

I said, "I need Mike."

The guy behind the counter said loud, "Mike—hey—problem"—buzzed the guy with the card through the inside door, and he went up the stairs and Mike came out of the back.

"David—" Mike said. "Out of here, now," and I said fast, "The tape"—pointed behind Mike, some viddie-boxes on the shelf—"There's a tape I wanna get"—and the counterguy lifted up a part of the counter and started to come over to my side and Mike grabbed his shoulders, stopped him, and I said, "The tape's me, it's mine"—

then the counterguy got his counter back down, got back and Mike said, "It's in a shit-pile, it's not even played anymore, you oughta know that."

I said, "Yeah, okay, whatever," and Mike said, "But I'll look," turned, went in the back and Branch came up from the back, stood behind the counterguy and they both watched me. Branch got his arms up and folded them on his chest and said, "Mike's got a deal lined up with a couple guys comin' up from Corvallis—two college profs—and they want us—" and I said, "Branch—me and Nikki—we're not coming back"—and Branch said, "Yeah, well, these guys won't be in town for a week yet," looked at the counterguy and smiled, then both of them looked back at me, laughed a little.

Mike came back, handed me a videotape, no cover, and I looked at it, turned it over, looked at the other side.

"That's it," Mike said, and I quit looking at the tape, turned and reached for the door and Branch said, "There's other copies around town, dumbass," and Mike said, "Yeah, that's right. Probably not in real high demand but still around," and the counterguy said, "Hard Times used to run it," then Mike said, "It's played out. But there's other copies. David, you know that."

I didn't turn around, kept my hand on the knob, said, "I know, but I want this one out of here," and I opened the door and Nikki—on the curb, back to me, turned, looked at me—and I stepped out and Branch said, "Don't dull up my blade"—laughed—then the metal door closed and I was back on Stark with Nikki. She had the pack around her shoulders and she stood up, back to me, and I unzipped it, put the tape in, zipped it up, then patted it, said, "This way," got us moving up Stark.

Nikki said, "This park is colder," when the guy with the house on the hill dropped me off, at the bathrooms, back in Volunteer Park, at night, and she got up from the bench by the mens' side, holding her arms tight for warmth, and I said Seattle was higher than Portland, we were further north, and summer was close to over, then, when the guy's car was fairly far down the exit road, she asked me how it went and I said that I got my first regular, plus a good lead on getting a beeper, and she looked around the park, asked where to crash and I said I wasn't sleepy, looked down at Seattle night-lights, said it was still early, we needed food, and I had to get more batteries and music, and Nikki hit the pack on my back, said, "We're heavy already," and I said, "One more disc, okay?" and she said, "Your money," started down the sidewalk, a car, going by her, slowed at me, but I shook my head at him, walked.

On Broadway, I bought Nikki a Snickers in a 7-Eleven, said to go ahead and down the whole thing because I wasn't really that hungry and wanted to find a music place first and she said she could've waited for food and I said no, that I'd heard her stomach making noise, and going out the 7-Eleven doors, some sole came loose off the front of my left boot and I stumbled, stopped, got my boot up, looked at and flicked the loose sole-piece, and then I looked down at Nikki's boots as she walked up to me, and she stopped and chewed a candy-bar bite and said, "What?"

Both of her boot-toes were scratched and the bottoms were worn down but not loose at all, anywhere, and the pink-polish streaks didn't look scraped or even faded and I said, "How come your boots aren't close to shot?"

"You've been running too much in yours," she said, "You need to just walk."

I dropped my boot, turned, walked further up Broadway, and she said loud, "Well, you asked me," and a while later, still on Broadway, she threw the Snickers wrapper in a trash-can in front of a CD store, asked if I was sure I didn't want any of what was left and I said no, so she put the last part in her mouth, opened the store-door and I stepped in and my boot-sole slapped loud on the wood floor, slapped with every step to the "F" section and Nikki giggled, then said, "Wait."

I said, "What?" and she came up, said, "I know it's your money and you said you're just gettin' the one, but this is the new-shit section, can you get it used?" and I looked back, saw the used table, other side of the store, said, "Yeah, you're right," looked at her and said, "All I make after this is for us, totally for us," and she said, "And you're gonna quit bitin' at me and bein' a dick," and I said, "Yeah," and she said, "Okay, we're lookin' for who?" and I said, "Foo." She turned, went to the used table, started thumbing through the F's and then fast, she said, "Hey, here, found one—and cheap," then stepped back—said, "Oh, Davy," held the CD up tight, backwards, cover to her tits.

I said, "Is it less than eight bucks?"

She said, "I've seen this," looked at me, held it out, said, "It's his,"

and I took it and looked at the front and over the toy-gun barrel, under
the words "Foo Fighters" was a crack, short and not deep and not curved
a lot, like a pulled-out W, and I nodded, looked up, and Nikki, running
up to the counterguy, said, "Do you know who sold—that?" and I held
up the CD.

The counterguy squinted, said, "Cracked Fighters? Yeah—actually—
I do—it was a kid, in the afternoon, and he just had that," then the guy
rubbed his face, laughed low, said, "He said he didn't have anything to
play it in, his ride left," and Nikki said to me, "Davy—he's breathing,"
and I nodded again, got the CD down, ran some fingers up and down
the crack, and pushed flat a curled corner of the white price-sticker that
said "USED, $8.95," Band-Aiding the top of the split so it wouldn't get
bigger.

Nobody's anything alone.

Absolute, infinite thanks to Edward Hibbert, David Bergman, and Matthew Stadler, for their time, honesty, bottomless wisdom, and fearless support; Will Schwalbe for his guidance and the great chance to do it all right; Richard Lyons and Barbara Gates for their very early encouragement; Kay Braun, Jeff Lutman, Patrick Hanna, and Robert Ball for their stories, Stolis, speech patterns, and silent inspiration; Jack and Fran Williams and Arlan Smith and the OPH crew; Jeannie and Emilee Martin, goddess and godchild, respectively; Ma—a roof, food, cable, and coffee change; and Kevin G. Litle, super-friend, soundtrack consultant, and Sunday night chauffeur.